PACIFIC
HOMICIDE

Dedicated to
Misty, Danny Boy, Aristede, Miss Scarlett, Dottie, PJ,
Tigger-Boo, Scooter, and Riley
For making my world a better place

Praise for *Pacific Homicide*

"Terrific! The classic cop story goes contemporary in this suspenseful, riveting thriller. Instantly cinematic and completely authentic—LAPD's tough and savvy Davie Richards will capture your heart. It's a page-turner from moment one."

—Hank Phillippi Ryan, Agatha Award–winning author of *Truth Be Told*

"In *The Third Man*, Graham Greene used the underground river—the sewer—of post-war Vienna for both a memorable chase scene and a larger metaphor. Now, in *Pacific Homicide*, Patricia Smiley, at the top of her form in this multi-layered thriller, investigates the grisly murder of a young Russian beauty found in the 6,500 miles of sewer pipelines under Los Angeles. Smiley knows the LAPD from the inside out and writes with the authenticity of Joseph Wambaugh. This is the first of a series featuring the tough-gal detective Davie Richards. I can't wait for the second one."

—Paul Levine, bestselling author of *Bum Rap*

"Crackling with wit and suspense, Patricia Smiley's *Pacific Homicide* is a classic police procedural told with flair, imagination, and the deep authenticity of an author who knows the LAPD from firsthand experience. You're in the hands of a master storyteller as you follow beleaguered heroine Detective Davie Richards—struggling to track the murderer of a young Russian model through the glitter and the dark underbelly of Los Angeles, while battling an internal affairs zealot bent on destroying her. This one kept me reading through the night."

—Bonnie MacBird, author of *Art in the Blood: A Sherlock Holmes Adventure*

"Fans of the classic police procedural will love Davie Richards, the LAPD detective at the heart of this novel … Readers will discover Smiley's nimble talents for understated wit, unsentimental affection, and the emotional wounds that drive the best of cops to buck the system in search of justice."

—Kim Fay, Edgar Award finalist for *The Map of Lost Memories*

"*Pacific Homicide* combines an insider's knowledge of the LAPD with a clear-eyed, no-nonsense heroine and an entertaining dry wit. Davie Richards is easy to fall in love with and her story is full of surprising twists."

—Matt Witten, writer and producer for
Pretty Little Liars, Law & Order, and *Homicide*

"With taut style, unfailing ear, and unflinching honesty, Patricia Smiley's *Pacific Homicide* puts a fresh, deeply emotional spin on the police procedural."

—Craig Faustus Buck, author of *Go Down Hard*

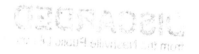

PATRICIA SMILEY

PACIFIC HOMICIDE

A

MYSTERY

MIDNIGHT INK
WOODBURY, MINNESOTA

FIRST EDITION
First Printing, 2016

Book format by Bob Gaul
Cover design by Lisa Novak
Cover art by iStockphoto.com/54877942/©rmbarricarte
Editing by Nicole Nugent

Midnight Ink, an imprint of Llewellyn Worldwide Ltd.

Library of Congress Cataloging-in-Publication Data
Names: Smiley, Patricia, author.
Title: Pacific homicide: a mystery / Patricia Smiley.
Description: First edition. | Woodbury, Minnesota: Midnight Ink, [2016] |
 Series: A Pacific homicide mystery; #1
Identifiers: LCCN 2016026049 (print) | LCCN 2016033631 (ebook) | ISBN
 9780738750217 | ISBN 9780738751306 (ebook)
Subjects: | GSAFD: Mystery fiction.
Classification: LCC PS3619.M49 P33 2016 (print) | LCC PS3619.M49 (ebook) |
 DDC 813/.6—dc23
LC record available at https://lccn.loc.gov/2016026049

Midnight Ink
Llewellyn Worldwide Ltd.
2143 Wooddale Drive
Woodbury, MN 55125-2989
www.midnightinkbooks.com

Printed in the United States of America

Acknowledgments

I owe a debt of gratitude to many people who offered their wisdom and support during the long journey to complete this novel, including: Elizabeth George, Lee Goldberg, Karen E. Olson, Charlotte Herscher, Bonnie MacBird, Harley Jane Kozak, Matt Witten, Craig Faustus Buck, Linda Burrows, Bob Shane, Jonathan Beggs, Jamie Diamond, Sandy Harding, and Michael Levin. Thanks also to my attorney Jonathan Kirsch and to all the people at Midnight Ink, especially my editor Terri Bischoff, for transforming my manuscript pages into a real book.

While researching this novel, I interacted with many officers and detectives of the Los Angeles Police Department. Thanks to all who answered my questions and regaled me with their stories, especially Homicide Detective Michael D. DePasquale, who inspired me in countless ways. Any mistakes you may find in police procedures are mine alone. Things change, including the law and LAPD policies. For example, Homicide detectives have been moved out of area squad rooms and are now consolidated at regional Bureaus. That makes sense in the real world, because it's a more efficient use of personnel. However, this is a work of fiction, so I chose to leave Pacific Homicide detectives where I first encountered them, in the Pacific Area squad room.

DETECTIVE DAVIE RICHARDS ARRIVED at Hyperion Sewage Treatment Plant near Dockweiler Beach on Tuesday morning at seven forty-five, shortly after an employee found what appeared to be a white female wedged between the claws of a rotating grinder.

Davie stood near the collection trough, studying what was left of the body. Part of the woman's face was missing as well as her left arm and right leg. Clumps of long blonde hair surged in the cloudy water. Davie shifted her gaze, forcing herself to think of the wreckage as a discarded mannequin from a department store window and not as somebody whose loved ones were hoping for better news.

The air in the sewage plant had an oppressive chemical odor. She glanced at her partner, Jason Vaughn, as he pulled a tube of menthol vapor rub from the jacket pocket of his designer suit, which was more Wall Street bond trader than Homicide detective. All it would take was one bloody crime scene and those expensive threads would be history. He didn't seem to care.

Vaughn dabbed the gel under his nose to mask the smell. "Good thing it's the coroner's job to dig her out of there. This could get messy."

Davie had seen plenty of dead bodies before. She had been with the Los Angeles Police Department nine years—eight in patrol and one year as a detective. Some nights working mid–p.m. watch in Southeast patrol, she had raced from one homicide to the next like her hair was on fire, barely able to distinguish one victim from another when the DA's office subpoenaed her to testify in court.

But she wasn't likely to forget this crime scene.

She squatted next to the trough, arcing her gaze across the victim's body for clues to her identity. The woman's remaining limbs looked waxy and frail, as if she might have been anorexic. Her fingers were long and thin. No ring. No jewelry of any kind. It was difficult to determine her age, but judging by the length of her thighbone, she appeared to be an adult.

Her mouth was open and flaccid. Her parted lips exposed some sort of metal in her mouth. Braces. Davie remembered the pain from the wires she wore as a teenager. Being forced to wear braces as a teen was one thing; wearing them as an adult was quite another. She would eventually find out why the woman had waited so long to straighten her teeth. It was her job to learn everything she could about a victim. Cops often solved crimes because they noticed some small detail— minutiae—that didn't fit the pattern.

She raised her voice over the rumble of machinery and wastewater flowing into the facility as she pointed toward the body. "Take a look at her elbow."

Vaughn moved toward the trough in one lanky, fluid motion. "Looks like a tattoo."

"A spiderweb. That's a prison tat. If she was in stir, she's got a rap sheet."

"Maybe she's just a gangster wannabe. I wouldn't spend too much time on this one, partner. She obviously committed suicide."

"How do you figure?"

"She's nude. In my experience, members of the female tribe always strip down before they pull the plug. You people just can't face eternity in any outfit that goes out of style."

"I doubt death by sewer will catch on with my so-called tribe."

Vaughn's grin was cocky. "Too bad you don't qualify as a spokesperson, Davie. You're not a woman. You're a machine, a ghetto gunslinger, a red-haired ninja. I mean that in a good way, of course."

"I'm sure you do."

She knew her partner was teasing. It was the way they related to each other. She also knew he was wise to be cautious. Back in his patrol days, a female officer had filed a mouth beef against him over a dumb-blonde joke. The personnel complaint had cost him an eight-day suspension for sexual harassment. He hadn't been promoted for five years after that, a standard department punishment.

"Call the coroner," she said, "and SID. Ask them to send a photographer."

"Why the paparazzi? Even if the vic was murdered, I doubt it happened here. The body looks like it's been on the road for a while. Take a few shots with the camera in your war bag and call it a day."

She made no attempt to conceal her irritation. "That's why we have a Scientific Investigation Division, Jason. They have people who can take pictures of the body before the coroner moves it. Stop whining and make the call, okay?"

He held up his hands in surrender. "Whatever you say, partner."

Vaughn was probably right. The LAPD's crime scene mantra of "Look around, don't walk around" didn't apply here. It was unlikely she'd find any evidence to collect at the plant, but this was her first call-out as lead Investigative Officer at Pacific Homicide, and she couldn't afford any screw-ups. She was already under investigation for an officer-involved shooting that had happened six months before. The LAPD brass had ruled the shooting was within policy, but until the police commission agreed with that decision, she felt like she was balancing on the sharp edge of a knife.

The air inside the building felt cold. Davie raised her shoulders toward her ears, wondering why that gesture always quelled a chill. Was it scientific or just her imagination? A moment later she heard footsteps and turned to see a black man in a hard hat walking toward her, carrying a large roll of paper under his arm.

The man towered over her by at least a foot. Six-two, she guessed. He looked to be in his early fifties, judging by the slouch of his shoulders, and the fat around his gut. A wedding band cut into his flesh. He'd probably gained weight over the years but never had the ring resized. Maybe he was superstitious about taking it off his finger or maybe he just couldn't get it off.

As they exchanged introductions, engineer Casper Blount's gaze swept down her size-zero black polyester pantsuit to her rubber-soled Oakley boots. Vaughn called them Special Ed shoes, but she could run in them and that's all that mattered. She knew the Smith & Wesson .45-caliber pistol holstered on her belt looked like a cannon against her small frame, but she'd chosen it over the department-issued weapon because it made a statement: I might be small but I'm a force to be reckoned with.

Blount's brown eyes lingered for a moment on the detective badge hanging from her belt. She didn't need psychic powers to read his mind. He thought she looked like a teenager playing dress up. At least he was smart enough to keep his opinions to himself.

"Has a body ever surfaced at the plant before?" she said.

"Not that I remember. This has been quite a shock. One of my employees called about an hour ago. Said there was something caught in the machine and could I come down and take a look. That's when we found her."

"How do you think she got in the grinder?"

Blount explained in detail how gravity propelled sewage through the system of pipes and connectors while Davie made Sewer 101 notes on her chronological report.

"Your partner asked me to show you a map of the plant," he said, "to help you understand the layout."

Blount bent toward her to compensate for the difference in their heights as he unrolled the tube of paper. He pointed to an aerial drawing of the Hyperion facility that reminded her of a hodgepodge of circles and squares on a high school geometry quiz.

"The facility receives four hundred fifty million gallons of effluent on a normal day, more when it rains." As he spoke, his finger traced over the four major sewer lines that merged into a tunnel under Imperial Highway and eventually surfaced as a river at Hyperion.

"Why didn't the equipment process the body and move it on?"

"There are several mechanisms to remove solids," he said. "The rotating grinder macerates oversized particles. Screens and bars remove what's left. In this case, the grinder couldn't handle the body. That's why it jammed."

"Could she be an employee?"

"I checked. All of our people are accounted for."

Davie saw Vaughn standing near a round tank a short distance away, holding his cell phone. He shook his head, indicating he was still waiting for word about the photographer.

"The victim probably didn't die here," Davie said. "If this turns out to be a homicide, I need to trace the body back to the place where she entered the sewer system. Can you calculate how fast the waste-water travels through the tunnels and give me a timeline?"

Blount frowned as he rolled up the drawing. "I'm afraid that's not possible."

With all the math and science in the world, Davie wondered why one sewer geek couldn't figure out how fast shit traveled.

"Why is that?"

Blount straightened his spine, widening the distance between them. "The wastewater system serves almost four million people in Los Angeles plus twenty-seven surrounding cities. There are more than sixty-five hundred miles of sewer pipelines. She could have entered almost anywhere. The path of debris isn't always straightforward. As for the timeline, the body could have snagged on one of the underground ladders and stayed there until the force of the flow broke her loose. That could have taken hours or days."

"Could that force tear a body apart?"

"Possibly."

"So we're back to square one. How could she get into the sewer?"

"There are only two ways," Blount said. "Somebody could have thrown her into an open pipe while the line was under construction, but that's unlikely. Those areas are generally blocked off. More likely, somebody dropped the body into a manhole. It slipped through the grates and entered the system. There are thousands of manholes, and they're easily accessible to the public. Some of the covers weigh up to three hundred pounds and require a special tool to open them, but most can be lifted by one person."

"I need a list of locations."

He hesitated before responding. "All of them?"

Davie understood it would be a challenge to find the body's point of entry, but it was her job to try.

"Yes," she said. "*All* of them."

He took in a breath, holding the air for a moment before letting it out. "I have maps. They're in my office."

Blount left the room just as Vaughn's cell phone rang. He listened a moment before ending the call.

"Doctor Death and the photog just arrived," he said, walking toward her. "Prepare to be underwhelmed."

While her partner interviewed Hyperion employees, Davie supervised the photographer and watched as the coroner's investigator extracted the remains from the grinder. The body revealed no obvious clue as to cause of death. She could only hope the medical examiner could sort that out at the autopsy. Davie jotted notes in her log as the tech bagged and tagged the victim as Jane Doe #3, the third unidentified female to die in Los Angeles County since the beginning of the year, just one week ago.

There was only one chance to process a crime scene. Once the yellow tape was removed, people would walk through the area and contaminate any remaining evidence. But contamination wasn't a factor here. Even though she had assigned a patrol officer at the door to keep out unauthorized personnel, it was mostly for show. There were no blood spatters or shell casings to collect and nothing to fingerprint, so at nine forty-five a.m., two hours after she had arrived, Davie notified Blount that she had finished collecting evidence at Hyperion and officially closed the crime scene.

The gurney's wheels bumped over the floor as the techs transported the body from the building. Davie thought about Blount's lecture: four hundred and fifty million gallons of daily sewage flowing in rivers of brown sludge beneath the streets of Los Angeles. Flushing toilets sent effluent surging into wastewater pipes four inches in diameter, which then gushed through sewer mains eight inches wide. The mains flowed into sixteen-inch laterals. Gravity propelled the waste into pipes, collectors, trunk lines, and then interceptors eleven feet across, spilling to downstream outfalls up to twelve and a half feet wide. All that waste was destined for four sewage treatment plants, one of them being the Hyperion location. Tumbling, cascading torrents of bacteria-filled muck and the body of one young woman known only as Jane Doe #3.

Davie felt perspiration form on her chest. It was certainly not the temperature in the room that made her sweat, but the image of the woman flailing in a dark tunnel as raw sewage swept her toward the sea. She closed her eyes to redirect her thoughts, hoping for the victim's sake that she had been dead before she went underground.

2

THE OCEAN BORDERING PLAYA del Rey was the same shade of flinty gray as the sky as Davie left Hyperion and drove back to the station in the only car that had been available that morning, a beat-up VW Jetta she had borrowed from Vice detectives.

A winter cold front from Alaska had blown into town for an unwelcome stay. People from Chicago joked when Angelenos complained about forty-degree weather, but Davie figured the hairs in your nose didn't have to freeze and break off before you could call the weather what it was: chilly.

Vaughn sat in the passenger seat checking the value of his stock portfolio on an iPhone. She didn't ask how he transitioned so easily between death and price-to-earnings ratios. It didn't matter. Vaughn was the closest thing she had to a friend in the department. They were the same age, thirty-one. They had graduated from the same academy class and had stayed in touch over the years. They hadn't worked together until recently, but Vaughn had her back, and that made him as close to perfect as a partner could get. Besides, she appreciated the silence. It gave her time to think. With luck, someone had reported the victim missing. Even with that information, learning how she had died might be difficult. Davie refused to say impossible because cynicism was a detective's enemy.

Davie entered the driveway from Culver Boulevard, pressed her ID to the security sensor, and waited for the gate to retreat. For the past month, she had been assigned to Pacific Division, which was number fourteen of twenty-one decentralized police stations. It covered 25.74 square miles carved out of the 468 square miles comprising the city of Los Angeles. The station served about 200,000 Westside vegans, movie stars, and gangbangers in the neighborhoods of Venice Beach, Oakwood, Mar Vista, Playa del Rey, Playa Vista, Palms, and Westchester. Its western border was the Pacific Ocean with Culver City to the east, the Los Angeles International Airport to the south, and National Boulevard to the north.

After the 1992 Rodney King riots, politicians decided that *division* sounded too militant. The next chief adopted a community-policing model and Pacific Division became Pacific Area Community Police Station. Subsequent regimes lopped off words until the brass and the politicians settled on Pacific Area Police Station. Most cops still called it Pacific Division. Burglaries and thefts topped the list of crimes in the hood, but homicides kept four full-time detectives occupied and Davie was grateful to be one of them.

Vaughn lingered in the parking lot to make a phone call. Davie entered through the back door. Before heading to her desk, she ducked into Records to pick up a blue three-ring binder and a set of twenty-six dividers that would make up the guts of Jane Doe's Murder Book. All LAPD Murder Books were organized the same way. Only the victims were unique.

None of the binders on the shelf were new. The city was broke. Some days, detectives were lucky to find an ink cartridge for the printer. Davie selected the binder with the least wear, but the shabbiness of the castoff annoyed her. Jane Doe deserved better.

The air in the detective squad room smelled of a TV dinner rotating in the microwave. Something Italian. Lasagna. Davie heard the radio dispatcher broadcasting a 211-robbery call and saw three Burglary detectives huddled outside the door to the Situation Room, probably calculating how to survive the mountain of Category II cases that landed on their desks each day, the ones with no fingerprints, no witnesses, no forensic evidence, and no hope of ever being solved.

She glanced to her left. Through the glass window of his office, she saw Lt. Ivan Bellows sitting at the conference table, talking to somebody she couldn't see. Davie had only been at Pacific for a month, but it was long enough to know that detectives in the squad room considered Bellows a soulless bean counter who only seemed to care about statistics. He had never worked as a detective. Some thought he didn't understand the mindset. She didn't know him well enough to judge.

As she headed to her desk, her boss, Det-3 Frank Giordano, braced his hands on the arms of his chair and hoisted himself up to greet her. He let out a groan, breathing deeply to control his pain. He had torn the ligaments in his knee during the takedown of a suspect in the Oakwood projects two months ago. Davie figured at his age he should have known better. Chasing bad guys was a young cop's game.

She set her notebook and the binder on her desk. "You okay, sir?"

"Peachy."

Giordano limped toward her, his bulk casting a shadow over her desk. His starched white shirt crinkled as he rested his arm on the cubicle partition. "Solve the case yet, kid?"

"No, sir, but I'm working on it." She filled him in on what she and Vaughn had learned at Hyperion. "I'm hoping Missing Persons can tell me who she is," Davie said.

"Tough case, but you need the experience if you want to be a good Homicide dick. You haven't paid your dues until you've taken at least five or six cases to trial and sweated it out on the witness stand while some defense attorney treats you like *you're* on trial."

She slid the dividers onto the rings of the binder and filed her chrono notes on the Blount interview under Section #1. "Yes, sir."

"And stop calling me sir. Makes me feel old. Call me Frank."

From the shelf above her gray cubicle, she pulled out a list of telephone numbers she had compiled in her years on the job. The movement caused the collapse of several softbound manuals she also kept on the shelf, including two volumes of the California Penal Code, a Homicide Investigation manual, and a dog-eared paperback edition of *The American Heritage Dictionary* she'd had since college. All the information in the manuals could be found online, but she preferred the tactile experience of holding a real book in her hands. She rearranged the manuals and made a mental note to buy a set of bookends.

"Yes, sir."

Giordano leaned toward her and lowered his voice. "You've been here a month, Richards, so by now you should know I don't allow any sissies, babies, pussies, or thin-skinned peeps on my team. If you turn out to be a Lone Ranger with a chip on your shoulder, I'll boot your ass out of Homicide before you have time to join the coffee pool."

She suppressed the urge to return fire. Maybe this was just a belated welcome-aboard speech he gave to all his detectives. If not, this assignment was going to be a long bumpy ride. "Roger that."

"One more thing," he continued. "Robbery-Homicide Division may get all the glory, but divisional detectives are the best in the department because we don't cherry-pick our cases. We investigate every murder that comes our way, and we don't bitch, moan, or expect rock star treatment. How does that sound to you?"

"Like an old *Dragnet* episode, *Frank*."

She immediately regretted the comment. Before coming to the division, she had asked around about Giordano. People who had worked with him told her he was a smart, fair-minded supervisor who backed his detectives. After hearing that, she lobbied Giordano to consider her for a vacant slot in Homicide. When a position opened, he'd called her. Another supervisor might have accepted her because he needed a woman on his table to avoid any affirmative action shit that might roll downhill from headquarters and land on his desk. Not Giordano. Instead, he had assigned her as IO on the Jane Doe case. She needed to prove to him he'd made the right decision.

"I'm glad we understand each other," he said.

As he turned and limped toward the lieutenant's office, she thought she saw Giordano smile, which made her think she had passed some sort of test.

Davie dialed the number for the Missing Persons Unit. A female answered and delivered the greeting verbatim from the LAPD manual: "Good afternoon. Los Angeles Police Department Missing Persons Unit, Detective Kim speaking. May I help you?"

Few detectives used the canned civility, but Davie let it stand without comment. She gave Kim what stats she had on Jane Doe #3, including the braces and the spiderweb tat on her right elbow.

"How long has she been dead?" Kim asked.

"Hard to say."

"You have any idea how many adults are reported missing in this city?"

"I only need to find one of them."

Kim let out a throaty sigh. "How tall is she?"

Davie thought of the woman's long slender bones and calculated based on proportions. "Can't be sure because of the condition of the body, but I'd guess five-seven or -eight."

"I'll look through the reports, but we're short-handed at the moment. I'll have to call you back."

"I'll hold."

Davie waited through several seconds of silence. Finally, Kim said, "Suit yourself." The line went quiet.

The irritated tone in Kim's voice made it clear she felt inconvenienced. Davie wondered if Kim would try to punish her with a long payback hold. Just in case, she made a note of the time. If Kim decided to play games, Davie would have proof of the delay tactic in the Murder Book. She was surprised when Kim returned to the line a few minutes later.

"Here's something interesting. This report was filed two days ago but we just got our copy this morning. I haven't had time to follow up yet. If the chief would kick loose a little overtime pay, maybe we'd get more done around here."

Davie wasn't interested in budget issues. "Who is she?"

She heard papers rustling.

"Name's Anya Nosova. Her boyfriend reported her missing, a guy named Andre Lucien. His California driver's license states he's forty-three. She's nineteen. Big age difference. She's five-eight, one hundred pounds, long blonde hair. She wears braces and has a spiderweb tattoo on her right elbow."

The click of puzzle pieces falling into place was always a good sound. "That's her. That's my victim."

"Lucien claims the two had a fight and she walked out on him. She's from Kiev, Ukraine. Doesn't have any friends or relatives in the area, so when she didn't come back to their apartment, he got worried and contacted police."

"Where does he live?"

"That's the interesting part. He filed the report at Devonshire Division but he lives in 90293. Isn't that zip in Pacific?"

"Yeah, Westchester. Body was found at Hyperion, just a few miles away. Did he call in the report?"

"Nope. He signed the paperwork himself. Odd that he drove over thirty miles to report her missing when he could have gone to a station less than four miles from his apartment."

"Maybe he wanted to delay the investigation," Davie said.

"If he killed her, why report her missing at all?"

"Hedging his bets. The victim must have friends or relatives somewhere. Eventually they'd start asking questions. If her body turned up, he'd look like a concerned boyfriend. If it didn't turn up, he'd still look like a concerned boyfriend."

"Good luck proving that."

"Prisons are filled with criminals who underestimated the police."

If the victim was Anya Nosova, Davie doubted the girl had thrown herself into the sewer over a fight with a boyfriend. Somebody had murdered her. If so, that made Lucien a person of interest in Nosova's death. She needed him to interview him as soon as possible.

Davie grabbed Kim's report as soon as it slid into the fax tray and hurried back to her desk computer. Anya Nosova didn't appear in any of the law enforcement databases, but Andre Lucien had a rap sheet. No domestic battery charges had been filed against him, no violent crimes at all, only a couple of drug-possession arrests with no convictions. She couldn't find any recent employment records, but Lucien owned a BMW and he lived in a decent neighborhood, so he had to have some source of income. Based on his arrest record, she wondered if he was supporting himself by selling drugs.

"Hey, partner," she said. "Let's roll. We have a lead in the Jane Doe case."

Vaughn stood in the gray cubicle across from hers, staring over her shoulder. "Don't look around, Davie. You won't like what you see."

Davie turned to see Det. Spencer Hall strolling out of the lieutenant's office, flashing a boyish grin as he scanned the squad room, searching for an audience. The overhead lights caught strands of premature gray in Hall's blond hair, making them seem translucent. Under his navy V-neck sweater, he'd undone the top button of his white oxford shirt and loosened the knot of the rep tie. The getup made him look like an overgrown Catholic-school boy.

Her gaze glided down his trim frame. He'd lost weight. She'd heard he'd recently reconciled with his wife. The broccoli Nazi must have put him on a diet.

"I wonder what he's doing here," Davie said.

"He's the new man on the Burglary table."

She stared at Vaughn, looking for any indication he was joking. "Pacific Burglary?"

"Sorry. I should have told you. The transfer list for the new DP came out yesterday."

The transfer list outlined changes in duty assignments for each twenty-eight-day deployment period. Hall was joining Pacific in a few days and that meant only one thing for her—trouble.

Six months ago, she and Spencer Hall had been detectives assigned to Southeast Division, she in Burglary, and he in Major Assault Crimes. Hall's partner had been in court, so Davie went with him on a routine follow-up call for one of his domestic battery cases. When they arrived at the house, the suspect was in the bedroom, beating his wife. As Hall pulled the man away from the victim, the man grabbed Hall's gun. Davie killed him to save Hall's life.

After the shooting, the LAPD had prodded, analyzed, and questioned everything from Davie's judgment to her sanity. Hall thought they should stop communicating until the OIS investigation was over. She felt that would show a lack of solidarity but he was adamant, so she agreed.

Then buzz began to spread along the Blue Grapevine that Hall had had the situation under control when Davie panicked. She assumed Hall had started the rumors. Maybe the pressure of the investigation had been too much for him or maybe he felt a need to shore up his reputation as a tough guy who didn't need a woman's protection. She had no proof Hall was behind the trash talk. Some things you could never prove. It was the detective's curse.

She had never defended herself against those lies, at least not in public, deciding instead to fight them with competence. Soon after the shooting, Hall moved to Hollywood station. He hadn't spoken to her since. She had remained in Southeast until her recent transfer to Pacific.

Once Hall arrived at Pacific, avoiding him wouldn't be an option. The squad room was too small for that. Everybody would sense the tension. Everybody would be watching.

"Forget about Hall," she said. "Let's roll. I'll sign out the shop."

Davie opened Giordano's desk drawer and logged out the keys to a dual-purpose Crown Victoria. The ride was a standard police sedan but in case they got into trouble, it was also equipped with lights and a siren.

Vaughn winked. "Like I said before, partner, you're a machine."

He was wrong. She wasn't a machine, but she had worked too hard to let Spencer Hall destroy her career. She would confront him before he got to the division. She just had to find the right time.

17

3

IT WAS TUESDAY MORNING and Malcolm Harrington stood in his sixth floor office at Figueroa Plaza in downtown L.A. surrounded by the detritus of a dead man's life. He brushed a speck of lint from the sleeve of his custom-made suit and glanced out the window to the concrete below. The view was dismal compared to the panorama of Santa Monica Bay from his former deep-carpet law office in Century City, but Harrington was content.

Three days ago, his photograph had appeared on the front page of the *Los Angeles Times*, accepting a handshake from Mayor Lloyd Gossett and the job of Inspector General of the Los Angeles Police Commission. He had replaced the former IG, who died in a scuba diving accident. The man had gone in the water alone, a miscalculation that proved fatal. Unfortunate as his death was, it had provided Harrington with the opportunity of a lifetime, so he felt a measure of gratitude to the man.

A tentative tap on the door interrupted his musings. His new assistant, Maggie Perez, stepped into the room holding two empty boxes and a roll of packing tape. She was attractive but not beautiful, from the X generation or perhaps a millennial. He could never remember what came after Baby Boomers, his own generation. The skirt of Perez's business suit was too short and the jacket too tight for his taste. Nonetheless, the girl seemed smart and eager to please. He'd wait a few days before counseling her about professional office attire.

"Sorry to bother you," she said. "I need to remove some things from your desk."

Perez had an annoying habit of ending her sentences on a high note, like she was asking a question. That, too, had to change.

He motioned her inside. "I've already emptied some of the clutter. It's in the trash can."

Perez seemed confused for a moment and then reached into the wastebasket and retrieved an abalone shell filled with paperclips and a photograph of a model-thin blonde woman with three tow-headed children. She gently placed both into one of the boxes.

"There are some files you need to look at," she said. "There was no time to sign them before he—" Her voice rose to high C and then broke off. "You might want to review them while I'm packing, in case you have any questions."

Harrington checked his Patek Philippe watch, a gift to himself after his first million-dollar jury award as a civil litigator. He had a meeting at noon, but there was enough time to review the files.

"Fine," he said. "Bring them in."

Perez left the room and returned shortly with a stack of file folders, which she separated into two piles on his desk. She pointed to the smaller stack. "These cases are closed. They just need your signature. The others ... well, you'll see from my notes."

He glanced at the closed files, hoping to dispense with them before the day was out. As he read the labels, he saw a familiar name on an officer-involved shooting case—Davina Richards.

Davina, Davie for short. He was surprised to learn that she had become an LAPD detective just like her old man but not surprised that she was in trouble with the department. When Harrington last saw her fifteen years ago she'd been a teenager, but he hadn't forgotten that cloud of red hair and those green eyes, shooting death darts at him from the bench behind the defense table in a courtroom in downtown L.A.

"Why is the Richards case in the closed pile?" he asked.

"The LAPD ruled the shooting was within policy. The Police Commission agreed. You just need to sign off on it and I'll do the rest."

"I'm not going to rubber-stamp someone else's decision. I have the final say now."

Perez stared at the folders to hide her discomfort. "Of course. It's your call. Are you familiar with the case?"

"No, are you?"

"Somewhat." She picked up the file and opened it to refresh her memory. "Richards was a Burglary detective. Hall worked Major Assault Crimes. They were on a routine follow-up call on a domestic violence case. When Hall entered the house, he found Abel Hurtado beating up his—"

Harrington felt the hair stiffen on the back of his neck. "Excuse me? Are you saying Detective Richards wasn't assigned to MAC?"

Perez ran her finger down the page. "The report says she was assigned to Burglary."

"Then why was she with Hall?"

Perez looked up. "There was only one other MAC detective on duty that day, Hall's partner, but he'd been subpoenaed to testify in court. There was nobody else available, so Detective Richards volunteered to go on the call. Why? Is it important?"

"Maybe. I knew her father, William Richards. I tried a case against him and the LAPD years ago in civil court."

Perez returned the file to the desk. "Her dad's a cop too?"

Harrington stared at her without responding.

"Sorry," she continued. "My mother always tells me I'm too nosy."

Perez's gaze was direct and unflinching. She didn't look sorry; she looked ambitious, a good quality in an employee as long as it was paired with loyalty. Only time would tell if she had either trait.

Harrington held up his hand to stop any further apology. "You work for a man whose job it is to ask questions. My history with William Richards is no secret. Fifteen years ago, he worked as a gang detective. During a drug bust, he shot a sixteen-year-old named Daniel Luna and left him permanently confined to a wheelchair. Richards claimed the boy reached inside his waistband for a weapon, but no weapon was found. The LAPD brass ruled the shooting was within policy."

"You disagreed?"

"I believe the LAPD ignored evidence against Richards because Daniel was a gang member and a known drug dealer."

Harrington had taken the case pro bono because Daniel's mother, Maria Luna, begged for his help. All these years later, he still remembered her perfect caramel skin and the sheen of her thick black hair cascading down her back. The way she looked at him in court—adoration bordering on hero worship—unleashed a chorus of hosannas that made the Mormon Tabernacle choir seem like humming off key in the shower.

Perez opened a nearby file drawer and pulled out a box of Godiva chocolates. "Yours?"

Harrington had just turned sixty-one, but he prided himself on keeping fit. He leaned back in the chair with his hands behind his head, exposing a stomach flat from running and lifting weights. "Do I look like a man who indulges in sweets?"

Perez shrugged and put the chocolates in the box. "Do you know Davina Richards?"

"Only from seeing her in court every day. She was a piece of work."

"What happened with the case?"

"William Richards took the stand and claimed he was innocent. The jury believed him. They decided neither the LAPD nor Richards was liable for Luna's injuries."

Perez had filled one box with her former boss's property and began taping it shut. "Must have been disappointing."

That's a gross understatement, he thought. For a long time after the trial, the injustice of the verdict burned Harrington's stomach like molten lava. He began soliciting clients who had been wronged by the police, vowing to never lose another righteous case. Over the years, he had filed numerous lawsuits against the LAPD. His supporters called him a watchdog. Detractors called him a zealot. He thought of himself as the conscience of cops who didn't have one of their own.

"I believe Richards was testilying—perjuring himself on the witness stand."

Harrington remembered the look on Davie Richards's face when the verdict was announced. It was a combination of relief and anger. Understandable. She was a teenager supporting her father. He had almost felt compassion toward her until she shot him a hostile stare as he followed Maria Luna out of the courtroom. He couldn't be sure, but he thought he heard her mumble the word *asshole*. He shouldn't have let it bother him, but he had just watched Maria's adoration for him crumble and in his memory, Davie Richards's *asshole* had turned to *loser*, a word that stung.

"Do you think the daughter could be lying about why she shot Mr. Hurtado?"

"Anything's possible. Even back then, she was a hothead who had no respect for authority."

"Whatever happened to William Richards?"

"The LAPD pressured him to resign, but that was no comfort to Daniel's mother. Her son was still a paraplegic with no medical insurance and no future."

Perez lifted the framed law degree from a hook on the wall and placed it in the remaining box. "What are you going to do?"

The position of IG had been created because of the LAPD's history of corruption and abuse of power. Harrington now had God-like power over all police records and personnel to aid any investigation into police misconduct. With one telephone call he could have anything he needed to put Davie Richards under the microscope.

"I'm going to take a fresh look at the investigation."

Harrington didn't have to read the reports to know he was going to reopen the case. Maybe the shooting had been within policy, but he had to know for sure. Davie Richards's old man was a dirty cop who'd gotten away with attempted murder. If his daughter's OIS case didn't hold up to scrutiny, he would use the full power of his office to make sure she ended up behind bars.

But before he did anything, he was obligated to inform the Chief of Police of his plans. He didn't anticipate a warm reception. Chief Juno defended his troops like a gung-ho general.

Harrington gestured toward the boxes. "Save the packing for later. I need to make a call."

4

DAVIE MANEUVERED THE CROWN Victoria through the crush of traffic on Manchester Boulevard, straining to read the street numbers. She had forgotten her dark glasses, and rays from the afternoon sun pierced the windshield, cutting into her eyes like shards of glass.

Vaughn looked up from the missing person report and glanced out the window. "Pull over. That's Lucien's place over there."

Davie a saw a three-story apartment building with a beige stucco exterior, a flat roof, and balconies that were barely long enough for a napping St. Bernard. The place had as much appeal as bad wine in a plastic glass.

"Let's park on the side street," she said. "If Lucien sees a police ride pull up in front of his place, he might get hinky." She pressed the transmit button on her Rover handheld radio. "Fourteen William sixty-six. Code six at five-eight-two-three Manchester Boulevard."

"Roger, fourteen William sixty-six," the dispatcher said, repeating the relevant information.

Davie glanced at her watch. It was twelve fifteen. Department regulations required her to call in a Code 6 whenever she left the car for a field investigation, especially when it was with a possible suspect in a homicide case. She had an hour to let the dispatcher know she was safe. No call and she might get a testy reminder, maybe two. No response after that, the dispatcher would call in the cavalry. Davie couldn't risk Armageddon over a missed radio call.

As she approached Andre Lucien's ground-floor unit, she motioned Vaughn to move behind a bush to the side of the door where he could watch unobserved. If anything went wrong, he would be out of the line of fire and ready to react.

While her partner scanned the area for potential trouble, Davie pressed her shoulder to the wall near the door with her hand poised on her gun. Andre Lucien might not pose a threat, but only Superman could see through a closed door. She pounded her fist on the wood. There was no response. She knocked again, louder this time.

"Los Angeles Police Department. Open the door. We'd like to talk to you."

She stood near the door listening but heard no sounds coming from inside the apartment.

"Dude's not home," Vaughn said.

Davie waited a moment longer, just to be sure, before clearing Code 6 with dispatch. "Let's door-knock the manager," she said to Vaughn.

According to the mailbox tags in the apartment's lobby, the manager's name was John Bell. He occupied the second-floor unit at the opposite end of the building from Lucien's place.

Bell answered the door in a plaid flannel bathrobe and a Dodgers baseball cap but not much else if his hairy legs and bare feet were any indicator. Davie guessed he was around fifty, wearing an affable smile, and a crumpled mantle of defeat. She introduced herself and told him she had some questions about Anya Nosova.

"Andre told me she didn't come home last Saturday. I hope she's okay."

Davie wanted to find out what Bell knew before telling him Anya was dead. "We have some promising leads."

Bell gestured them inside. "Cool. Lay 'em on me."

Davie stepped over the threshold into a small living room separated from the kitchen by a half wall. A black leather recliner, an end table, and a love seat formed a neat L. In one corner of the room, a stack of what looked like movie scripts bundled together with brass-colored brackets formed a column nearly six feet high. Books with titles like *How to Create Compelling Characters* and *The Screenwriters Handbook* were strewn across the end table. Hundreds of multicolored three-by-five cards covered the kitchen counter and the beige carpet. Others were pinned to the walls next to photographs of people, which appeared to have been ripped from magazines. The collage reminded Davie of a stalker collecting information on his latest obsession.

"What's that on the walls?" she asked.

"Story ideas and pictures of my characters. I got the idea from one of my screenwriting books. It helps me stay organized."

Bell scooped up a fan of cards from the love seat's cushions and gestured for Davie to sit. Vaughn remained standing but Bell didn't seem to notice. He pointed toward an open laptop computer on a footstool in front of the chair.

"I'm installing a new operating system, but don't worry, I can talk and download at the same time."

Davie glanced around the room. "Are you alone?"

He winked. "Not anymore." He slumped into the chair, shifting his baseball cap so the bill was backwards, as if he thought that made him look sexy. Davie ignored the gesture. Vaughn moved down the hallway, looking into each room to make sure Bell wasn't lying about being alone.

Davie kept her expression neutral as she filled out a Field Interview card with information Bell provided, including his height, weight, date of birth, and California driver's license number. He told her he was a screenwriter who had managed the apartment complex for the past seven years. When she asked if he had any tattoos or distinguishing marks, he said he had a mole on his ass. She declined his invitation to verify in the field.

"What's the plate number on your vehicle?" she asked.

"Don't have one. Everything is within walking distance. If I need wheels, I borrow my buddy's Olds. It's one of the last ones they made, and it's a honey. I'd be happy to take you for a spin sometime."

"Does your buddy have a name?"

Bell glanced at his computer screen, perhaps searching for the answer to her question. "Jerry Forrester."

"You have a contact number for Mr. Forrester?"

Bell rattled it off but paused before continuing. "It's a coincidence you showing up today, because I'm writing a spec script about an alcoholic detective who's afraid of guns. Do you people really call each other dicks, or did some pulp fiction writer make that up? Just curious because I used it in the script, and I don't want a real detective like yourself rolling her eyes, especially when they're as beautiful as yours."

Davie shifted her gaze to Vaughn who had been peering into a room off the hallway. He had obviously heard Bell's comment because he slapped his palm to his forehead.

"Don't worry," she said. "We call each other dicks all the time."

Vaughn used his middle finger to scratch an imaginary itch on his cheek to indicate what he thought of her attempt at humor before moving on to clear another room.

Bell picked up a bowl of popcorn from the floor and thrust it toward her. "Want some? It's organic."

"No thanks. How long has Andre Lucien lived in the building?"

Bell grabbed a fist full of kernels and stuffed them into his mouth. "A couple of years. Anya moved in about three or four months ago." He swallowed and nodded his head toward her gun. "So, how do you like your Glock?"

"It's a Smith & Wesson. Forty-five."

Bell looked disappointed. "Really? Somebody told me the LAPD issued Glocks."

"Not anymore," she said. "The official duty weapon is a Smith & Wesson M&P."

Bell hesitated, still thinking about Glocks, no doubt. Davie saw Vaughn in the hallway, walking toward her. He gave her a thumbs-up sign, signaling he had cleared the apartment.

"Do you have a photo of Ms. Nosova?" Vaughn said.

Bell glanced over his shoulder. He looked surprised, as if he had been so focused on Davie that he had forgotten Vaughn was in the apartment.

"A while back I took some snapshots so she could send one to her dad. She's an only child and he missed her a lot. I think I printed an extra copy."

"Do you have her dad's contact information?" Davie asked.

"He lives in Ukraine. Her mother lives in Moscow. They're divorced. Andre must have the phone numbers."

"Does Anya have a cell phone?"

"Sure." Davie wrote down the number, noting that Bell recited it from memory.

Bell walked to a card table in the kitchen that bowed under the weight of stacks of paper. "You guys have a BOLO out for Anya? Or is it called an APB?"

"For now," Vaughn said, "all we have is a missing person report."

Bell sorted through the papers on the table until he found the photo. He walked back into the living room and handed it to Davie. The surface of the paper was greasy with a substance that smelled like butter.

Davie stared at the image of a young woman squinting against the sun. A strand of windblown blonde hair was caught in her lip gloss. Matchstick arms poked out of a tank top. Her features were symmetrical and flawless, but the wariness in her eyes confirmed that beauty alone did not always make for a happy life. Her elbow wasn't in the picture, so Davie couldn't tell if it was inked with a spiderweb tattoo. She wanted to believe Anya Nosova was somewhere safe and happy, but science would almost certainly prove otherwise. At least now there was a face to the investigation.

"Is this the only picture you have of her?" Davie asked.

Bell hesitated. "No, but that's the best one. Sometimes it takes a few shots before you get it right."

"Where are the others?"

"I deleted them. Digital, you know." Bell paused. "She's almost as pretty as you are."

Davie glanced up from the photo, unsure of how long she'd been trapped in her thoughts. "Pardon?"

"Anya. She's a looker. I told her she should get an agent, do some film work. She has the bones. She told me she came to the US to be a model, but she didn't like it. Her mom was a prima ballerina with the Bolshoi. Anya traveled all over the world with the company to watch her mom perform, so she'd had enough of celebrity."

Vaughn took the photo from Davie's hand but remained standing. "Who did Anya model for?"

"She never said."

"She's skinny," Vaughn went on. "Does she have an eating disorder? A drug habit?"

Bell shrugged. "We all have our demons."

Vaughn's tone sharpened. "Which one did *she* have, Mr. Bell?"

"Neither that I know of."

"Why did she ask you to take her photo instead of Mr. Lucien?" Davie asked.

"I don't know. Maybe Andre didn't have a camera."

"Or maybe the photos were your idea because you had a thing for her," Davie said.

Bell's facial muscles slackened. "Why would you say that?"

She changed the subject, hoping to throw him off balance. "How would you describe Mr. Lucien's and Ms. Nosova's relationship?"

"He didn't treat her right. They argued a lot. He was always pushing her to get pregnant but she didn't want to have a baby outside of marriage. Money was an issue too."

"Is Mr. Lucien employed?"

"I don't know where Andre gets his scratch. He pays the rent on time. The rest is none of my business."

Bell's computer dinged. He leaned over and pressed something on the keyboard. "This shouldn't be taking so long." He was still looking at the screen so Davie figured he was talking about the download, not the interview.

"Did she have any friends in the area other than Mr. Lucien?" Davie asked.

"None that I know about."

Vaughn stood near the door scrutinizing Bell. "When was the last time you saw Ms. Nosova?"

Bell pressed another key and the screen flashed shades of purple and blue, like it had suffered a direct hit from a meteor. Davie sat back and waited.

"Around eight o'clock last Saturday night. I hit a wall with my writing, so I walked to the grocery store to buy a bottle of Glenfiddich. That's the drink of choice for the dick in my script. Research, you know. I got back just as Anya was getting into a taxi. She looked like she was dressed for a night of clubbing."

"Do you remember the name of the cab company?" Davie said.

He thought for a moment. "Sorry. It was dark outside. I didn't see the name. Couldn't even tell what color the car was."

"Did you notice if she came back to the apartment that night?" Vaughn said.

"Huh-uh. I had a couple of drinks and went to bed. Even without the booze I sleep like the dead."

"Did you ever have any problems with Mr. Lucien?" she said.

Bell leaned back in the chair. "Depends what you mean by *problems*."

"It means anything you want it to mean."

"I don't want you to think I'm a whiner."

"I'd never think that, Mr. Bell."

He smiled. "Okay. Cool. So here's the deal. Andre has visitors that come to the apartment at all hours of the day and night. It's annoying because they park in my space right in front of the No Parking sign. I've complained to him a million times that I need that space for official apartment visitors but nothing changes." Bell leaned toward Davie with an earnest look on his face. "You're an expert on the law. Isn't that harassment? Maybe we could have dinner some night and talk about my options."

Davie ignored the lame come-on. "What kind of cars?"

He sighed, frustrated that his Don Juan routine wasn't scoring points. "Expensive ones. BMW. Mercedes. You name it. Anyway, it happened again last Saturday night. When I got back from the market there was a black Lexus SUV parked in my space. I was about to use my cell to call a tow truck when some guy walked out of Andre's apartment and got into the driver's seat."

"Who left first?" Davie asked. "The driver or Ms. Nosova?"

Bell closed the lid of his laptop. "Anya."

"So you think the Lexus driver was in the apartment with Anya before she got into the cab?"

"He had to be."

"Did you notice which direction he took when he drove away?"

Bell seemed confused by all her rapid-fire questions. "Same direction as the cab."

"Could you identify the driver from a photo lineup?"

Bell told her the man was of medium height with a thin build but added, "I didn't see his face, only his hair. It was shoulder-length. Sort of golden blond. Curly."

"Did you notice the license plate number?"

"Actually, I wrote it down—you know, for the tow truck driver." Bell gazed at Davie. "Hey, I made you smile. That must be worth at least a coffee date."

5

AS SOON AS DAVIE and Vaughn returned to the station, her partner began writing a search warrant for Anya Nosova's cell phone records. The telephone company didn't have to return the warrant for ten days, but homicides were usually given priority. She hoped to have the information back by the following day.

"Bell is weird," Vaughn said over the partition wall. "All that shit pasted on his walls."

"He definitely has a thing for colored note cards and cop trivia."

"And why did it take him so long to tell us about the last time he saw Nosova?" Vaughn said. "I think he had a thing for her. Maybe he wanted to take it to the next level and when she told him to take a hike, he killed her."

"Maybe."

"He seemed to have a thing for you too."

"He's worth looking at," she said, "but I'm guessing he's just a horny screenwriter who needs to get a life."

While Vaughn drove to court to find a judge to sign the warrant, Davie ran a criminal records search on John Bell. His name popped up several times—but as a victim, not a suspect. He had filed half a dozen 459-burglary reports for break-ins at the apartment's swimming pool cabana and also at his personal storage unit. Other than that, his record was clean. She found that Bell had a driver's license and confirmed he had no vehicle registered in his name.

At nine that night, eleven hours after she had closed the Hyperion crime scene, Davie was still at her desk in the squad room. Earlier in the day she had called every cab company on the Westside and finally found the cabbie that picked up Anya the night she disappeared. All he could tell Davie was that he had dropped her off at a street corner in Hollywood but he had no idea where she'd gone after that.

For the past several hours, Davie had focused on the license plate number Bell had scrawled across one of his three-by-five cards. When she didn't get a hit on the first try, she realized he had made a mistake somewhere in the alphanumeric combination. She started over, substituting the letter *T* from Bell's version for a *J* and then an *I* and so on. She was beginning to worry she would have to repeat the process for every letter and number on the seven-digit plate, because no matter how many ways she manipulated the data, she could not locate the registered owner of the black Lexus SUV that had been parked near Anya Nosova's apartment the night she disappeared. The effort had made her vision blurry and her fingers stiff from pressing the computer keys.

Dinner had consisted of a bag of M&Ms from a vending machine and a cup of bitter coffee she found reducing to sludge on the warmer. Vaughn had left hours before. Except for two blue-suits watching a high-speed freeway chase on the squad room television set and a night detective auditing a stack of arrest packages, she was alone.

Heavy footsteps fractured her concentration. She glanced over her shoulder and saw Detective Giordano lumber through the door of the squad room, rubbing his hands, warming them from the cold.

"What are you doing here so late?" she said.

"A good Homicide detective has no life." He removed his overcoat and slung it across a chair. "I just left Sergeant White's retirement party. Bunch of maudlin shit. It was pitiful. Reminded me of a funeral."

Giordano was on the verge of retirement and Davie sensed he was not looking forward to his last end of watch.

"How many days before you pull the plug?"

"Ninety or so. I don't keep track." Giordano glanced around the room. "Where's your partner?"

"He went home to catch some Zs."

"When did he leave?"

"Around sixteen-hundred hours."

Giordano glanced at his watch. "That was five hours ago. Not even a two-year-old needs that much sleep."

She didn't like having to defend somebody else's work ethic, but Vaughn was her partner, so she cut him some slack. "He signed in at oh-dark-thirty this morning. He'll be back in the morning."

"He damn well better be." Giordano lowered himself into a chair across from her and stretched out his bum knee. "Any leads in the Nosova case?"

"The boyfriend wasn't home and so far he isn't answering his phone. I'll keep trying."

Giordano leaned back in the chair, which groaned against his weight. "What else?"

"I found the cabbie who picked up Nosova last Saturday night, but it wasn't easy."

"Nobody said it would be."

"He claims he dropped her off at the corner of Santa Monica and Las Palmas in Hollywood but he didn't pay attention to where she went after that. Most of the businesses in the area are closed now. I'll canvass the neighborhood tomorrow."

"Anything else?"

"The apartment manager saw a white male leaving the victim's apartment Saturday night. He wrote down the license plate number of the guy's SUV, but it's no good."

Giordano glanced at her computer screen and frowned. "You can always send the information to DMV headquarters in Sacto and wait till some computer nerd sends back a phone book–sized list of possible license numbers, but it'll take you until the next millennium to check it out."

"I don't have time for Sacramento," she said. "There has to be a smarter way to do this."

"Sometimes lucky is better than smart." After a period of silence, he continued. "So how's it going for you at the division? Any problems?"

Davie interpreted his concerned tone as an invitation to confess something. She just didn't know what. If he knew she had come to Pacific riding a beef, he also knew those troubles involved Spencer Hall. The department had already ruled her shooting within policy, but the Police Commission hadn't cleared her of wrongdoing. To complicate matters, the mayor had just appointed a new Inspector General of the Police Commission, a man with an old grudge against her father. She worried he might reopen her OIS case, which could put her job in jeopardy. She appreciated Giordano's concern but he wasn't allowed to ask about the details, and she wasn't supposed to volunteer information until the case had been fully adjudicated.

"Things are fine," she said.

Giordano leaned on the workstation desk for support and stood. "Just so you know, I support my peeps even when they screw up. Anybody needs to talk, they can call me twenty-four/seven."

He put on his coat and limped toward the squad room door. Before stepping into the hallway, he turned toward her. "Good work today, kid. Congratulations." Without waiting for a reply, he ambled toward the back door.

Davie heard the patrol officers groan and then laugh. She glanced at the TV and saw the suspect's car roll over and skid into the center divider like an overturned turtle. The man climbed out of the driver's-side window and ran down the carpool lane followed by at least twenty black-and-white patrol cars. Davie wanted to tell the guy, *When the hole gets too deep, stop digging.*

She continued entering more combinations into the license plate database until the characters on the screen seemed to float like letters in a bowl of alphabet soup. She wondered if her vision would ever recover.

Hinges creaked as she leaned back in her chair. She closed her eyes and thought about the driver of that SUV. He obviously didn't believe the rules applied to him. Not only did he ignore the No Parking sign but he also left his vehicle unattended for at least half an hour, according to Bell, as if any consequences were worth the risk. In her experience, older people were less likely to flaunt laws, so she guessed the driver was younger than sixty, especially since Bell described his hair as long and blond.

Bell had also told her there was a constant stream of people driving expensive cars who had visited Andre Lucien's apartment. The Lexus might have been in the neighborhood before that night. She checked for parking citations, but no massaging of the information produced results.

Fighting exhaustion, she stepped outside, hoping the cold night air would revive her. At the far side of the parking lot, the garage was dark. The mechanics had gone home hours ago. Her gaze swept the area to the two rows of detective cars on her left. Directly below the overhead light was a Crown Victoria. She remembered the first time she used the car. The tag on the keys identified it as green. After spending fifteen minutes looking for the ride and passing it multiple times, she realized the green was so dark the car looked black, even in daylight. Maybe Bell had misjudged the color of the SUV. He told her it was so dark that night, he couldn't tell the color of the taxi that had picked up Anya Nosova.

She jogged inside to her computer and opened the vehicle description database. A partial plate number was enough information to conduct a search, so she entered the first two letters from Bell's three-by-five card into the plate sequence, followed by a series of hyphens, representing unknown data. The known sex of the driver was male. Davie estimated the age range as 25 to 55. She entered the LAPD reporting district assigned to Bell's address, and the make of the SUV. Bell had been sure the Lexus was new, so she also entered the age of the vehicle as the current year. Instead of black, she entered the color as green. The search netted nothing. She repeated the process, substituting any primary color that might have a dark hue until she got to blue. A moment later, she got a hit.

She studied the plate number and saw where Bell had gotten it wrong. He had recorded one of the numbers as a six instead of a nine. Before she could celebrate her success, she entered the plate number in the DMV database and waited until the name of the registered owner appeared.

Davie stared at the screen. Her sense of unease had turned the M&Ms and coffee in her stomach into battery acid. She searched the Internet for the telephone number she needed. It wasn't hard to find. She punched in the numbers on her desk phone keypad and left a message she knew nobody would return. She paused to consider her next move.

Then she grabbed the Jetta keys and hurried toward the back door. Traffic should be light at this late hour; it wouldn't take long to get where she had to go.

6

TEN MINUTES LATER DAVIE stepped out of the Jetta onto the small parking lot next to the Lucky Duck bar, inhaling the aroma of greasy fried tortillas from the Mexican restaurant across the street. She drew her suit jacket around her neck to block the chilly air, trying but failing to stave off the anxiety she had carried with her from the station.

The Duck sat on not-quite-prime real estate in a section of Culver City she thought of as "hip adjacent." The building was a windowless box, its dark wood exterior bathed in white light from the neon sign above the door.

Three teenaged girls sauntered along the sidewalk, arm in arm, all wearing black skinny jeans and gray hoodies—a trio of pigeons huddled against the wind. They were singing and laughing. Davie thought back to her teenage years but could not recall ever feeling that carefree. There had been too much drama back then with her father's legal troubles, her mother's affair, the divorce, her subsequent remarriage, and her brother's betrayal, which had shattered Davie's trust in him. At times, Davie felt as if the entire weight of preserving the family had rested on her shoulders and she had failed in her duty.

Rusty hinges groaned as she nudged open the door with her shoulder. Inside, cool air blunted the odor of spilled beer and ancient dust. As she crossed the threshold, she glanced at the familiar sign near the front door: *Was a woman who led me down the road to drink. I never wrote to thank her.* One of the regulars, a woman in her fifties with a weathered face and lowered expectations, was playing pool in the adjacent room with three men who looked like insurance agents out for a night of slumming.

The woman waved her stick at Davie. "Hey, D-Dogg. What's shakin'?"

"Not much, Suzanne. What's up with you?"

"Just showing these tadpoles who's got the balls in this place." Suzanne laughed as her stick cracked against the cue ball, sending red number three slamming into the side pocket.

On the far side of the room, Davie saw a lone man perched on a stool at the bar. He was wearing a Metro tux: police boots, a white T-shirt, and the black uniform pants worn by the LAPD's elite Metro unit. His uniform shirt and weapon were probably stowed in the trunk of his car, but he had come into the bar still wearing his superior attitude. Davie could see the outline of his abdominal muscles through the tight T-shirt. The guy was ripped and he wanted everyone to know it.

Her father stood behind the bar. A neon Budweiser sign on the wall cast a fitful shadow on the purple XXL Lakers jersey stretched across his broad back. Most of the world called him William Richards. She called him Bear and had since she was a child, after listening to him read her the story of Goldilocks. He didn't seem to mind the name, so it stuck.

Bear had a towel draped over his shoulder. One of his hands cradled a dainty glass. The other held a pitcher of frothy liquid that looked like a Pink Lady, probably for Suzanne, who still appreciated a classic drink now and then.

He looked up and nodded. "Hey, Ace. Be right with you."

Davie slid onto a stool at the end of the bar as far away from Metro Tux as possible. She waited on the stool's cracked leather cushion as her father ambled to the pool table and handed Suzanne the drink.

"Thanks, Doll," Suzanne said. "Put it on my tab?"

"Like always, Suzie-Q."

Back behind the bar, he turned to Davie. "What can I get you?"

"*Agua libre* on the rocks."

"Coming up," he said, dispensing ice and water into a highball glass. "This one's on the house. The next one comes out of your allowance."

Davie scanned the room. "Where's PJ?"

"In the can putting on her game face. She could wipe out the national debt with the money she spends on cosmetics."

Peggy June Jordan was one of the Lucky Duck's bartenders. She had worked behind the bar long before her father bought the place and was infamous for the cranky, profane way she had of slicing through trouble with a flick of her sharp tongue. Davie suspected Peggy June had a crush on her dad and secretly hoped she would corner him in the beer cooler one day and make her feelings known. After all these years, she figured that was unlikely to happen.

"You look tired," he said. "Job getting you down?"

"I love my job. You know that."

"Like I told you before, Ace—you can love the job, but the job will never love you."

She had heard that old saw a million times before and she didn't want to hear to again tonight. He usually followed that bromide with a lecture about getting a life and settling down. If there was a formula for figuring that out, he hadn't perfected it.

"I just stopped by to pick your brain," she said.

"Not much left of it, but what I got is yours."

At the far end of the bar, Metro Tux picked at the label on his bottle of Miller Genuine Draft. The din in the place would likely scramble their conversation, but nonetheless she kept her voice low. "A witness gave me a license plate number for a Lexus SUV. He wrote it down wrong. I couldn't match it to a vehicle."

Her father dipped a cocktail shaker into the bar sink and swished it around in the soapy water. "Lot of those rigs out there. Keep trying."

"I did. The vehicle belongs to Ray Anthony Falcon."

Bear pulled the bar towel from his shoulder and wiped the shaker. "That doper movie star?"

Falcon was an A-list actor known for his big talent and even bigger drug habit. He had been in and out of celebrity rehab centers at least three times in the past several years.

"He's high profile. I don't want to screw up the interview."

"You're not even sure it's him. I'd guess lots of people have access to his cars."

"The witness estimated the guy's height and weight. It matched information on Falcon's driver's license. He also said the driver had shoulder-length curly blond hair. Falcon's photo showed his hair as brown, but he's an actor. His hair must change every time he's cast in a new role."

"What did this wit supposedly see him do?"

Davie glanced around to make sure there was no one within earshot. "He saw the guy leaving the apartment of a suspected drug dealer whose girlfriend just turned up dead."

"Why am I not surprised?"

Metro Tux signaled for another MGD. Her father pulled a bottle from the refrigerator and slid it down the bar toward him. Then he washed and dried wine glasses until he had six of them lined up on the back counter like soldiers guarding some lonely outpost.

"I left a message for his talent agent, but I doubt Falcon will get it. I was hoping you could give me advice about how to approach him."

He grabbed the pitcher and dipped it in the water. "If he gets a whiff you want to talk to him, especially about drugs, he'll tell you to go pound sand, or more likely, his lawyer will do it for him."

"A woman is dead."

"Even more reason to kiss off an interview with the cops." Her father threw the wet towel in a basket on the floor and pulled a clean one from underneath the counter. "You're smart enough to figure out how to interview a celebrity. Why are you asking me?"

"Once a cop, always a cop."

"So they say," he said as he studied her expression. "There's something else on your mind."

She swirled the ice in her glass. "Malcolm Harrington. The mayor just appointed him IG of the Police Commission."

Davie was fifteen when Harrington sued her father in civil court for negligence in the on-duty shooting of a local gangbanger. The case was bogus; the jury saw that, but even though they ruled Bear was not liable for damages, the department pressured him to retire. After that everybody took sides. A lot of people abandoned Bear, including her mother and brother and several of his so-called friends in the department. Davie had stood by his side throughout the ordeal, but the stress hadn't been easy on either of them.

"I read that in the paper," he said, drying the pitcher. "The mayor will regret his decision."

43

"Maybe, but that still puts Harrington in charge of my shooting case."

"I thought the investigation was closed."

"It was but the former IG died before he signed the papers. It's up to Harrington now. I'm worried. I remember what he did to you."

Her father slammed the pitcher on the bar. "You think I forgot? I think about it every damn day. I risked my life for this city for sixteen years. If it weren't for one cop-hating lawyer named Malcolm Harrington, I'd be collecting my full pension right now instead of working my ass off just to make ends meet."

"I know. I was there. Remember?"

Bear raked his hand through the stubble of his self-inflicted crew cut. "Look, Ace, once he finds out you're my kid and you were involved in a shooting, he'll screw you over just like he did me and nobody from the Big Blue Machine will do shit to help you."

"I'm going to make a few phone calls. See what I can find out."

The clamor of voices had ramped up a couple of notches. Davie heard laughter and the clack of a cue stick slamming a ball across the pool table. She watched her father's face and saw a subtle shift in his expression.

"Just watch your back."

She nodded and slid off the barstool. "Thanks, Bear. I'll do that."

7

JUST AFTER ONE A.M., Davie drove her car through the security gates toward her rented guest cottage in Bel-Air, part of the so-called Platinum Triangle that also included Beverly Hills and Holmby Hills.

At the end of the long driveway she pulled the Camaro into the carport at the back of the house. Gravity propelled her fatigued body out of the car and into a crisp night air filled with the aroma of cedar trees and a silence that only extreme wealth could buy. There was no entrance to the cottage from the back of the house, which she considered a design flaw. Out of habit, she scanned the area before walking around to the arched entryway.

The cottage was 581 square feet, 449 on the main floor and 132 on the upper floor loft, which had twin dormer windows and was accessed by a spiral staircase. There was one bathroom off the bedroom. That may have been inconvenient for guests but so far, none of her friends had complained.

A wood bench sat to the right of the front door near a round table and three chairs positioned on the flagstone patio. She opened the door, which was a wood and wrought iron affair that reminded her of a medieval castle.

Once inside the cottage, she flipped on the Tiffany lamp and dropped her car keys onto the eighteenth-century Chippendale walnut dressing table. A stark watercolor by Andrew Wyeth hung above the table. In it, one leafless windswept tree stood alone in a meadow, its limbs reaching out of the shadows toward a stand of evergreens in the distance, pleading its case. She didn't know much about art, but she understood loneliness and the harsh landscape never failed to draw her in.

Her boots made no sound on the hardwood floors as she walked through the small living room, veering left into her bedroom. She set her notebook on an armchair and placed her gun and badge in the top drawer of the bedside table.

Her father believed Malcolm Harrington would screw her over in some sort of twisted revenge plot, but she had found that people were generally more complex than that. It was possible Harrington had become a decent guy who had forgotten about her family long ago. But until she knew which Malcolm Harrington she was dealing with, she had to remain vigilant.

Tension constricted her muscles. She wouldn't be able to sleep, so she decided to go for a swim. Her pantsuit landed in the laundry basket, barely grazing the rim. The outfit was one of three siblings, all black, all size zero, and all machine washable. Her clothes were among the few items in the house that were hers. Everything else belonged to her landlord, Alexander Camden.

A year ago, Alex had served as an art consultant on one of her cases, shortly after she'd made detective. She'd been working Southeast Division Burglary, investigating a theft from an antiques store. The only item stolen was a rare eighteenth-century French vase, which told Davie the thief had targeted the item. The department's art unit suggested she contact Alex, who had been helpful to them in the past.

Using his client list, she located a collector who had been approached by the thief with an offer to sell the vase. Davie set up an undercover sting, recovered the vase, and arrested a former store employee.

A month later, she called to tell Alex he was being subpoenaed to testify in the case. During the conversation, she mentioned she had to move because her apartment was being converted into a condo. He offered to rent her the guesthouse. It was furnished, which was convenient because she had little furniture of her own and none that was worth keeping. Acquiring things had never been a priority for her.

In the months since she'd moved in, they had developed a symbiotic relationship. She loved to hear about his travels to exotic places in pursuit of art and antiques for his wealthy clients. He liked that a cop lived in his guesthouse, and he kept the rent low to make sure she stayed.

Davie slipped a parka over her swimsuit and made her way through the rose garden along the flagstone path toward the pool. Vincent and Leonardo were barking in the distance, which meant Alex was home. A moment later, she felt two cold noses sniffing her legs and two warm tongues licking the backs of her hands.

"Hey, Leo. Hey, Vinny," she said, ruffling the golden retrievers' coats until the dogs were satiated with the attention and willing to lead her to the edge of the pool. She dipped her toe in the water, knowing that in summer or winter Alex always kept the thermostat fixed at eighty degrees.

Through vapors of steam rising from the water, she saw Alex lying on a chaise longue holding a martini glass and wearing a navy sports jacket, charcoal slacks, and a Burberry plaid scarf knotted around his neck. He had gray hair and claimed he'd earned every one them. His chiseled features reminded her of an aging version of Michelangelo's David.

"Good evening, Davina. Care to join me for a nightcap?"

She had never liked her name, but Alex made it palatable because he spoke it with affection. Her brother, Robbie, had been named after her mother's older brother, who'd died in the Battle of Duc Lap in the early days of the Vietnam War. Her mother had picked the name Davina at random from a book of baby names. It meant "the beloved one." Davie was sure her mother had forgotten the meaning long ago.

"I'll have a Pellegrino," she said.

"I must be clairvoyant." He pointed his martini glass toward a mahogany cart that held an emerald bottle in a champagne bucket. "One day I hope to win you over to a more elegant choice—a dry martini or Scotch. I have a twenty-five-year-old Macallan that will cure anything that ails you."

She twisted off the bottle cap and flopped onto the chair across from him. Vincent rested his head on her foot while Leonardo settled into a futon near the spa.

"You're up late," she said.

"I just got home from a meeting with a difficult client and noticed you weren't back yet."

"Worried?"

"I'm used to your odd hours, but I'm still human."

"What's your client's problem?"

"He's a billionaire but he still wants a Mona Lisa for the price of a velvet Elvis. I've tried to disabuse him of that notion, but he remains immune to logic. I've also been warned he'll try to stiff me on my final bill."

"You don't have to work with him."

Alex sipped his drink. "I'll find some way to accommodate him. He's one of those rich tech entrepreneurs who might recommend me to his equally rich friends. It's in my best interests to make nice. What about you? Are you working a case?"

Davie gave him a few generalities about Anya Nosova, mostly details that would likely appear in the morning newspaper.

"I hope the boyfriend didn't do it," he said. "It's so clichéd."

Davie held the water bottle to her temple to ease her budding headache. "Seventy-five percent of victims are killed by somebody they know."

Alex raised his glass in a toast. "To choosing your friends wisely."

"I'll drink to that."

"I read in the *Times* the mayor appointed a new Inspector General of the Police Commission. Will that delay your OIS case?"

"I don't know. The former IG was ready to close the case, but Malcolm Harrington will decide now and that could be a problem."

She gave Alex the short version of her father's fifteen-year-old troubles with Harrington and Bear's fears that he would cause trouble for her as well.

"Perhaps my rich client can speed things up by buying him off."

"I don't think he's for sale."

Alex studied her over the rim of his glass. "My dear Davina, at the right price, everyone's for sale."

"I wish it were that simple."

"What's happening with that Spencer Hall person? Still spreading nasty rumors about you?"

"Like I said before, I'm not sure he's behind the rumors, Alex. I hope not, because I just found out he's transferring to Pacific."

Alex pushed himself into a sitting position. "Why would the department do that?" The dogs seemed to notice the tension in his voice because they padded over to him for reassurance.

"They wouldn't have unless he requested the transfer."

He petted the dogs until they settled at his feet. "What are you going to do?"

"Talk to him."

Alex retrieved the olive from his glass and dropped it into his mouth. "Be careful. As Voltaire said, 'It is the flash which appears, the thunderbolt will follow.'"

He finished his martini and took the dogs inside the main house for the night. Davie left the unfinished Pellegrino on the cart as she dropped her jacket on the chair and slid into the deep end of the pool.

Since she'd first entered the police academy, she had lived by the credo posted above the gym door: *The more you sweat, the less you bleed.* That was at the forefront of her mind as she sliced the water with her strokes until exhaustion overtook her. She dragged herself from the pool and returned to the guesthouse to shower.

As she lay in bed, she thought about Spencer Hall's transfer to Pacific and Malcolm Harrington's newfound control over her and the impact each might have on her future. Memories from the day of the shooting flashed through her mind in a kaleidoscope of sensory images: The taste of the Cheez-its she'd eaten in the car mixed with the fragrance of gardenia blossoms carried on a sullen summer breeze. The woman screaming from inside the house. The echo of knuckles pounding on the hollow wood door. The smell of sour milk radiating from the T-shirt of the five-year-old girl who had let them into the house. Her mother's face reduced to pulp. Her father's fist, dripping blood onto the flowered bedsheet. Rough leather abrading Davie's finger as she unsnapped the gun from its holster. The deafening explosion. The fog of gunpowder hanging on the stagnant air. The suspect's dilated pupils black as spilled ink. A child's screams casting a pall over everything.

Sometime in the early morning hours she fell into a deep sleep as Voltaire's words clawed at the edge of her dreams.

8

MALCOLM HARRINGTON SAT ON a leather chair in Mayor Lloyd Gossett's office at City Hall, still upset over his telephone conversation the previous day with Chief of Police Chad Juno. He had not expected the chief to be pleased with his decision to reopen the Davie Richards officer-involved shooting case, but he had not anticipated a vitriolic rant either.

Gossett sat at a wood desk the size of an aircraft carrier. Behind him was a painting depicting an abbreviated Los Angeles cityscape that spanned from the ocean to the mountains. The mayor preened as a young Asian woman manicured his fingernails in preparation for a *People* magazine photo shoot later that day.

"Did old Cotton Balls bring up my name?" Gossett said.

Harrington could almost see the waves of bitterness radiating off Gossett's spray-on tan, a hue that made his skin seem more Big Bird yellow than San Tropez bronze.

"Chief Juno understands you and I are friends. His term is up next fall and he thinks you're pressuring me to reopen the Richards case to make him look bad."

"I'd love to fire Juno," Gossett said, "but I'm up for reelection. I can't afford more enemies."

"If things go my way, this investigation could be the *pièce de résistance* of your campaign."

"What makes you think anybody cares?" Gossett asked in a tone that was poised and self-assured. "Last year the city slashed Juno's budget by twenty percent. He still cut homicides in half. The city council thinks he's Kobe, Cesar Chavez, and the Pope all rolled into one."

The manicurist lifted Gossett's soapy hand from the dish and patted it dry. Harrington didn't like the idea of having her as a witness to this conversation, but he was lucky to have engineered an appointment with Gossett on such short notice. The mayor's executive assistant had dragged him through hell until Gossett interceded on his behalf. Friendship had its benefits.

"Juno claims to be a reformer," Harrington said. "He'll go along with my investigation once he knows you've endorsed it. If he's really on the side of justice, he'll understand it's the right thing to do for the department and the city."

Gossett's ramrod-straight torso seemed staked to the chair. "Juno's no reformer; he's an enabler. His record of disciplining officers is pathetic at best. I appointed you to keep him in check. He knows that and he's not happy about it."

The manicurist began sweeping a file across Gossett's nails as if she were wielding a saw. The *skritch-skritch-skritch* sound was making Harrington testy.

"I don't want to be left swinging in the wind," Harrington said. "I need to know I have your support."

Gossett inspected his squared-off fingernails. "Is Davie Richards a rogue cop? Is the department covering it up? *Those* things would get me excited."

The mayor's resistance was hiking Harrington's blood pressure. "Her old man was dirty. Who knows what I might uncover about her when I start digging?"

The manicurist squeezed oil from a bottle onto the mayor's cuticles, releasing the syrupy scent of almonds into the still air. Gossett seemed to be in a trance with his eyes closed.

"A jury ruled William Richards was not liable for Daniel Luna's injuries," Gossett said. "And unlike you, they weren't the slightest bit upset that a beautiful woman like Maria Luna was going to spend the rest of her life in some dingy apartment with ten relatives, listening to her son bitch about his fate."

Harrington felt his face flush with anger. "Politics has made you timid, Lloyd. Richards shot an unarmed teenager and lied about it under oath. He should have been prosecuted for attempted murder. Instead, he walked away with no consequences."

"He lost his job."

"A small nod to justice."

The manicurist struggled to open a jar of buffing powder. Gossett sensed the movement and opened his eyes. He took the vessel from her hand and gave the cap a violent twist before returning it to the table.

"Your investigation has to be meticulous," he said. "I don't want anybody thinking I'm out to get the Richards family. If you can't make a slam-dunk case against this woman, you will quietly drop the whole thing. Understood?"

Righteous indignation churned Harrington's gut as he stared at the US and California flags, standing like silent sentinels behind Gossett's desk.

"Every investigation I undertake is meticulous."

"Be cool, Malcolm. You made big bucks suing the LAPD. The brothers in South Central may dig you sticking it to the Man, but my constituents on the Westside think you're out to destroy the department. They gave me flak for appointing you. I don't want the Richards case to give them ammunition to shoot down my chances for a second term."

"Then I have your backing?"

The mayor nodded. "Just don't screw this up."

For a fleeting moment Harrington wondered if Lloyd Gossett's tepid endorsement might come back to bite him in the ass, but he quickly dismissed his concerns. After all, if you couldn't count on your friends, then whom could you count on?

Still, his pulse raced as he thought of the telephone call that would ignite the firestorm.

9

WEDNESDAY MORNING DAVIE DROVE the Crown Victoria into the rear parking lot of the Los Angeles County Coroner's office with Vaughn in the passenger's seat. The call confirming the autopsy had come in shortly after she arrived at work. She was surprised the post mortem had been scheduled so quickly. Sometimes it took days for a body to be examined.

Even before they stepped outside the car, a noxious odor began seeping through the windows, squeezing the air from her lungs. Vaughn reached for the tube of vapor rub in his jacket pocket, dabbing a generous amount of gel under his nose.

"They must have a decomp," he said. "I hope the ME doesn't keep us here all day."

Davie's father had once told her that in the old days, you could smell the dead from a block away. The county had cleaned up the place since then. Now the aromas were mostly chemical, but on the days they received a decomposing body, there were no compounds in the world strong enough to mask the stench. She had always been hypersensitive to unpleasant odors, so she forced herself to take a deep breath, knowing if she could keep it together now she would probably survive the ordeal.

They followed two technicians wheeling a bagged body on a gurney up the ramp and into the building. Vaughn entered their names in the sign-in book in the reception area before they proceeded down the hall to suit up in blue paper protective clothing: pants, shirt, booties, an apron tied in the back like a hospital gown, gloves, and a face mask. Even though it was unlikely the medical examiner would ask Davie to touch the corpse, she would be standing over his shoulder watching as he made the cuts, so it was necessary to shield her body from any fluids.

The elevator descended one floor to the windowless basement. When the doors opened, the overpowering crush of death was everywhere. So many bodies in one place, dozens of them lying on gurneys parked in the hallway at haphazard angles, like discarded grocery carts.

A short distance down the hall was a rectangular autopsy room with five stations spaced a few feet apart, each with its own stainless steel table and sink. Once inside the room, Davie saw flashes of light from a photographer's camera and heard the low rumble of conversation from the mix of detectives, lab technicians, and medical examiners standing near the bodies, which were each identified by a toe tag.

Two post mortems were already under way. A toddler as pale as a porcelain doll lay on one autopsy table. A young Latino lay nearby. Five bullet holes had pierced his back, nearly obliterating the tattoo of a skeleton wearing a fedora and a fur coat, which Davie recognized as the symbol of *Las Avenidas*, the Avenues, a violent street gang associated with the Mexican mafia.

Davie turned her gaze to her victim's body, at least what was left of it. She lay on a table at the far end of the room near a wall shelf lined with jars holding a variety of parasites preserved in formalin. The collection belonged to Medical Examiner Jay Wray. Detectives called him "The Worm" because of the intestinal vermiform he'd collected over the years from bodies he had autopsied. Davie paused in front of a container that held a tangle of white worms, each more than a foot long.

"As soon as the post is over," Vaughn said, "let's do lunch. I know a great Italian place ... "

"I see you're still the resident comedian, Detective Vaughn." Davie turned and saw Doctor Wray walking toward them, swathed head to toe in a plastic suit that hung like a tent on his trim frame. Tucked under one arm was a matching hood. Under the other was a file folder. He adjusted his bookish glasses and gazed at the jars.

"Those are *Ascaris lumbricoides*—roundworms to you non-bug people. I extracted those beauties from the small intestine of a tourist who made the mistake of drinking water from a contaminated well in Guyana."

Vaughn nodded toward the body. "I don't think our girl will add to your collection. Not much left of her."

"I can see that," Wray said as he assessed Davie with his bronze-colored eyes. "You must be Detective Richards."

She nodded.

"Just so you know. This is my world and these are my rules. Don't tell me how to conduct an autopsy and I won't tell you how to investigate a murder. Stick with the program, we'll get along just fine."

"Thanks for the warm welcome."

"My pleasure. From your briefing on the telephone this morning, I gather this post has two goals: get DNA samples to compare with your missing person and find the cause of death. Right?"

Davie was sure the victim was Anya Nosova. The braces, the tattoo, the fragile bone structure all matched the description from the missing persons report and the photo John Bell had given her. If Andre Lucien could identify the victim from the crime scene photos, DNA comparison would be a formality she would need only when the case went to trial.

"I'm hoping you can find proof she was murdered."

"I saw the article about your Jane Doe in the *Times* this morning. The reporter claimed the death was due to 'foul play.' I'll give you the benefit of the doubt and assume she made that up. I make no guarantees that I'll rule this as a homicide, but let's get started."

Wray called in the photographer. As the lead investigator on the case, Davie guided him through the shots she needed for the investigation and later for trial.

Wray placed the hood over his head and connected a hose from an oxygen canister to his breathing mask to avoid inhaling fragments of blood and bone. The getup made him look like an astronaut bound for the moon. Davie took notes as he measured, weighed, and inspected every part of the body.

"There are no obvious bullet holes or stab wounds," he said. "No ligature marks on the neck. Right arm is missing. No needle tracks on her left arm to suggest she was an intravenous drug user. We'll do a toxicology work up, of course. In case she died from an overdose."

"That would simplify things," Vaughn said.

Overdose or not, Davie still didn't believe the woman had stripped naked and jumped into a sewer voluntarily. Somebody dumped her there, either before or after she was dead.

"She was murdered," she said.

The plastic hood could not mask Wray's irritation. "I don't fudge facts so you can make a case, detective."

"You'll find the truth," she said.

"Whose truth?"

Davie pointed toward the body. "Hers."

"Good. Then we're on the same page."

Starting at each shoulder, Wray guided his scalpel toward a point at midchest and then continued down the center of the torso, forming a neat Y.

When the cut was completed, Wray looked up. "How's Frank Giordano? Don't see him around here much anymore. Have you put him out to pasture yet?"

"He's supposed to retire in ninety days," Vaughn said, "but on his last end of watch I expect to find him superglued to his chair."

Wray set the scalpel down and picked up what looked like a three-foot branch trimmer. "Frank loves the job. Leaving won't be easy for him."

He cut through the victim's ribs, pulling the breastbone back to expose the chest cavity and releasing a fetid odor of rot that blossomed in the air. Davie felt her stomach churn. She glanced at the sink, wondering if she would have to make a run for it. Breathing through her mouth was an option, but filling her lungs with death vapors was more unsettling than breathing through her nose. As she blinked away the moisture that had accumulated in her eyes, she felt Vaughn's elbow in her ribs. She glanced up and saw his outstretched hand holding the tube of menthol gel. She swiped some under her nose.

Using a large syringe, Wray extracted blood from the heart. "The lab can use this to create a DNA profile. When will you have a sample from the missing woman for comparison?"

"This afternoon," Davie said.

She planned to drive to Andre Lucien's apartment immediately after the autopsy and collect any DNA samples—hair, saliva, or blood—Anya might have left in the apartment. If he wasn't home or if he refused to cooperate, she would not be able to meet that deadline unless she found a judge to sign a search warrant.

Wray took out each organ and weighed it until the chest cavity looked like a carved out canoe. "No obvious abnormalities so far."

Davie's paper suit crackled as she leaned over his shoulder. "What about those scratches on her face and chest?"

"They're definitely antemortem."

Davie moved in closer. "So she was beaten before she died?"

"I doubt that. The abrasions are superficial."

"But they could be consistent with some sort of physical attack, like somebody shoving her against a rough surface?"

"Perhaps, but if she was alive when she went into the sewer, debris could have just as easily abraded her skin."

Vaughn smirked. "Maybe it's a rug burn."

She figured Vaughn's juvenile humor was some sort of coping mechanism, but his lame jokes were interrupting her train of thought.

"Chill, partner," she warned.

"Lighten up, Davie. I'm just trying to get through my day."

The pungent odor of scorched bone filled the air as Wray circumscribed the head with an oscillating saw. The remnant piece of skull made a sucking sound as he separated it from the head. A moment later, he removed the brain and held it up to the light.

"No signs of trauma, so she wasn't bludgeoned to death."

Davie continued peppering Wray with questions and pointing to oddities she didn't understand until he grew impatient. Her hopes ebbed as the post dragged on. If he failed to rule the death a homicide, Giordano would assign her to another case. Anya Nosova's death would be filed away and forgotten except by those who loved her.

Vaughn looked at his watch. "About done, doc?"

"He'll tell you when he's done," she said.

Vaughn shot her a guarded look.

Wray continued examining Jane Doe, probing around the neck.

"Interesting," he said.

Davie focused on his gloved hands. "What?"

"The cricoid cartilage appears to be fractured. I don't know how I missed that before."

"Lay it on us, doc," Vaughn said in a flat tone. "We're on the edge of our seats."

Wray straightened his spine and turned toward Davie. "You'll get my complete report in about six weeks, but for now I'm going to rule that the cause of death was manual strangulation and that a person or persons unknown dumped the body in the sewer postmortem. Congratulations, Detective Richards, your case is now officially a homicide." He paused as he took off his mask. "And one more thing: your girl was pregnant."

10

VAUGHN DRUMMED HIS FINGERS on the dashboard of the car. "The zygote changes everything. How's this sound? Lucien wanted Anya to get pregnant, but after he knocked her up, he changed his mind. They fought and he killed her. Once the Worm types the kid's DNA, we'll nail him for Murder One."

"Interesting theory, but even if Lucien is the baby's father, we still have to prove he killed Anya. Let's hope he gives consent to search his apartment."

Davie jockeyed the Crown Vic through light traffic on their way to Andre Lucien's place. Twenty minutes later they arrived in Westchester. Vaughn grabbed a small bag from the trunk of the car. It held a camera, gloves, evidence bags, and vials in case they found anything to collect for DNA analysis.

This time when Davie knocked on the door she heard movement inside the apartment. A moment later, the dead bolt turned and the door cracked open as far as the security chain would allow, exposing a hollow-eyed and unshaven man. A moment later, the pungent odor of sweat rolled over her like a tsunami.

"Are you Andre Lucien?" she said.

"What do you want?" Despite Lucien's French-sounding name, his accent was pure L.A.

She held up her badge. "I want to talk to you about Anya Nosova. Can we come in?"

Lucien glanced over his shoulder as if he were consulting someone inside the apartment. "Not now. The place is a mess."

"Is somebody with you?" Davie asked.

"What difference does that make?"

"Would you mind stepping outside, sir?"

"I can't talk right now. You should have called first. You'll have to come back tomorrow."

"I have a few questions. They won't take long."

"I'm not feeling well."

Davie noted the shift in his story. Lucien's behavior was setting off alarm bells. She wondered if he was in the processing of destroying evidence of a murder. The urge to kick down the door and search the place was strong, but as much as she wanted to hook him and book him, she needed probable cause to force her way into the apartment. Right now she had no proof Lucien had done anything but report his girlfriend missing. Her only option was to keep him talking and hope he would invite them inside.

She struggled to keep a measured tone. "If you're not feeling well, maybe you should come outside. Get some fresh air."

"I don't want fresh air. I want to be left alone."

"You reported your girlfriend missing," she said. "Why won't you talk to us? Don't you care what happened to her?"

"You cops are all alike. Always hassling people."

"You told Missing Persons that Ms. Nosova had a spiderweb tattoo on her elbow," Davie said. "Did she serve time in prison? Maybe in Ukraine?"

Lucien moved to close the door. Davie jammed her shoe into the opening, pushing with her shoulder to test the strength of the security chain.

"We found the body of a young female," she said. "We think it's Ms. Nosova. We need you to identify her." Davie pushed harder on the door. The chain pulled away from its mooring and the door swung open.

Lucien lost his balance. He groaned as he hit the ground.

"Jeez, partner," Vaughn said under his breath. "Leave the guy some dignity."

The apartment reeked of unwashed clothes and the faint odor of marijuana. Davie reached out to help Lucien to his feet. His hand was spongy, almost boneless. His tremor vibrated up Davie's arm.

Lucien's driver's license listed his age as forty-three, but his stooped posture made him seem older. Dark circles under his eyes were in harsh contrast to the pasty white of his unshaven face. It was hard to imagine why Anya Nosova had found him attractive.

Lucien massaged his lower back. "She's dead?"

Davie slipped the Hyperion crime scene photos from her notebook. "I have to warn you, Mr. Lucien, these are hard to look at, but we're hoping you can tell us if the woman in the photos is Anya Nosova."

Lucien grimaced as he stared at the photos. A moment later, he handed them back to Davie. "It's her. It's Anya. What happened?"

"She was murdered," Davie said. "Any idea who might have wanted to harm her?"

He stared into midspace, his face muscles slack. "I found a letter on the dresser this morning. I checked my computer. It was typed on Saturday, the night she disappeared."

"Where is it?"

Lucien didn't answer right away. "She was leaving me. I assumed she hooked up with her old boyfriend. He was upset when she dumped him for me. He told her if he couldn't have her nobody could. If she was murdered, you should talk to Troy Gallway."

"Today is Wednesday," Vaughn said. "She disappeared on Saturday. That's four days ago. Why didn't you notice the letter before?"

"I've been gone for a few days." Lucien picked up a piece of paper from the kitchen counter and handed it to Davie.

It was definitely a Dear John note, but it was computer-generated and unsigned. The language on the page was stilted and awkward, as if the writer wasn't a native English speaker. The message claimed Anya had found love elsewhere, but Gallway's name wasn't mentioned. Davie glanced toward the kitchen and saw a laptop computer and printer on the table.

"How do I know you didn't type this yourself?" she said.

"Why would I do that?"

"Because maybe you know more about your girlfriend's death than you're telling us."

The tremor she had felt in his handshake seemed to have spread to his entire body, rattling the timbre of his voice. "She was the best thing that ever happened to me. I would never hurt her."

"What do you do for a living, Mr. Lucien?" Vaughn said.

He hesitated. "Sales."

Vaughn moved closer to Lucien in an attempt to intimidate him. "Pharmaceutical sales?"

"I know you checked my rap sheet, but those were misdemeanor possession charges. That was a long time ago. I don't do drugs anymore. I sell rebuilt computers."

"To clients like Ray Anthony Falcon?" Davie said.

"The movie star? I don't play in his sandbox."

"Are you telling us you don't know him?"

Lucien's face was glazed with sweat. "Only from the tabloids."

"A witness saw him at your apartment the night Anya disappeared."

He wouldn't meet Davie's gaze. "I wouldn't know anything about that. I wasn't home Saturday night."

Vaughn scanned the living room and adjoining kitchen. "Where's your inventory? All I see is one computer."

"I'm low on product at the moment."

"Who else was Anya sleeping with?" Vaughn said.

"Nobody. Before me there was just Gallway."

"How do you know?" Davie said.

"That's what she told me and I believed her."

Lucien seemed sincere, but Davie knew men sometimes anesthetized their insecurities with chemicals and denial.

"Mind if I have a look at your computer?" Vaughn said.

Lucien bolted toward the table and closed the lid of his laptop. "Yes, I do mind."

"I can call a judge and get a warrant," Davie said, "or you can give Detective Vaughn permission to check the date and time Ms. Nosova wrote the letter. What's the harm if you have nothing to hide?"

Lucien paused a moment to weigh the pros and cons of the offer. "Okay. Just don't screw up my files."

While Vaughn searched the computer's hard drive, Lucien gave consent for Davie to explore the rest of the apartment and collect anything she needed for DNA comparison. She grabbed a handful of evidence envelopes from the bag Vaughn had brought from the car and headed down the hallway. Lucien seemed torn between watching Vaughn and monitoring Davie. He eventually stationed himself in the hallway between the two of them.

Neither Anya nor Lucien appeared adept at housecleaning. The apartment had only one bathroom and judging from a hairy fringe attached to the toilet bowl at the water line, the place hadn't been cleaned since Thomas Crapper filed his first patent. Toothpaste oozed from a tube onto the countertop. The medicine cabinet held over-the-counter meds but no drugs, not even prescriptions. Two toothbrushes lay on the counter.

Davie poked her head into the hall. "Hey, Mr. Lucien. Which one of these toothbrushes belonged to Ms. Nosova?"

"The red one."

"You ever use it?"

"No. That's gross."

"Anybody else been in your bathroom since Saturday?"

"Just me."

Davie gloved up and dropped the red toothbrush into a paper evidence bag, hoping it might contain enough saliva for DNA testing.

At the end of the narrow hallway, she entered a small bedroom. Taped to the walls in random order were red construction-paper hearts that looked like a child had made them for a grade school Valentine party. It reminded her of the three-by-five cards plastered to the walls of John Bell's living room. She pulled back the covers on the double bed but found no visible bloodstains on the sheets or mattress.

Men's clothing occupied most of the closet space. Hanging at one end was what appeared to be the tank top Anya wore in Bell's snapshot and a pair of jeans that looked too big for a slender woman like Anya Nosova. Pink-flowered flip-flops rested on the closet floor. Anya must have brought more outfits than that when she moved to L.A. from Ukraine. Davie wondered what had happened to them.

On the low-slung dresser was a brush that contained long blonde hairs. Several appeared to have roots attached. SID would need at least a hundred of them for accurate testing, preferably from different areas of Anya's head. Davie doubted there were enough for that, but she pulled the hairs from the brush and dropped them into a paper bindle. Then she folded the bindle and dropped it into a paper evidence bag, along with the brush.

A search of the dresser revealed a stash of men's T-shirts, socks, and a couple of sweaters. Tucked in a corner of a drawer, Davie found several pairs of women's underwear wrapped around a collection of heart-shaped collectibles, including a small candle and a handkerchief embroidered with a trio of hearts. Davie wasn't sure where a person could buy a woman's handkerchief these days. Maybe Anya had brought it to the US from her home in Kiev. There was also a business card for Inky Dink Tattoos in Venice. The owner had one of those Scandinavian names impossible to pronounce: Karen Skjelstad.

Davie studied the heart-themed items cradled in her hand and the paper hearts taped to the wall. She wondered if they spoke of a young girl's naïve faith in romance or something darker—a woman with a prison tat and a drug-dealer boyfriend who died knowing love was just an illusion.

Davie photographed the wall collage. Then she bagged the heart items and returned to the living room just as Vaughn was closing the lid of Lucien's laptop.

"The note is time-stamped just after seven p.m. last Saturday," he said, "the day Nosova disappeared. Our wit says she left the apartment at eight, so she could have typed it."

Davie stared at Lucien. "Where were you Saturday night?"

Lucien collapsed onto the sofa. "I took my mother to dinner and a movie on Saturday. I left my apartment at about three and slept at her house in Simi Valley that night. I was bummed about Anya, so I stayed at my mom's house until yesterday afternoon. I swear I never saw Anya again."

Davie wrote down his mother's name and phone number so she could verify his alibi.

"Where are Anya's clothes?"

"She didn't have much when she moved in. Her old apartment was burglarized. I was going to buy her new stuff, but she didn't like to go shopping. I got her a new cell phone, though. The old one was stolen."

Davie stood at the kitchen counter looking through a pile of mail. "Who paid for her braces?"

He seemed confused, as if he'd never considered the question before. "I don't know. She had them when I met her."

"And where was that?"

"At Café Brew in Venice."

Davie held up the Inky Dink card. "Is this where she got her tattoo?"

He shrugged. "Maybe."

"Where did she get the money for a tat?"

"Not from me. I hated it. Told her it made her look like a lowlife."

Davie showed him the bag of heart-themed items. "Where did Anya get these?"

"Bought them, I guess. She had a thing for hearts."

"Mind if I take them for evidence?"

"Go ahead."

"Are any of Anya's things missing?"

He inhaled deeply and then blew out the air. "A black cocktail dress and a red coat. She must have been wearing them the night she left. A red heart-shaped purse too. Beaded. And a locket, shaped like a heart. She never took that off, not even in bed."

Vaughn changed the subject to keep Lucien off balance. "Why did you file the missing person report in Devonshire Division?"

He buried his head in his hands. His shoulders trembled. "Like I told you, I went to my mom's place on Saturday. I tried to call Anya all night and all day Sunday, but she didn't pick up. I was worried. Mom told me to report it to the police. Devonshire was the closest station to her house."

Vaughn pulled a tissue from a box on the counter and let it float into Lucien's lap. "Did your mommy know she was about to become a grandma?"

Lucien wiped his nose with the tissue. "I don't know what you're talking about."

"Come on, Mr. Lucien," he said. "You must have known your girl-friend was pregnant. That's what you wanted, right?"

Lucien sat in silence, as if digesting the words. "I didn't get her pregnant."

Vaughn looked like his bullshit meter had just overloaded. "Don't tell me. You had a vasectomy."

"I had mumps when I was eighteen. It blew out my gonads. My mom said having children was overrated, so I was glad when Anya told me she didn't want them, either."

Davie glanced at Vaughn. Bell had told them Lucien wanted a child but Anya didn't. Somebody was lying.

A few minutes later, Lucien located the phone number for Anya's father in Kiev and they headed back to the car.

"Let's drive to Venice and interview the tattoo shop owner," Davie said.

"No use both of us spending all night doing paperwork. You talk to Karen Skajello or Skajellabad or however the hell you pronounce her name. I'll go back to the station, book the evidence, and find Troy Gallway. I'll also ask RACR to track down a Russian translator. "

Vaughn was right. They couldn't afford to waste time. Finding Gallway was a priority. She was confident the Real-Time Analysis and

Critical Response Division could find a translator among the department's nearly ten thousand ethnically and culturally diverse officers.

Fifteen minutes later, she dropped her partner at the front door of the station and headed to Venice.

11

VENICE BEACH WAS SECOND only to Disneyland as L.A.'s biggest tourist destination. By the time Davie arrived, the flotsam and jetsam of society's fringe had washed onto the boardwalk and were hustling a busload of Japanese tourists. Con artists, panhandlers, and psychics pitched their services to the uninitiated. Local shop owners hawked T-shirts and L.A. souvenirs made in China.

A homeless junkie slumped against the building. Mylar strips hung from his watch cap like a carwash for heads, which Davie guessed he needed, from the look of his matted hair.

"Hey, pretty lady," he said. "I could use a bite to eat. Can you help me out?"

She stopped in front of him. "You know I'm a cop. Right?"

He cocked his head, as if listening to a sound only he could hear. "Sure. But that doesn't mean you don't feel for a war vet down on his luck."

"What war is that, sir? The war on drugs?"

"Grenada."

Davie continued walking. "There's a shelter down the street. Maybe they'll give you lunch and a more creative sales pitch."

"It's okay if you're a little short today," he shouted after her. "Jesus loves you anyway."

His blessing triggered a deep racking cough. Davie figured it was God's warning that neither name-dropping nor begging would get this junkie any closer to the pearly gates. She wondered if redemption were even possible for a drug addict circling the drain.

Maybe it was the flicker of intelligence in his eyes that hinted at the man he once was or maybe it was just because he'd called her pretty, but she stopped and walked back to where he was sitting. She pulled out a five-dollar bill from her ID-card holder.

"Here," she said. "Don't spend this on drugs. Okay?"

"I'm not going to lie to you, pretty lady. I'll do my best, but I can't promise."

Davie rolled her eyes as she walked toward the pink neon Inky Dink Tattoos sign and headed up the narrow flight of stairs. Framed photos of skin art lined both sides of the walls, mostly skeletons with ghoulish smiles, lethal-looking snakes, scorpions, and fire-breathing dragons. As she opened the door, she heard a bell tinkle, a gentle sound that seemed incongruous in the company of all those moody reptiles.

The waiting room was dressed in gunmetal gray walls and black leather chairs that looked expensive even in the dim light. Behind a three-panel partition, a reclining chair and a massage-type table stood empty. A dozen or so tattoo needles hung from a metal rod on the wall above a shelf holding bottles of colored ink.

"Today's your lucky day. I just had a cancellation."

Davie turned toward the voice. A woman sat on a chair, wearing an orange do-rag tied over her electric blue hair. Her neck was unadorned, exposing skin as pale and rich as clotted cream. Inked on her right arm was a koi swimming in a pool of lotus flowers. On the left arm was a geisha with a flirtatious smile just visible above her fan. The woman had a brown tabby pinned down on her lap. If the nail clipper in her right hand was any clue, the cat was about to get a manicure.

"I'm not here for a tattoo." Davie pulled the Inky Dink business card from her pocket and pointed to the name. "Is this you?"

"It's pronounced *Shellstad*," she said, "just so you don't embarrass yourself." The woman's gaze swept Davie's black pantsuit, stopping at the bulge of the Smith & Wesson under her jacket. "My bad. I should know a girl never covers her body art. I can see now the only thing you have under that polyester is a gun and a badge."

Davie doubted the woman's gift for identifying synthetic fabric would lead to clues in Anya Nosova's death, but she decided to reserve judgment. She pulled the victim's photo from her notebook.

"Do you recognize this woman?"

Skjelstad glanced at the snapshot as she rested her forearm over the cat's neck and squeezed its right front paw between her thumb and forefinger. "Yeah. Anya Nosova. Strange little chick. What did she do?"

Davie thought it interesting that the woman immediately assumed Anya had done something wrong. "Strange how?"

Skjelstad acknowledged Davie's unresponsiveness with a shrug. "She used to sit on the bench in front of my shop, staring at the ocean. One day I went out and told her I was going to charge rent if she didn't buy something. I was joking, but she started to cry."

"Did you do her tattoo?"

Skjelstad kissed the cat's head and squeezed the clipper. A piece of nail took flight and landed on the floor. "I have a bad habit of taking in strays, so I invited her in. After that, she stopped by almost every day.

She thought my art was genius. She told me her mother worked for the Louvre in Paris. She wanted to set up an exhibition of my designs."

Anya had told John Bell that her mother was a dancer with the Bolshoi. Davie doubted she was also a curator in a famous museum. Somebody had a faulty memory or else Anya was a compulsive liar.

"Did you take her up on the offer?"

Skjelstad chuckled. "Are you kidding me? The Louvre? She was playing me, but I didn't care because she was good at it, a real charmer. One day business was slow so I offered to give her a freebie."

"Why a spiderweb? That's a prison tat. It usually means the person killed somebody."

"I told her it would give some people the wrong idea, but she insisted."

"Did she say why?"

Skjelstad hesitated. "You got some sort of ID?"

Davie showed Skjelstad her department ID and also handed her a business card. The woman studied the card. When she looked up, her eyes were moist.

"This says you're a homicide detective. The girl's dead, isn't she?"

Davie nodded. "I hope you can help me find the person who killed her."

Skjelstad didn't respond right away. She finished clipping the nails on one paw and started on the other. Both she and the cat seemed restless.

"I got the impression Anya hooked up with some bad people in L.A. I don't know the details, but I wouldn't be surprised if she had a long list of folks she wanted dead. Maybe the spiderweb was just credit in advance."

"Did she mention any names?"

She tucked a wisp of blue hair under her do-rag. "But she nearly jumped out of her skin every time my shop door opened. I told her to call the cops if somebody was hassling her, but I don't think she ever did."

"Did she tell you she was pregnant?"

"She didn't have to. She was skinny like you, only taller. She wasn't that far along but her baby bump looked like an olive stuck in a straw."

"Who was the father?"

Skjelstad snipped the last two nails. The cat jumped to the floor and headed toward its food dish, whirring like a margarita blender. "I just know it wasn't her boyfriend, because she told me he was shooting blanks."

Anya must have lied to John Bell about Andre Lucien pressuring her to have kids because she already knew he was sterile. Maybe she was playing Bell to get his sympathy, because she knew he was attracted to her. Anya seemed to have a knack for telling people what they wanted to hear, just like her fib to Skjelstad. Lying with flattery was a common tool of sociopaths and survivors.

"Anything else you remember?"

Skjelstad shook her head. "I've known a few clients who've been murdered. Some of them deserved to die, but not Anya. I hope you get the bastard who killed her."

Davie hoped so too.

The junkie was gone when Davie left the shop, probably on the nod in an alley somewhere courtesy of her five bucks. She made her way back to the car and headed for the station.

12

RAGS DROPPED THE FIVE-DOLLAR bill from the pretty-lady cop into his backpack and headed down Pacific Avenue toward his go-to newspaper box near the beach. He had told her the truth: he might use the money to buy drugs, because he had a King Kong habit for Mexican black tar heroin that eclipsed fear or common sense. Brown Sugar. Horse. Caca. His need for the drug was nearly as vast as his bad luck.

Cold air seeped into the joints of his fingers, making them stiff as he jimmied the lock on the coin box of the newspaper stand. He brushed the coins into his palm—a disappointing three dollars and twenty-five cents—not even close to the money he'd need to buy heroin.

Rags used to read the paper, but he was losing his vision. Even when he squinted, he couldn't see the small print anymore. Maybe someone at the homeless shelter could fit him with a pair of glasses. He needed twenty-twenty to see the evil in a man's eyes.

He thought about grabbing a couple more newspapers to protect his chest from the cold, because surviving winter, even in sunny California, meant dressing in layers. After careful consideration, he decided to keep the paper he was already wearing. It had a color photo splashed across the front page—men wearing business suits and phony smiles. It reminded Rags he had to protect himself against the forces of evil.

The coins dropped into the bottom of his backpack with a muted jingle. Rags preferred to shoot up alone because life on the street had taught him to distrust people in general and drug addicts in particular, but his need for a fix coupled with his current monetary shortfall had forced him to look for business partners.

He shuffled along the boardwalk scouting for kindred spirits, moving with caution to avoid detection by government agents who had him under surveillance twenty-four/seven. As an added precaution, he had lined his watch cap with strips of Mylar to scramble the government's global positioning satellites.

The cold weather held foot traffic to a minimum, so it took fifteen minutes before he spotted two men huddled against the side of a building. Arnie was a black man he knew from the shelter. His mind was dust from too many drugs and too many days on the street. Cysts covered his face. He scratched at them constantly. It drove Rags crazy. Still, the two remained friendly because Rags saw no evil in Arnie's eyes.

The other man was a stranger and white, like Rags. Arnie introduced him as Beau Fischer. When Beau spoke, Rags was sure he heard the whirring of a tape recorder beneath that bulky parka of his, feeding every word he said into a database at the Pentagon. The voices in his head warned him that Beau was bad news, but this time he didn't listen because Arnie announced he had a little over seventeen dollars. Add that to the five from the lady cop and the three twenty-five from the coin box, they had enough cash to score some H. Beau, though he claimed to have no cash, knew a dealer in the area who could provide the goods.

They bought the H, but the dealer didn't have any spare syringes, so Rags let Beau and Arnie use his to inject their share of the heroin. Three hypes on a spike was like playing Russian roulette, but Rags's need for the drug compelled him to spin that cylinder.

As soon as Beau and Arnie nodded off, Rags stashed the remaining heroin in his backpack and headed to Pacific Avenue, where, for the past several nights, he had slept in the alley behind an appliance store in a cardboard box that had once housed a Sub-Zero refrigerator.

It took effort to crawl into the box because of the mountains of scar tissue in the crooks of his arms. Once inside, he took the drug paraphernalia from his backpack: the bottom half of a soda can, a disposable lighter, and the used syringe. He placed the brown rocks of heroin into the can and melted it with the lighter. When the H was cooked he filled the syringe, anticipating the warmth that would flush his skin. His chin would drop to his chest, and his eyelids would flutter and struggle to stay open. A moment later he would be floating, his limbs sagging in surrender. *Sweet Jesus*, he thought. *Take me home.*

It was impossible to find a vein in either arm. He had blown those long ago. He opened the box's north-facing flap to get some light. He pulled off his shoe and guided the needle toward the skin between his toes, but the point was too dull to penetrate the scar tissue. His hand trembled. The need was gaining strength.

The muffled roar of a vehicle entering the alley stole his attention. Cars sometimes nosed into the lane, but once they saw the orange LADWP barricades blocking the exit, they usually turned around. This vehicle crept forward. *More bad luck,* he thought.

It wasn't G-men. They couldn't have found his hideaway—he was too clever for them—but it might be the cops. He wondered if the owner of the appliance store had called to complain about him. Rags had failed several stints in rehab. The judge would send him to jail this time, maybe for a long time. He couldn't survive that.

He weighed his need for the drug against another arrest on his rap sheet and knew he had to get rid of the heroin. There was nowhere to hide the syringe and he was too sick to run. He pitched the soda can, needle and lighter into the alley as far as his stiff arm could manage, hoping it would fall shy of the street where a passerby might steal it. Maybe the cops would just roust him from the box and leave so he could get the syringe before the need consumed him. For now, there was nothing to do but wait.

The vehicle drove past his box and stopped near the barricades at the end of the alley. Rags heard a car door open. He suppressed the urge to cough. Despite the frigid air, sweat formed on his chest, saturating the newspapers under his clothes.

Rags gathered his courage and peered out of the south-facing flap of the box. An SUV was parked at the end of the alley near the street. It wasn't a cop car. Even undercover rides were never that new or that clean. His body trembled as he remembered the SUV from a few nights ago and wondered if it were the same one. The driver might have come back to kill him for what he saw.

He heard a car door close and shoes scrape across the pavement. He focused on those footsteps. Light gait. A clicking sound. A woman's high heels. Then he saw her. She was wearing a dress and carrying a box toward the back entrance of a shop. Not like the other night.

Rags agitated the Mylar on his watch cap but it didn't cleanse his mind of the memories of that other SUV. It had driven into the alley just like this one. A man dressed in blue jeans and a dark hooded sweatshirt struggled with something pale and limp at the rear door of the vehicle. A moment later, the object fell to the ground with a thud. At first glance, the thing had looked like a giant octopus with seaweed tangled around its tentacles, but there were only four appendages. An octopus had eight. The need had made it difficult for him to concentrate.

Rags remembered squinting until his vision cleared. That's when he saw a woman lying on the ground at the rear of the SUV. She had long blonde hair tangled around her torso. She was naked. Unconscious. Maybe dead.

His heart had felt as if it might explode. He wanted to help the woman, but the voices in his head screamed a warning about the powerful forces aligned against him and that he would survive only with constant vigilance. He wanted to tell the voices to shut up, but his parched tongue was too thick to form words. He had retreated into a far corner of the refrigerator box, trying without success to control his trembling. From the alley, he had heard the man grunting from exertion and the scraping of metal against pavement. Then something heavy hit the ground with the force of an aftershock.

After the SUV had left, Rags made a slow turn to look for the woman but she was gone. He felt bad about not helping her. He didn't know if the man had taken her away, or if she had left on her own two feet. Even now, he wondered if he had imagined the whole thing.

The woman with the package was taking her own sweet time in the shop. Rags was beside himself by the time she backed the SUV down the alley and disappeared into traffic. He had to get his heroin back. He crawled out of the box and staggered toward the syringe, only to find that the woman's SUV had crushed it beneath its wheels. He scooped the heroin residue into his hand and licked it from his palm, knowing it would not be enough to feed his hunger.

The screaming in his head escalated until the sound was unbearable. He yanked his watch cap over his ears and slumped to the ground, tapping his fingers on the pavement and humming tonelessly, hoping to block spy satellites from reading his thoughts.

13

FIFTEEN MINUTES AFTER LEAVING Inky Dink Tattoos, Davie arrived at the station. Vaughn wasn't at his desk. The books on her shelf had fallen over again. She rearranged them before slipping the Karen Skjelstad interview notes into the Murder Book. She was reaching for her cell phone to text Vaughn when she heard him call her name. She looked up to see him walking toward her with a paper coffee cup in his hand—a latte, she suspected.

"We can scratch Andre Lucien off the suspect list," Vaughn said. "I talked to his mommy. She claims little Andy was at her place last weekend from about four on Saturday afternoon until Tuesday at about two. He was never out of her sight and she'll swear to that in court."

Lucien was an obvious suspect, but clearing him meant Davie had to look beyond the obvious and find the loose thread, some piece of minutiae that unraveled the case.

Vaughn held up a set of cars keys. "Here's the good news. I found Troy Gallway. You can tell me how brilliant I am on the way to his crib."

It took twenty minutes to steer the car from the station to the Wilshire exit of the freeway, past the Westwood Boulevard intersection to Gallway's condominium. She was relieved when Vaughn asked her to drive so he could answer his emails. Her partner was easily distracted. She always felt safer when she was behind the wheel.

Vaughn looked up from his phone. "RACR found a Russian speaker. Since Lucien identified the body, I told the translator to meet us at the station tomorrow to help interview Anya's father."

"The father doesn't know Anya's dead."

"He will soon enough."

The car smelled of cinnamon sprinkled on top of the latte Vaughn had wedged between his knees. His thumbs sped across the keypad of his cell phone, likely texting his latest love interest, a P-3 who worked in the West L.A. Community Relations Office, a unit everybody in the department shortened to its initials and pronounced "crow."

"How'd you find Gallway?"

"Everything you ever wanted to know about him is on his Facebook page."

Vaughn rattled off the bullet points of Gallway's bio: has an MFA from Yale in Graphic Design, works as a graphic artist, specializes in creating corporate identities, designs movie posters for various Hollywood studios. A link on his page led to an art gallery on Melrose that sold his oil paintings. Gallway had accomplished much in his life. Davie wondered if his talents included murder.

Vaughn hadn't told Gallway that Anya had been murdered, only that she was missing. Davie wanted to watch his reaction when she broke the news, to study his body language for signs that he already knew she was dead.

Rays from the winter sun filtered through gauzy clouds, casting muted shadows on the high-rise condominiums that lined Wilshire

Boulevard. A flock of crows banked over a row of palm trees and landed on a patch of grass, pecking the soil for brunch—out-of-towners wintering in L.A.

"I love this part of the boulevard," Vaughn said. "No parked cars. No telephone lines. No trash. Neat and clean. Back in the eighties I hear you could get a free Rolls Royce if you bought a penthouse in one of these places."

"Maybe there's a unit for sale in Gallway's building. I could see you living in this hood."

"If we nail him for the Nosova caper maybe I can buy his place in the fire sale. You think he's Anya's baby daddy?"

"The Worm said Anya was about two months along. According to John Bell, she'd been living with Andre Lucien for three or four months, but it's possible she was still seeing Gallway on the side."

"Let's say Anya was doing both of them. She knew about Lucien's mumps problem, so when she got pregnant she knew the baby wasn't his. She had to weigh her options—a one-bedroom apartment in Westchester or an upscale condo on Wilshire Boulevard. Even I can figure out that one. Maybe she told Gallway the baby was his and expected a ring, but a wife and baby weren't part of his game plan so he pressured her to have an abortion. She said *nyet*. They argued. It got loud. He tried to shut her up and bam! One dead Russian girl."

Squelch from her radio interrupted the conversation. The dispatcher was calling for all available units to respond to a 459 in progress in Playa del Rey. She lowered the volume.

"This morning I would have said Lucien was lying," she said, "putting a case on the ex to take heat off himself. Now that his mother confirmed his alibi … "

"Nobody tells the truth anymore."

"Did they ever?"

There was no parking on Wilshire Boulevard, so Davie maneuvered the car to a side street and tossed the plastic city-parking permit onto the dusty dashboard to avoid a ticket. Vaughn reluctantly abandoned his latte on the passenger-side floor.

Gallway's condo was in a twenty-story glass-and-marble monolith with a circular driveway edged with pink and purple pansies. Inside the lobby, the concierge located their names on the list of approved visitors and directed them to the elevator.

A slim man in his early thirties answered the door of unit 1844, assessing Davie with raised eyebrows. Her red hair and petite figure blindsided some people, but she had learned to use lowered expectations to her advantage.

They exchanged formal introductions, but Davie already knew it was Troy Gallway from the driver's license photo she had accessed at the station. He was tanned and toned with the sun-bleached blond hair of a California surfer boy who'd successfully transitioned from the beaches of Malibu to the hair salons of Beverly Hills. She wasn't a fashionista, but she noted the understated elegance of his clothes and imagined the getup had cost a bundle.

"I've been worried about Anya ever since you called," he said. "I assume you've contacted her family to see if she went back to Ukraine?"

"We haven't spoken to her parents yet, but we don't believe she's there."

"How long has she been missing?"

"Since last Saturday."

"Look, I'm happy to answer your questions, but it's been so long since I've seen her. I don't think I can be of much help."

Gallway opened the door wide in an unspoken invitation. When Davie stepped into the entry hall, she noticed a painting on the wall of a young blonde female whose fragile arms held a cello in a lover's embrace. The artist had peeled back the façade to expose a complex array of emotions: passion, pain, and perhaps a glimmer of hope. The woman's true thoughts were unknowable but her identity was not. It was Anya Nosova.

"Cool picture," Vaughn said. "Who's the artist?"

Gallway paused to study the image. "I am. It turned out rather well, I think."

"I thought you made movie posters," Vaughn said.

Gallway's smile confirmed he took no offense. "Movie posters pay the mortgage, but painting is my passion."

"How much does that picture go for?" Vaughn asked.

"That one's not for sale but something similar might be priced at ten to twenty thousand."

Vaughn inspected the brush strokes on the cello. "Maybe I should sign up for art classes. How long does it take to whip up one of these babies?"

Her partner liked to needle people, push them off balance in hopes they would say something incriminating. It wasn't her style, but he got results and she couldn't argue with that.

Gallway must have considered Vaughn's question rhetorical, because he didn't respond. Instead, he led them down the hall and around a corner into the living room. Behind his back, she saw Vaughn pick up a small crystal bowl from an end table and turn it over to read the markings on the bottom. He looked duly impressed as he mouthed the word *Lalique*. Davie didn't know a Lalique from a Ball jar but wasn't surprised that her partner did. He gravitated to the finer things in life. From cell phone conversations she'd overheard, Vaughn seemed to be on a first name basis with the entire sales force of Tiffany & Co.

A large window commanded a spectacular vista of Santa Monica Bay and the hazy form of Santa Catalina Island thirty odd miles out to sea. Davie glanced around the room but didn't see the cello Anya had been holding in the painting. Maybe it was just a prop Gallway had borrowed from the philharmonic.

Vaughn leaned on the wet bar and gazed out the window. "Awesome view," he said.

In fact, everything in the condo from the view to the artwork to the furnishings attested to Gallway's reverence for beauty. Davie compared the childlike construction-paper hearts taped to Anya's walls to the elegance of Troy Gallway's world and concluded that the two lovers were an odd match. She wondered what Gallway had seen in Anya beyond her physical beauty. Maybe that had been enough.

Davie sat facing the window on a couch covered with some sort of knobby fabric that prickled the palms of her hands. Vaughn lingered by the wet bar to inspect a terra cotta sculpture of a nude male.

"I was about to make espresso," Gallway said. "Would either of you care to join me?"

Davie noticed the disappointment on Vaughn's face when she said, "No thanks. We're fine."

Gallway walked into the kitchen a few feet away, poured beans from a gold bag into a grinder, and flipped a switch. There was a high-pitched whir followed by the pungent aroma of coffee.

"I assume you've spoken to Andre," Gallway said. "Doesn't he know where she is?"

Davie waited for Gallway's admission that he and Anya had gotten back together, but his question hung in the air and eventually died.

"Where did you meet Anya?" she said.

"At the Westwood farmers' market. She was sitting on a curb eating a *vatrushki* she'd brought from one of the vendors. She looked gangly and lost. She was extraordinarily beautiful, but there was also something contradictory about her. She seemed like an old soul in a child's body. I couldn't take my eyes off her, so I walked over and asked if she needed help."

"What's *vatrushki*?" Vaughn asked.

"It's a cottage cheese pastry made with raisins and rum. She used to go to the Volga Bakery in Hollywood once a week to buy one and to speak Russian with the owner. She said the place reminded her of home."

"Was she alone the day you met her?" Davie said.

He nodded as he spooned the ground beans into a metal cup and slid it into the espresso machine. "She told me she and her roommate had an argument. She left the apartment to cool down and when she got back, the roommate was gone, along with all of her possessions."

"So you took her home with you?" Davie said.

Gallway pushed a button on the machine and thick espresso streamed into a porcelain cup. "Yes, but the plan was just until she found the roommate. A couple of hours at most."

"But it turned into more than a couple of hours."

"Anya said the roommate took her cell phone too. I let her use mine, but she couldn't reach the woman. I invited her to sleep in my guest room that night. She felt guilty for imposing, so she insisted on cooking dinner. The meal was awful. She told me her father was a famous chef at a restaurant in Moscow. He did all the cooking at home so she had never learned how. We enjoyed each other's company. After a couple of days it was clear she needed money, so I asked if she would pose for a live drawing."

Vaughn had been unusually quiet, but when he heard that he abandoned the sculpture. "What's a live drawing?"

Gallway pulled a carton of milk from the refrigerator. "A model poses nude while I sketch. Every fifteen minutes or so she moves to a different position. It's a great way for an artist to study the human body."

"I'll bet," Vaughn said. "How much did you pay her?"

"A hundred dollars and all the food she could eat, which wasn't much."

"Did that include dessert?" Vaughn asked.

Red splotches appeared on Gallway's cheeks. "What exactly are you implying, detective?"

Davie fired off a question to cut the tension. "How long did she stay?"

"About a month."

"Why did she leave? Did you two have a falling out?"

"More like a falling in. Anya fell in love."

"With Andre Lucien?"

Gallway poured milk into a metal cup and held it up to a metal arm attached to the machine. The frothing produced a strangling sound, the sound Anya must have made when somebody's hands closed around her neck and choked away her life. She studied Gallway's long agile fingers. They seemed delicate, but they might still be strong enough to end a woman's life.

"She met him at the beach," Gallway said. "Apparently, she found him irresistible."

"How did you feel about that?" Davie asked.

Gallway poured the milky foam into the cup. "I was happy for her."

She studied his expression but saw no sign he was lying. Still, no man liked getting dumped, especially a successful man like Gallway who might expect gratitude for taking in a homeless waif like Anya Nosova.

Davie waited until he carried the cappuccino to the leather chair across from her. "When was the last time you saw her?"

He took a deep breath and exhaled slowly. "The day she moved out. I didn't hear from her again until a week ago. She called and asked if she could move back in with me. She told me she was pregnant but the father didn't want the baby. She needed a place to get away and think. I told her I was in a new relationship and it wouldn't be convenient."

"How did she take the news?"

"She cried. I felt terrible. When I first met Anya I got the impression all she ever wanted was to be a wife and mother. To me it seemed hopelessly old-fashioned, especially for a beautiful young girl with her whole life ahead of her. But that's why she wanted braces."

"Braces might get you married and pregnant in Vladivostok," Vaughn said, "but not in L.A. How'd she figure?"

Gallway's jaw muscles tensed as he wheeled around to meet Vaughn's pointed stare. "Her teeth were crooked. She thought if she had straight teeth her children would, too, and that would make her a more attractive marriage partner. I told her it didn't work that way, but she didn't believe me. Her naïveté was charming, so I referred her to orthodontist friend of mine."

From what Davie was learning about Anya Nosova, she guessed the woman's yearning for braces was less charming naïveté and more posturing for free orthodontia.

"Who paid the dentist?"

He shrugged. "I think he did the work for free."

Anya had a knack for tapping into the kindness of strangers: Skjelstad, Lucien, Gallway, and now the dentist. She was sounding more and more like a modern-day Blanche DuBois.

Davie wrote the orthodontist's contact information in her notebook. "Who was the baby's father?"

He took a sip of the cappuccino. "I assumed it was Andre. You must have asked him. What did he say?"

"That the baby wasn't his."

He leaned toward, his face strained. "Then whose was it? You have to find him. They're probably together." He set the cup on the coffee table. "Look, I've answered all your questions. You've ignored most of mine. There's something you're not telling me. What's happened to Anya?"

Gallway's concern seemed genuine. Either he was an accomplished actor as well as an artist or he didn't know that Anya was dead. Telling somebody that a loved one had been killed was always the worse part of the job for Davie, but there was no reason to withhold the bad news any longer.

"Anya's been murdered," she said.

There was silence and then a sharp intake of breath. Gallway's shoulders slumped and anguish settled into the lines of his tanned face. There was no *surely you don't think I did it.* He seemed unaware that she and Vaughn might consider him a suspect. Still, there had to be a reason a sophisticated man like Gallway was interested in a naïve girl like Anya. It was a small detail that didn't fit the pattern. There was something he wasn't telling her.

Nobody tells the truth anymore.

"Where were you last Saturday night?" she asked.

"Santa Barbara," Gallway said. "We were at the Biltmore all weekend."

Before she could ask another question, she heard the outside door open and footsteps advance toward the living room. Vaughn moved toward the hall with his hand on his weapon just as a man in his twenties rounded the corner. He was dressed in Spandex cycling gear and had a helmet tucked under one arm. He looked sweaty and physically taxed, as if he had just battled Lance Armstrong up L'Alpe d'Huez.

Vaughn's sudden movement apparently unnerved Gallway because his tone became shrill. "It's okay. It's Rod."

At first, she thought Rod was just another model arriving at the condo to pose nude, but when he reached for the Lalique bowl that Vaughn had moved and centered it perfectly inside the dust-free circle on the table, she knew he had intimate knowledge of this place.

"I have horrible news," Gallway said, extending his hand toward the young man. "Anya's been murdered."

The helmet fell to the floor with a hollow thud. A moment later, Rod knelt in front of Gallway, surrounding him with an intimate, comforting embrace.

Anya had told Lucien that Gallway had been her lover, but that was another lie in what was becoming a long list of them. Davie wondered why Gallway hadn't admitted upfront that the two had never slept together. Maybe he assumed she and Vaughn already knew.

There was someone else in Anya's life, then. A secret lover whose identity she had hidden from everyone. Secrets didn't remain secret forever. Someone knew. People talked. Davie hoped Anya's telephone records would lead her to the baby's father and possibly to her killer.

14

VAUGHN RESCUED HIS LATTE from the floor of the car moments before Davie pulled away from Gallway's condo. As they approached the entrance to the 405, Vaughn's cell phone rang. Davie could tell from listening to her partner's side of the conversation that there had been another homicide in Pacific Division.

He ended the call and turned to her. "That was Giordano. He wants us back at the station—pronto."

"What happened?"

"A tourist in Venice stumbled over a body in an alley off Main. He's assigning me as IO, so you're on your own, partner."

"Where are Garcia and Montes?"

Vaughn took a sip of his latte. "Garcia is off until Monday, Montes is in court. It's just you and me for now."

Davie entered the freeway on the Wilshire onramp. "The second murder in the division and it's still January. That's a regular crime wave. Who's the vic?"

"A homeless junkie named Beau Fischer. Giordano says he hung out mostly in Venice, but Santa Monica PD scooped him up a couple times on drug charges and ADW."

Davie wasn't surprised. Assault with a Deadly Weapon and drugs were common in the homeless community. "Any suspects?"

"Another hype probably killed him over dope. Just my luck, you get *vatrushkis* and movie stars, and I get to do a bum sweep in Venice, looking for witnesses."

"We need all kinds of experience if we want to be good detectives."

Vaughn made a drama out of swiveling toward the backseat. "I hear an echo. Is Giordano in the car?"

She let Vaughn off at the sidewalk in front of the station. Then she headed east toward the Volga Bakery, knowing there was one stop she had to make first.

———

The building's dull brick façade seemed to sag under the burden of an ornate sign: GARDEN VISTA ASSISTED LIVING APARTMENTS. Davie parked in the garage and made her way to the front desk. She jotted her name on the log and waited while the ancient elevator groaned to the second floor. At the end of the hallway, she used a key to enter unit 221. The room was filled with remnants of a life well-lived: a chintz loveseat, a grandfather clock, and a rogue's gallery of family photos clustered together in silver-toned frames mounted on the wall.

"Who's there?"

It was a woman's voice, quivery and frail. A cloud of snowy hair rested against the back of a blue recliner as the footrest retreated, leaving the woman in a sitting position.

"It's me, Grammy. I just stopped by to say hello."

"Davie? Is Robbie with you?"

Her grandmother couldn't see that Davie's brother wasn't in the room. Macular degeneration had stolen nearly all of her sight.

"I came alone."

The slight slump of her shoulders conveyed disappointment, but she disguised it with practiced cheer. "How lovely."

Davie leaned over so her grandmother's outstretched hand could touch her face. Grammy's hand felt soft and cool against her skin. It smelled of Jergens lotion, triggering childhood memories of weekends at her grandparents' house, when Poppy was still alive and all things seemed possible.

"Your mother was just here. I'm sorry you missed her."

Davie didn't respond. There was nothing to say. She hadn't seen her mother in six months and that was fine with her. After her father was forced out of the LAPD, he descended into a dark pit of despair. Her mother found Bear's depression impossibly dreary. She said she had to get out of the house or she'd go crazy. A gym membership was just what she needed to clear her head. Soon after, she had exercised her buff new body into the bed of a wealthy real estate developer. The two married before the ink was dry on her parents' divorce papers. At fifteen, Davie was left to deal with her mother's betrayal and her father's shattered psyche. Bear had recovered; the relationship between Davie and her mother had not.

After a long silence, her grandmother said, "I know Evelyn has her faults, but she's still my daughter."

"She's lucky to have you in her corner."

"I'm in your corner, too, Davie."

"I know, Grammy."

It was almost four thirty p.m. One of the aides would arrive soon to take her grandmother to eat in the community dining room. Grammy was still in her slippers, so Davie brought her shoes and support stockings from the bedroom and knelt by her chair. The stockings were tight, so it took some tugging to get them onto her feet and pulled up to her knees.

"Are you still living alone in that man's guesthouse?"

"His name is Alexander Camden. He's a good guy. Don't worry."

"What happened to that nice young man you were dating?"

"It didn't work out."

"I'm sorry. I liked him."

"I know, but not every man is Poppy."

"I suppose not," she said. "Your grandfather was special, but I worry there's nobody around that place for you to talk to. Not like at an apartment house where you bump into people at the Dumpster. Don't you get lonely?"

"I get together with friends when I can. Right now there's not much time for that. I'm always at work."

"Even on the weekends?"

Davie slipped the shoes onto her grandmother's feet and fastened the Velcro straps. "Sometimes."

"But sometimes you're at home. Maybe you need a dog to keep you company."

"I can't take care of a dog right now, Grammy."

She sighed. "You're probably right. Dogs get bored without their people. A cat?"

Davie picked up a comb from the end table and used the rat-tail to refresh the curls on her grandmother's head.

"Someday, maybe."

"I worry that you're alone. It makes me think about the thing that happened to you."

Her grandmother called her officer-involved shooting "The Thing," for the same reason the people of Northern Ireland referred to their history as "The Troubles"—because surviving violence gives you license to abbreviate. Davie was still angry that her mother had burdened Grammy about details of Abel Hurtado's death. It was just another of her piss-poor decisions.

"That was months ago, Grammy. Nothing like that will ever happen to me again."

"There are a lot of bad people in this world, Davie. Sometimes it's hard to pick them out of a crowd."

Years of training and experience as a cop had taught her how to pick bad guys out of a crowd. At least she hoped so. Anya Nosova hadn't been so lucky.

Davie kissed the wrinkles creasing her grandmother's forehead. "I have to get back to work now."

Her grandmother patted Davie's cheek. "I wish you could stay for dinner. It's always a treat to watch Mrs. Edelstein drool in her tapioca."

"Sounds like fun. How about a rain check?" Davie stood. "I may not be able to stop by tomorrow, but I'll call for sure."

"I know you will. You always do."

Davie paused at the door. "Bye, Grammy. Love you."

"Love you much."

It was the same goodbye script the two had repeated for as long as Davie could remember. A rush of emotion filled her chest. Some might have called it love, but she had learned that certain things were too pure to dilute with labels.

The elevator lumbered to the ground floor. When the doors opened, she signed out and headed for her car. Parked just outside the front door in the loading zone was a dusty cable company van. The dirt was unusual. Most companies kept their vehicles clean because, to many customers, clean equaled high-quality product and good service. Even Pacific detectives were expected to wash city vehicles in the car wash next to the station's garage.

She glanced up and caught the driver watching her. The guy looked normal enough—buff, blond, and neat in his company polo shirt—but his eyes were narrowed and calculating. Grammy was right. Picking bad guys out of a crowd wasn't easy. It took practice.

A moment later, the cable guy broke eye contact and Davie returned to the car. A dirty van was a small detail that probably meant nothing, but a lot of men had served time in prison because of her. Call it intuition. She had learned not to ignore those feelings. During the drive across town to the Volga Bakery, she kept checking her rear-view window for any signs she was being followed.

15

"Skål!" **Malcolm Harrington clinked** glasses with his host Thor Amdahl in the dining room of the Sons of Norway Lodge, a converted house in a Van Nuys residential neighborhood of low-slung homes and squat apartment buildings.

Harrington was still feeling buoyed after his successful meeting with the mayor, so while waiting for the dinner meeting to begin, he downed a glass of aquavit and dutifully admired the lodge's gift shop filled with all things Norsk, including rosemalled plates, krumkake bakers, aebleskiver pans, and lefsa grills. His enthusiasm had earned him an invitation to the annual lutefisk and meatball dinner in November. Lye-soaked fish swimming in butter was not at all appealing, but excursions into the city's cultural backwater were part of his new job as Inspector General. The police commission's goal was to increase ethnic diversity in the ranks of the LAPD, and if any group qualified as a minority in the City of Angels, it was Norwegian-Americans. He doubted there was a single person in all of city government who knew the meaning of *uffda!*

Harrington felt his cell phone vibrating in his coat pocket. He checked the display and saw that the call was from LAPD Internal Affairs Investigator Alex Sloan. Shortly after speaking to the mayor, he had asked Sloan to reopen the Davie Richards investigation. He must have found something or he wouldn't be calling so soon.

"Sorry to interrupt, Thor, but I have to take this call."

Amdahl glanced at the women setting up the buffet. "Should we wait dinner for you then?"

"Why don't you start without me?"

"Oh boy, I'll save you a seat, but you'd better hurry up. The reindeer roast goes fast."

Harrington hurried outside the building before answering the call, hunching his shoulders against the cold air. "What is it, Alex? I'm up to my eyeballs in knackbrod and limpa."

"I'm parked across the street. We need to talk."

Harrington scanned the area and saw the flashing headlights of a city ride. He walked across a strip of dead grass in front of the building and made his way to the vehicle. As soon as he opened the passenger door, the collective reek of cigarette smoke and pine air freshener assaulted his senses. Hot air blasting through the vent only exaggerated the odor. Harrington slid into the passenger seat. He shut off the heater and lowered the window to get some fresh air.

Harrington had requested Sloan because the detective also worked off-duty as a private investigator. Harrington's law firm had hired him on a few cases and found him to be a loyal soldier even though the man's addiction to nicotine counted as a character flaw in Harrington's book.

"You've been smoking in the car again," he said. "You really should stop."

"I will."

"When?"

"When I'm ready."

Harrington accepted temporary defeat. "What did you find?"

"I checked out Richards senior. He keeps a low profile. Not even a traffic ticket in the past fifteen years. He owns a dive bar called the Lucky Duck, which gives him decent income but nothing to write home about. He also has a PI license. He works part-time for a small group of clients, mostly insurance companies."

Harrington felt let down by the news. He had hoped for more. "Anything on the daughter?"

"She's only worked Pacific Homicide for a short time. She keeps her head down, but I found people who were more than willing to talk trash about her."

"Regale me."

"In her patrol days in Southeast she earned a reputation as a cowgirl. Fearless, maybe too fearless."

"Any information about the shooting?"

"Just a rumor. People say Hall had the situation under control until she panicked and started shooting."

"Do you believe that?"

"It's doubtful. Doesn't fit her profile."

In his peripheral vision, Harrington saw Thor Amdahl on the front porch of the building holding a plate of food. A moment later, the Norwegian shrugged and walked back inside.

"I need more than rumors," Harrington said.

"That's why I paid a call on Abel Hurtado's widow."

"Is she still grieving?"

Sloan reached for the heater knob and turned it up a notch. "Not that you'd notice. The police report claims she didn't see what happened that night because she was prone on the bed getting the shit get kicked out of her. But her memory has gotten sharper since then."

101

Harrington felt a tingling sensation on his skin. "How so?"

Sloan turned the heater up again. "According to the widow, the two detectives were screaming before the shooting, calling each other names."

"Are you sure they weren't addressing her dearly departed husband?"

Sloan picked up a pack of cigarettes from the dashboard. He tapped one into his waiting hand and slid it between his lips. "She said they acted like there was some sort of beef between them."

"Don't even think about lighting up."

Sloan ignored the admonition. "After I left her place, I made a few phone calls and guess what? Davie Richards and Spencer Hall were having an affair. Hall was separated at the time and headed for divorce, but when his almost-ex-wife found out about the hookup, she wasn't amused. He recently got back together with the wife, so I had a talk with her. She told me she'd called her husband about financial issues connected with their divorce just before he and Richards left for Hurtado's house that day. He told her he had just ended his relationship with Richards."

"Don't you think that's odd? His telling his estranged wife about breaking up with his lover?"

"Wifey has control issues. I'm guessing she pressed him for information."

Harrington chuckled. "Maybe Richards was aiming at Hall and hit Hurtado by mistake."

"It's never smart to piss off a cowgirl," Sloan said, "especially if she carries a forty-five."

Harrington had merely been joking before, but now he steepled his fingers and considered the possibilities. "So, what's next?"

"Some ambulance-chasing attorney got wind of the case. He claims Mr. Hurtado was a good man and a good father. The guy wasn't beating his wife that night, only comforting her after she fell and smashed her face against the coffee table. The attorney claims Richards fabricated statements on the crime report to cover her ass. Now his poor client is left to raise a young daughter alone. Somebody has to pay. The lawyer is floating a settlement figure of ten mil."

Despite the chilly air flowing through the open window, the heater was making Harrington feel clammy and uncomfortable. "Does Mrs. Hurtado really think a jury will believe perjured testimony, especially with two detectives contradicting her story?"

Sloan pulled a lighter from his pocket. "Lying on the witness stand isn't limited to victims. As you know, cops lie too."

Just like William Richards lied, he thought. The civil jury's decision in the Richards trial still left a bitter taste in Harrington's mouth. He would never get another chance to right that wrong, but it was within his power to keep Davie Richards off the streets if he found credible evidence that she was dirty just like her old man.

"Police groupies on the jury are going to think Mrs. Hurtado is a typical battered woman," Harrington said, "excusing her abuser and turning against the cops who saved her life."

Sloan rolled his thumb across the lighter wheel, igniting a yellow flame. "The scent of money is a powerful perfume. The defense will hire a hack expert in repressed memory and paint the husband as a martyred saint."

Harrington studied Sloan's face, marking the moment, calculating the risks of pursuing felony charges against Davie Richards. The theory that Richards meant to kill Hall defied logic. There was no evidence she was stupid. On the other hand, he understood the pain of unrequited love. It could be unbearable. Davie Richards's lover dumped her just prior to the shooting. That may have caused sufficient mental instability that she lost control and killed a man. Once she realized she had screwed up, she convinced Hall to falsify the police report to cover it up. Conspiracy and collusion under color of authority were serious charges and, if proven, would end her career and possibly send her to prison.

He remembered Maria Luna's face when she heard the jury's verdict that William Richards was not financially responsible for her son's paralysis. It seemed like a cable broke on a theatre curtain and yards of fabric had crashed down, smothering her under its weight. Before she walked out of the courtroom, she had flashed him a look that could only be described as contempt. Seeing her like that had broken something inside of him. He wondered if Davie Richards had experienced similar feelings just before the shooting.

"What's Richards working on now?" Harrington asked.

"A Jane Doe found in the sewer. She's the lead Investigative Officer."

Harrington felt a chill on his back. "Do they know who the victim is?"

"Not that I've heard."

Harrington watched the flame of Sloan's lighter move closer to the cigarette. He counted the teardrops on the detective's paisley tie, considering what he was about to do. His pulse escalated as he thought about the peril to his career and possibly to his personal safety if things went sideways.

"Bring Hall in for questioning," he said. "Squeeze him until you get the truth."

16

THE VOLGA BAKERY WHERE Anya Nosova bought her *vatrushkis* was located mid-block on Las Palmas in Hollywood. It was not far from where the cab driver had dropped her off the Saturday night she disappeared.

The owner was squat and bald except for a fringe of wispy hair circling the back and sides of his head. The man's stooped shoulders and dark under-eye pouches signaled to Davie that he was a person whose weighty responsibilities kept him awake at night. His name was Pasha Kozlov and he was not happy to have an LAPD Homicide detective impeding commerce in a store full of paying customers.

According to Kozlov, he had kept the bakery open until nine p.m. the previous Saturday because it was a key weekend in the Russian New Year celebration and everybody wanted bread and pastries. Anya had come into the store at about eight forty p.m.

"Did she usually come in that late?" Davie said.

"She is dressed up. Fancy black dress. Red coat. High shoes. I think maybe she go to New Year's party."

"Have any idea where?"

A middle-aged couple walked out of the store without buying anything. Kozlov threw up his arms, apparently exasperated by the missed sale. "That night I have many customers. Like now. No time for Anya."

The implication was not lost on Davie. Kozlov had no time for her, either. She waited as he bagged a loaf of rye bread and a dozen cookies for an elderly woman wearing an old-fashioned *babushka* headscarf.

"Did Anya seem upset that night?"

A bell above the door tinkled as a young woman walked in with two small children. Kozlov seemed irritated that Davie was still buzzing around his store like an unwanted fly.

He shrugged. "She order one *vatrushki*. Her cell phone ring. She go outside. Talk, talk, talk."

As soon as the search warrant for phone records was returned, Davie could identify the person Anya had been talking to that night.

"Did you hear what she said?"

"I help customer. I turn around. Anya is gone."

"She left without paying?"

He tidied loaves of bread on the counter. "She left without *vatrushki*. Without purse. I wait. Nine o'clock, I close store."

"She never came back?"

"No."

"What did the purse look like?"

"Is like a red heart but with beads that sparkle."

"Where is the purse now?"

"I give to policeman. On Monday."

Davie felt tension radiate along her jaw. She doubted that anybody from the LAPD had picked up Anya's purse. Still, somebody had interfered with her investigation, possibly compromising evidence. She wondered who it had been and what she would do about it.

"Did he give you his name?"

A customer stood at the cash register drumming his fingers on the counter as he waited to pay for a bag of rolls. Kozlov frowned before pulling a business card from under the counter and handing it to Davie. It was a two-sided generic card printed in bulk by the Los Angeles Police Department. It had a blank line that allowed detectives to write in a name and telephone number, but there was nothing written on this card.

"What did the guy look like? Tall. Short. Fat. Thin."

"I see many men that day. Who knows if they are fat? Please, now you give me peace and quiet to run my store."

A thousand questions cycled through Davie's brain, the foremost of which was, Who had given that business card to Pasha Kozlov in exchange for Anya's purse? Any sworn or civilian personnel who worked for the department had access to those cards. They were handed out to dozens of people every day. Checking the card for fingerprints was probably a waste of time. Even if the paper surface were smooth enough to absorb prints, any number of people could have handled the card since Monday. Still, she slipped it into an evidence bag she pulled from her notebook.

At some point Anya must have realized she had left her purse at the bakery. She didn't have a car and she was wearing high heels. She must have eventually arrived at her final destination or she would have gone back for the purse. She might have sent someone to collect it, except the purse was picked up on Monday, two days after her disappearance. It had been Tuesday morning when Hyperion employees discovered her body. Until then, nobody knew she was dead, leaving Davie to wonder if it had been Anya's killer who had collected the purse, hoping to eliminate any evidence that might implicate him in her murder.

17

DAVIE STOOD ON THE sidewalk outside the bakery inhaling deeply. She wished she were a bloodhound capable of following Anya's scent, but all her brain registered were fumes from passing cars and the aroma of burnt sugar streaming from the bakery's exhaust pipes. Her gaze traveled along the pavement, but she saw no manhole covers capable of swallowing a body.

Anya hadn't taken a forty-dollar taxi ride to Hollywood just to buy pastries, so the bakery probably wasn't her final destination. Kozlov said Anya was dressed for a party. She had only ordered one *vatrushki*, so she wasn't buying for a crowd. She'd probably bought the pastry for herself before moving on to the evening's main event.

Storefront businesses huddled together on both sides of the street, including a frame shop, a dry cleaner, and a hair salon. She scanned each façade until she spotted a surveillance camera mounted at the roofline above a liquor store across the street. The lens appeared to be pointing toward the front door of the bakery. If luck were on her side, the video had captured shots of Anya arriving and leaving the bakery sometime before nine o'clock last Saturday night. The tape might also confirm who had left the LAPD business card the following Monday.

When the young man behind the counter heard Davie open the front door, he looked up from a physics book that was lying open in front of him. He had dark unruly hair, rimless eyeglasses smudged by fingerprints, and a faded maroon and gold hoodie emblazoned with the logo of the University of Southern California Trojans.

Davie looked around the store but saw no other customers. She showed her department ID. He told her his father owned the store. When she asked to see the surveillance tape he began to sweat, which soon produced the acrid odor of fear.

"I know how to work the system," he said, "but there's no film in the camera. We just keep it for show."

"That's not helpful if somebody robs the store."

"I have a good memory for faces. I could identify the robbers." His gaze darted below the counter. "And we have a gun. It's registered. I can show you the permit if you want."

"Who was working at eight thirty last Saturday night?"

He averted his gaze. "My father."

"When will he be in? I'd like to talk to him."

"He left for India Sunday morning—on business. He won't be back for a month."

"What time did he close the store on Saturday?"

He hesitated. "Actually, I closed the store that night."

"And what time was that?"

"Eight fifty."

Davie gave him a stony stare. "Don't play games with me. Why didn't you just tell me you were here that night?"

"You said eight thirty. I wasn't working at eight thirty. I didn't get here until eight fifty. Twenty minutes. That's a big difference."

"Did you see a woman in a red coat standing outside the bakery around that time?"

The clerk brushed sweat from his forehead with the sleeve of his hoodie. "Yeah, I saw her, but I heard her first. She was screaming. I thought she was being mugged so I went outside to check, but she was just yelling into her cell phone."

"What was she saying?"

"I don't know. I couldn't make out the words. I waved but when she saw me, she started running." He paused to moisten his lips. "The problem is I may have been holding the gun when I waved at her, but I didn't mean to scare her. Really, I didn't. I only took it with me because I thought she was in trouble. She reported me, didn't she? Please don't tell my father."

"Which way did she go when she left the bakery?"

"Toward Highland."

Davie held up Bell's photo of Anya. "Do you recognize this woman?"

The clerk glanced at the picture. "Yeah, she's the one I saw. Is she going to press charges? Please don't arrest me, I have a really important physics test next week. I have to ace it or I won't pass the class."

Davie didn't bother telling him that Anya Nosova was in no position to jeopardize his grade. Instead, she recited her standard lecture on gun safety and the penalties for Brandishing a Weapon. Then she advised him to load a tape into the store's surveillance camera or, better yet, upgrade to digital.

Back in the car, she thought about where a young girl might go for a Russian New Year's party. The neighborhood was dotted with small businesses and a few modest houses. One of the nearby residents might have hosted an event but if not, where else would Anya go to party? Restaurant. Club. Hotel.

She steered the car toward Highland, surveying both sides of the street for possible venues. She had driven only five blocks when she spotted a five-story boutique hotel with a row of taxis waiting by the curb. The sign read THE EDISON. She parked on a side street and went inside.

18

THE MANAGER OF THE Edison, who introduced himself as Charles Nyland, was in his early fifties, wearing the pinstriped suit and guarded demeanor of a company man. As soon as Davie told him she was looking for evidence that a murder victim had attended a party at his hotel, he hustled her to a quiet alcove adjacent to the lobby where no one could eavesdrop on their conversation.

"We did have a Russian New Year's party Saturday night," he said, "but the hotel has an exclusive clientele, and I can't give you any information about our guests without a search warrant."

"Look, Mr. Nyland, nobody wants to invade the privacy of your guests, but I need to look at your surveillance video to see if my victim was here. If I don't see her, I'll leave."

"You'd be spying on guests without their permission."

"If you don't want the footage to be seen, why do you have a security system?"

"It's strictly for guest safety."

Davie pulled out a piece of paper from her notebook, labeled *Homicide Investigation Notes*, and wrote the words *refuses to cooperate* large enough for Nyland to read them even upside down.

"Do you have children, Mr. Nyland?"

He stared at the words on the page. "Yes. Two."

"Someone killed Anya Nosova and dumped her body in the sewer. She was just nineteen years old and her parents' only child."

His face betrayed no emotion. "I'm sorry for their loss."

"Yeah, me too. No parent expects to outlive their child." Davie slowly closed her notebook. "With or without your cooperation I'm going to find out if she was at this hotel last Saturday night. If you want to play hardball, I'll come back with a search warrant. A judge will order you to give me details about every party and every guest registered at the hotel for the past year."

Davie knew no judge would grant her such a sweeping warrant, but Nyland didn't need to know that. There was a short silence before the manager cleared his throat.

"Perhaps I should check with our corporate office."

"Perhaps you should."

Davie waited fifteen minutes in the lobby under the spell of recessed lighting and a single iris impaled in a Zen flower dish centered on the lobby table. A band played dance music in a room down the hall. After what seemed like endless ABBA tunes, Davie heard the whisper of tulle and the click of high heels against marble tiles. She turned to see a woman walking toward her in a wedding dress. The bride headed toward the front door, pulling a cigarette and lighter from her cleavage. Wednesday was an unusual day for a wedding. Davie wondered if a film company was shooting a movie, but she saw no evidence of cameras or clapperboards.

When Nyland returned, he informed Davie that corporate had cleared her to view the video but not to copy it. He led her to a back office where monitors covered an entire wall and introduced her to the hotel's Director of Security, Cal Rogers.

"Show her the video," Nyland said. "Then escort her out of the hotel."

Rogers had the well-toned physique of an athlete. Wire-rimmed glasses failed to mask his ice blue eyes. His premature gray hair was tied in a ponytail at the nape of his neck with a string of black leather. His features were symmetrical and delicate, what some might call pretty.

A small desk abutted a back wall and displayed matching charcoal-colored containers for every office need: papers, pencils, paperclips, and business cards. On the desk was a small Lucite trophy embedded with a Los Angeles County Sheriff's star and the words *Deputy of the Year* awarded by an Elks Lodge. Davie had received a similar award as a patrol officer assigned to Southeast Division.

"How long were you on the job?" Davie said.

Rogers glanced at the trophy. "Four years, all on jail duty. I hated every minute of it. Now I bust people for smoking in the rooms and staying past checkout time, but I don't take my work home with me."

Rogers folded his muscular frame into one of two chairs in front of the wall of computer monitors. He motioned for Davie to sit in the other one. His long slim fingers tapped the keyboard until a view of the front door appeared, dated and time-stamped the previous Saturday night.

The action was in black and white but of good quality. Davie could clearly see a woman—thin, light-haired, and wearing a coat—enter the lobby at 9:10 p.m. She couldn't confirm that the coat was red, but the woman was definitely Anya Nosova.

"That's her. That's my victim."

Rogers switched to the reception-desk view. They saw Anya speaking to the clerk, gesturing. She appeared to be asking for directions.

"Have you ever seen her at the hotel before?"

Rogers stared at the screen. "Not me, but I can ask around."

"Where was the New Year's party held?"

"Fifth floor. Presidential Suite."

She thought about the man who flashed that LAPD business card when he picked up Anya's purse at the Volga Bakery on Monday.

"Any law enforcement types at the party?"

He glanced at her and frowned. "I was off that night but it's unlikely."

"Can you show me the shots from outside the suite?"

"We don't record beyond the elevators. Privacy issues."

Rogers changed the screen format so they could view four shots at once, including the fifth-floor landing. At 9:16 p.m., the elevator doors opened. Anya stepped out of the car and turned right.

"Which way is the Presidential Suite from the elevator?" Davie asked.

"It's the only suite on the floor. There would have been a sign near the landing, directing guests to the right."

"What's to the left?"

"The service entrance to the kitchen. Nobody uses that door except the caterer."

During the next few minutes, she and Rogers watched a parade of arriving guests, men with attitudes and women wearing enough flashy diamond jewelry to light up a runway at LAX. There were also a dozen or so beautiful young women in skimpy outfits who looked like hookers to Davie.

At 9:40 p.m., the elevator doors opened again. Four people exited, including a slim man with a buzz cut and an air of macho entitlement and a stocky guy with a Joseph Stalin mustache. Two tattooed knuckle draggers dressed in dark clothes shielded the men. They were probably private bodyguards, but they reminded her of extras in a 1940s gangster movie. One of the bodyguards scanned the hallway. When he saw the camera, he raised his hand to block the lens.

"Who are the two guys with the mouth breathers?"

Rogers leaned forward and lowered his voice. "Don't tell my boss I said this, but the thin guy is the host of the party, Grigory Satine. He has some sort of event at the hotel every couple of months for the local glitterati."

"Who's usually on the guest list?"

"Everybody from business tycoons to politicians."

"Anybody I'd know?"

"Maybe, but I can't give you any names. All I'll say is Satine spares no expense. Pricey booze. Gourmet food. Beautiful girls."

"Hookers or Hollywood starlets?"

"Is there a difference?"

"Where does he get his money?"

"He owns a nightclub in West Hollywood called Perestroika."

"Is he mafia?"

Rogers shrugged. "As far as I know, he's a local businessman who likes to entertain."

"Who's the stocky guy with the mustache?"

"Never seen him before."

Davie kept her gaze riveted on the screen. A few minutes later, she bolted upright in her chair when she saw Ray Anthony Falcon step out of the elevator car. For a moment he stood alone on the landing, fiddling nervously with his shoulder-length curly hair. She couldn't confirm the color but the tone was light. She guessed it was golden blond.

The hair all but confirmed Falcon was the man John Bell had seen at Anya's apartment earlier that evening. The two had left around at the same time but in separate vehicles. They were obviously heading to the same party. She wondered why he hadn't offered Anya a ride.

Falcon turned right and headed toward the party. Davie pointed to the actor. "Ever see that man at the hotel before?"

Rogers hesitated. "Not here. He's that movie star with the three names, right?"

Davie nodded and asked him to fast-forward through the next few hours of tape, looking for shots of Anya. But if she had left the fifth floor that night, she hadn't used the guest elevator.

"Is there another way off that floor?"

"The stairs, but we would have seen your girl walk past the camera to get to the door. She could have left by the service elevator in the kitchen, but only the catering manager and her staff have security key cards."

The video showed guests, including Falcon, moving toward the elevators until 2:23 a.m. After that, Davie saw no one in the hallway until 3:17. The action was speeding by so fast she almost missed it.

"Stop," she said. "Back up."

Rogers replayed the footage. A heavy-set man wearing a chef's coat pushed a cloth-covered cart down the hall toward the elevator. A baseball cap obscured his face.

"Looks like one of the kitchen staff," Rogers said. "I don't recognize him, but the caterer sometimes hires outside help for these events."

"Are they allowed to ride the guest elevator?"

"They're supposed to use the one in the kitchen, but at that hour nobody would complain. The catering manager should be able to identify the guy, but she won't be back until tomorrow morning."

"Run the video again."

Rogers complied and together they watched the action two more times.

"See anything odd about that cart?" she said.

"There's nothing on top of it."

"And we can't see what's under the tablecloth."

"Looks like a metal cart from the kitchen. There's usually a shelf below where they put dirty dishes."

Davie's mouth felt dry as she watched the waiter bend his body at a thirty-degree angle and prod the cart down the hallway with long slow strides.

"The guy's built like a brick shithouse," she said.

"Yeah. So?"

"So why is he struggling to push the cart?"

Rogers let out a soft whistle. "Good question."

"Could he have left the hotel without being seen?"

"Maybe by the side lobby door. There's no camera there."

Davie wanted to show Kozlov the surveillance video, hoping the man who'd picked up Anya's purse had been among the guests.

"I need a copy of the video."

"I can't give it to you. I'd lose my job."

"You're going to make me waste time getting a search warrant?"

"You have five more days before the system automatically tapes over itself. In case you have trouble with the judge, I'll ask Nyland if I can make a copy and hold it until you get the warrant. That's all I can do."

Davie was disappointed but not surprised. Taping over old footage was standard procedure, which meant she wouldn't be able to see if Anya had attended of any of Satine's previous parties.

Rogers stood. "I'll find Nyland. I'll meet you in the lobby in about ten minutes." Then he walked out of the room.

She wondered if he'd left her alone with the video equipment because he'd lost his edge or because he still remembered how hard it was for a cop to catch a break. Didn't matter. She decided to exploit the opportunity.

Davie's pulse drummed as she pulled her phone from her pocket and switched it to camera mode. Snapping photos on her cell might cause chain of custody issues when the case went to trial, but it was worth the risk if having the pictures led to an arrest.

She had watched Rogers reverse the video several times, so she followed his example and reversed it again. She repeatedly glanced at the doorknob to make sure it wasn't turning as she pushed play, fast-forwarding and stopping to snap photos of everyone who was at the party that night, including the man rolling the cart toward the elevator. Despite her fear, nobody burst through the door to confront her. When she was finished, she slipped the phone into her pocket and left the room. Rogers was waiting for her in the lobby.

"Nyland said it's okay to preserve the video, but he won't budge on letting you have a copy. I'll ask the catering manager if she recognizes the guy pushing the cart and give you a call tomorrow. I know you'll have to interview any witnesses yourself, but at least it's a start."

Davie slipped him a business card from her notebook. She hoped her gratitude was reflected in her tone. "Thanks."

His nod told her he understood. As she slid into the car, she noticed he was still standing by the hotel entrance, watching her.

Davie had no way of knowing if the party's host was a member of the Russian mafia, but from experience, she knew criminals often preyed on people of their own race or nationality. Los Angeles had a large Russian émigré population, and it appeared that Anya Nosova might have been hobnobbing with some of its shadier members.

A few months back, she had read an internal LAPD bulletin about several cases in Northern California involving the remains of young Russian prostitutes pulled from bodies of water. Police suspected the girls were victims of the Odessa mafia, but they couldn't prove it.

Anya was found in a river of sorts—the L.A. sewer system. She had been stranded in the city with little money. Yet she'd managed to collect benefactors as easily as seashells on the beach. Karen Skjelstad said Anya was hanging out with a bad crowd. Troy Gallway said she was ambitious. On Saturday night she attended a party hosted by a nightclub owner with other young women, some who looked like hookers. Davie wondered if Anya had turned to prostitution to keep herself supplied with *vatrushkis*.

Anya's murder might be unrelated to the cases in Northern California, but Davie planned to find an expert within the LAPD who could provide a conduit to L.A.'s Russian community.

In the meantime, she was going to have a chat with Grigory Satine. It was 9:13 p.m. The action at Perestroika was likely just getting started.

19

PERESTROIKA WAS LOCATED IN the middle of a nondescript block of storefronts on Santa Monica Boulevard near Plummer Park in West Hollywood. The only signage was a neon *P* to the left of what Davie assumed was the front door. Black curtains shrouded the entrance. About a dozen twenty-somethings, mostly dressed in black party attire, were lined up near the door, waiting to get in.

For the next few minutes Davie sat across the street in the Jetta, watching people advance to the front of the line and then disappear behind the curtains. The pace was slow, so she assumed there were gatekeepers but she couldn't see them from her vantage point in the car.

She didn't want to alert Satine by flashing her badge at the door, but if she got past the bouncers, she was sure she could talk to him. The line swelled to about twenty people before Davie shook her hair out of its knot. She smeared gloss over her lips, removed her gun belt and tucked her .45 inside her purse, along with Anya's photograph. As an afterthought, she undid the top two buttons of her oxford shirt, hoping to distract from a black polyester pantsuit that screamed *cop*. Then she strolled across the street and melted into the crowd.

When Davie reached the front of the line, she recognized the two massively built men standing at the entrance. They were the knuckle draggers she'd seen guarding Satine at the Edison New Year's party. The pair reminded her of Tweedle-Dee and Tweedle-Dum from the *Alice's Adventures in Wonderland* book that Bear had read to her as a child, except these two had matching buzz cuts and gold chains nestled on hairy tattooed chests. Each of their arms was the circumference of her waist. She wondered if they trained at the same gym or shared the same steroid needle.

The shorter of the two men had eyes that were feral and predatory. They reminded her of mythic beasts that killed not for food but for pleasure.

He thrust his hand toward Davie. "ID."

She flashed a smile as she held up her driver's license, hoping the gesture looked coquettish and not demented. "I look young but I'm old enough to know better, if you know what I mean." She would likely score more points if she batted her eyelashes, but she couldn't force herself to do it.

Davie's heart pounded as the beast pointed the beam of a flashlight on her card and studied it carefully.

"Let her in, Vlad. Perestroika is made for pretty girls."

Vlad's expression hardened. He shot back with a few angry words in Russian.

His partner's cupid's bow lips stretched into a smile. "You forget. We are lion tamers. This one is no more than a hundred pounds. If she causes us trouble, we will poke her with our chairs." He elbowed Vlad's tree-trunk arm and winked.

Vlad didn't seem appeased, but a moment later he motioned Davie inside. As she stepped over the threshold, she sensed Vlad's gaze fixed on her back like the laser beam of a hunting rifle.

Perestroika's interior lighting was dim. The air smelled of onions and strong perfume. As Davie's eyes adjusted to the dark, she noticed yellow, magenta, and red silk streamers billowing from a glittery disco ball mounted to the ceiling and flowing into the far corners of the room. Tables covered with food and bottles of vodka hugged the dance floor. A deejay on a riser played music for a pack of gyrating dancers. Suspended above his head, a woman danced in a cage, wearing knee-high black boots and black lingerie.

Grigory Satine stood near the bar on the left side of the room. His image on the Edison's surveillance cameras didn't do him justice. Davie guessed he was a few years shy of forty with short hair the color of summer wheat and sapphire eyes that were alive and engaged. His nose was flattened as if it had been broken, but that only made his face more interesting. An expensive-looking suit draped his trim frame like a second skin.

Satine's expression was confident, almost cocky, as he whispered in the ear of a thin blonde with oversized breasts that looked grotesque on her teenaged body. The young woman's gaze darted around the room with a haunted expression. A moment later, Satine walked into the crowd as an aging Baby Boomer slipped onto the stool next to the blonde. A forced smile ghosted across her lips as she moved her hand between the man's legs. A few minutes later, the pair stood and strolled toward the front door.

Anya had come to L.A. to be a model, but sometimes "model" was a euphemism for "prostitute." She imagined Anya sitting at the bar, hooking up with rheumy-eyed old men in order to line the pockets of Satine's custom-made suits. What Davie had learned so far about

Anya wasn't shaping up to fit the Hollywood cliché of the beautiful young girl lured into prostitution and then used, abused, and discarded like yesterday's garbage. Still, Davie felt troubled as she imagined Anya servicing men from this dimly lit bar.

She watched Satine stroll down a long hallway before following him, her hand in her purse, gripping the butt of her .45. Satine used a key to open a door toward the rear of the nightclub. His body tensed when he saw Davie walking toward him.

"If you're looking for the restroom, it's by the front door." His voice was smooth and mellow with only a hint of an accent.

"Actually, I was looking for you."

He cocked his head and smiled as she stepped past him into his office. The décor was a mix of modern metal furniture in shades of charcoal and black. One wall was accented with Russian religious icons all depicting the Virgin Mary. The icons looked old and valuable, maybe priceless. They added splashes of gold, carnelian, and peacock to an otherwise monochromatic room. She wondered how Satine had acquired them. A two-year associate degree from Santa Monica College hung on the wall behind Satine's desk, a small detail she found odd.

"Your frown tells me you are not impressed by my alma mater," he said.

"We can't all go to Harvard."

He gazed at the diploma. "I keep it to remind me that education is not always found in a classroom."

"Very philosophical."

Davie picked up a beveled frame on the credenza that held a photo of an old man wearing a Soviet-style military uniform that was weighted down with medals, gold epaulets, and a matching gold belt.

"The uniform looks World War II. He must have served with the Allied Forces," she said.

Satine closed the door and began circling her—a cheetah stalking a gazelle. "My grandfather. Can I offer you vodka? Or are you on duty?"

She wasn't surprised he'd pegged her as a cop. Her pantsuit was a dead giveaway. "I'm not much of a drinker."

He took the photo from her hand and returned it to the shelf. "Pity. What do you want with me, officer—or is it detective?"

She sat in the leather chair behind his desk, but if he were threatened by her invasion of his personal space, he didn't show it. If anything, he seemed amused.

"I'm looking for information about a Russian girl named Anya Nosova."

"Is that name supposed to mean something to me?"

She leaned back in the chair. "She probably didn't mean anything to you, but you knew her. She's dead and I'm hoping you can tell me how she got that way."

Davie pulled the girl's photo from her purse and held it up for Satine to see. He turned away from the image and picked up a shot glass from a wet bar next to the credenza.

"As I said, I don't know the girl."

"She was at your party at the Edison last Saturday night."

He poured vodka to the rim of the glass. "I make good parties. People beg me to invite them." He held up the glass to toast. "Maybe you will beg me someday too. That could be fun for both of us."

Davie repressed the impulse to shoot him where it would hurt the most. "I'd like to have a copy of your guest list."

"That would not be possible."

"I just saw a young blonde girl at the bar. I'm pretty sure she's a hooker. That's illegal, you know."

He shrugged. "A lifestyle choice. Who am I to judge?"

"Anya Nosova came to L.A. hoping for a modeling career. Instead, she ended up dead. Are you sure you never saw her at the bar, hustling johns?"

He brought the glass to his lips and downed the vodka. "Men who pay for sex confuse me. I've had hundreds of women in my bed. All of them were happy to be there."

"Men pay for sex all the time. From what I saw tonight, some of them are here at your nightclub."

Satine set the glass on the desk and strolled toward the door. "I have nothing against a vivid imagination, but yours is beginning to annoy me. It is time for you to go. I have work to do."

"You won't be happy when I come back."

He opened the door. "That is for me to say. *Spasibo*. Thanks for entertaining me. Next time maybe we can spend more time together. I know a place near Palm Springs where we can have privacy."

Palm Springs was in the Coachella Valley about 120 miles east of L.A. Murderers from Las Vegas to the Pacific Ocean and all stops in between also found privacy in the wide expanse of empty desert, especially as a dump site for dead bodies. Davie wondered if Satine's comment was a come-on or if he had just threatened her life.

20

DAVIE LEFT PERESTROIKA AND headed back to the station. It was late and she was exhausted, but she was determined to stay at her desk until she ran out of leads to follow.

She knew Ray Anthony Falcon had partied with Anya Nosova at the Edison hotel the night she disappeared. She needed to arrange an interview with the actor. Without an arrest warrant, there was nothing in the penal code to force Falcon to talk to her. It wasn't enough to drop by his place for a chat; housekeepers and security guards were paid to keep people away from movie stars. She would have to find another path to get to him.

She searched the Internet for information and found several online pieces, including one in the *Hollywood Reporter*. According to the article, Falcon had been cast to star in a film about General George Armstrong Custer's Civil War days as a cavalry commander before the so-called Indian Wars and his death at Little Bighorn. Filming was due to start in Montana the following Monday. The article claimed Custer was an aggressive commander of his Michigan infantry brigade who had fought with distinction at various battles, including Gettysburg. He was also reckless and narcissistic. From what Davie knew about Falcon, hiring him sounded like typecasting.

She also found several photos of Falcon on various tabloid sites: Falcon eating ice cream on the sidewalk of trendy Melrose Boulevard, baring his six-pack on the beach in Waikiki, and posing for a booking photo during his last drug arrest. All showed a man in his early forties with a deeply lined face and an air of edgy unpredictability.

People magazine featured a piece on how Falcon prepared for his roles, with sidebars about method acting and quoted passages from *An Actor Prepares* by Constantin Stanislavski. In another sidebar was a photo of a weatherworn and grim-looking man named Bud Stanton, who had been hired to teach Falcon to ride a horse for his current role.

Davie looked up Stanton's website. He had a stable at the Los Angeles Equestrian Center where he boarded horses and taught riding. It was after midnight, but she called the number listed on the home page. A woman answered.

"You're working late," Davie said.

The woman chuckled. "Horses don't know what time it is. They eat and poop twenty-four/seven. What can I do for you?"

"I'm calling for information."

"About riding or boarding?"

"Uh ... riding."

"When do you want to start?"

Davie debated whether to identify herself, but decided to be the rock in the stream and let the conversation find its own path around her. "How about tomorrow?"

"No can-do. Bud's working with a private client all day every day until next Sunday. I can refer you to another stable or you can wait till he's available. I recommend you wait. Bud's worth it."

"What if I came in early, before the private client gets there?"

"The guy gets here at nine and by the time he leaves at three, Bud's ready for a little R and R at the local watering hole. You get my drift? Have you ridden before?"

The closest Davie had ever been to horses was on the sidelines at the Rose Parade. "Not recently."

"How about ten o'clock Monday morning?"

Falcon would likely be in Montana shooting the Custer film on Monday, but if he was Bud's private client, as she suspected, it sounded as if he'd be polishing his riding skills until he boarded the plane.

"Let me check my schedule. I'll get back to you."

———

At seven thirty the next morning, Davie sat at her desk in the squad room calling the number Troy Gallway had given her for the orthodontist who had wired Anya's mouth with braces. The dentist told her he had found Anya charming and somewhat fragile. Gallway had warned him she had no money, so he offered to do the work gratis. That's why he had been annoyed when she didn't show up for her last appointment. Now that he knew why, he felt guilty about his reaction.

Davie asked him all her standard questions: did he know any of Anya's friends; did he know of any enemies who might want her dead; had she ever talked about any run-ins she'd had with strangers, boyfriends, or other people she knew. To all, he answered no.

She had already run his name through department databases and found no criminal history. She could do more digging into the wire bender's background but doubted he was involved in Anya's murder.

After ending the call, she entered her interview notes into the Murder Book. Then she left the station in search of Ray Anthony Falcon.

Just before nine a.m., Davie drove the Jetta through the gates of the Los Angeles Equestrian Center in Burbank and parked in the dirt next to a wooden fence. A few yards away, she saw a man standing by a trailer and heard the clang of his hammer beating a horseshoe into shape. Across the road, a truck fanned water onto a dusty field. Beyond the field lay Griffith Park's four thousand plus acres of urban wilderness. To Davie, the scene was bucolic and alien.

She walked through a loggia adjacent to the barn, inhaling the aroma of hay and horseshit. A Latino mucking a stall pointed her toward Stanton's stable.

As she stepped onto the road, she felt the thunder of hooves pounding the dirt. She spun toward the vibration and saw a horse galloping toward her. It was so large it seemed to block the low-slung winter sun. The rider wore a helmet and polished knee-high boots.

Davie squinted through her dark glasses until the man's face came into focus. It was Ray Anthony Falcon. Her pulse drummed in her ears as the horse came closer, forcing her to jump back to avoid getting trampled. Falcon reined the horse to a stop so close to her she felt froth from its mouth spatter her cheek.

Falcon's eyes were wide with panic. "Holy shit! You okay?"

The actor looked a lot like the photos she'd seen of Custer with his curly golden-blond hair. Davie assumed a makeup artist would paste a mustache and goatee on Falcon's face before filming started.

"Mr. Falcon, I'm Detective Richards, LAPD. I'd like to talk to you about Anya Nosova."

Falcon patted the horse's neck to calm its nerves or maybe his. "What about her?"

"Ms. Nosova was murdered."

"Too bad, but I barely knew the chick."

"Barely is good enough. I need your help."

Falcon's gaze swept the landscape, possibly looking for a getaway route. "Call my lawyer. He'll set something up."

"I have a witness who saw you coming out of Andre Lucien's apartment on the night Anya disappeared. I know you were with her at the Edison hotel later that night."

"I wasn't at Andre's place to buy drugs, so don't try to pin that on me, and I sure as hell didn't kill anybody."

"I'm just trying to get your side of the story. If you don't want to talk here, I can hook you up in front of your horsy friends and haul your ass back to the station."

He smiled as if he considered her statement merely pleasant foreplay. "My lawyer will have me out before you finish your silly little report."

"Maybe, but I'm guessing your lawyer warned you against associating with known drug dealers like Lucien. I know a hard-core deputy DA who believes that once a junkie, always a junkie. He might think you were desperate for a fix last Saturday night, so after the party at the Edison you took Anya back to her apartment hoping to score drugs. She declined your request, and you killed her because nobody says no to Ray Anthony Falcon."

He clapped his hands slowly. "Brava. I like my women sassy."

"I'm not one of your women."

He leaned toward her, resting his forearm on the saddle horn. His smirk said *not yet anyway*.

"Go ahead," she said. "Blow this off. Just so you know, there's no celebrity rehab for murder."

"Okay. I'll talk to you, but here's the deal. I start shooting in Montana next Monday. The trainer says my riding sucks, so if you want to talk, you'll ride."

"Do I look like Annie Oakley?"

"More like Howdy Dowdy. Is that red hair even real?"

She wanted to tell him to cut the personal insults or his date with Crazy Horse might be the best part of his day, but starting a pissing contest with a movie star would just delay the investigation, especially since he seemed willing to cooperate.

"Where's your trainer?" she said.

"Good old Bud is babysitting a sick horse. He told me to take a short ride to warm up. If the horse and I survive, he'll meet us in the arena in thirty minutes."

Falcon motioned to a groom from Stanton's stable and told him to saddle another horse. A few minutes later, the man led a spotted pony with a long red tail to a box with three steps and thrust the reins toward Davie.

"His name's Outlaw," the groom said. "He's an Appaloosa. Some Appys can be a pain in the ass. Just do what I tell you and don't irritate him."

Davie listened as the groom demonstrated some clicks and whistles that would make the horse trot and gallop. None of the information inspired her confidence. All she wanted to know was the click for stop.

Falcon had the reins gripped in his right hand, so Davie copied his form. Her stomach pitched as she mounted the steps and swung her leg over the saddle. Outlaw's hair prickled her palm as she patted the Appy's neck. She hoped the gesture assured the horse but it did nothing to calm her nerves. Without prodding, Outlaw followed Falcon's horse toward a trail on the far side of the arena, gaining ground until the two horses were side by side. For the next few minutes, all she heard was the distant hum of traffic on Interstate 5 and the rhythmic clopping of the horses' hooves.

"How did you meet Anya Nosova?" she said.

"Her boyfriend is a purveyor of high-end pharmaceuticals. I used to be one of his best customers. Let me repeat, *used* to be."

As suspected, Lucien had lied about not knowing Falcon. "What was your relationship with Anya?"

"There was no relationship. I'd seen her a few times at the apartment. That's all."

Once they entered the tree-lined mountain trail, Falcon's horse broke into a trot. Outlaw followed, slamming Davie's tailbone against the hard saddle. She calculated the pain she'd be in the next day.

Davie looked down. The ground seemed a mile away. "If you weren't at Lucien's to buy drugs, why did you go to his apartment last Saturday night?"

"Because I knew Anya was Russian. The producers needed more money for the Custer project. I have a financial stake in the picture, so I was invited to party with some starstruck investors. We were especially interested in hustling a Russian billionaire. I figured the guy might be more inclined to write a check if I introduced him to a fine-looking girl from the Motherland."

Davie was relieved when Falcon reined in his horse to cross a shallow stream. Outlaw picked his way across the rocky bed and trotted back to dry land. Only then did Davie realize she'd been holding her breath.

"Why didn't Anya ride to the hotel with you?"

"I had to run some errands. I gave her money for cab fare and told her to meet me there."

"Did anybody at the party show unusual interest in her?"

His gaze swept over Davie's body in one intimate pass. "Everybody's interested in a beautiful woman."

"Anybody show more interest than usual?"

Falcon reached out to push away a sapling that was intruding onto the narrow trail. "There was another Russian woman at the party.

Late thirties. Hard looking, like a hooker past her sell-by date. I saw her grab Anya's arm. Spit was flying."

Davie felt a tingling sensation on her scalp that signaled she was close to a discovery. "Any idea who she was?"

"Not a clue."

"What were they arguing about?"

"How should I know? They were talking Russian."

Falcon checked his watch and then turned the horse back toward the stables. Without prompting, Outlaw followed. Dust clouds from the dry earth had rained a film of brown grit onto Davie's black pants. Her mouth was dry and her knuckles white from gripping the reins. She pressed her heels into Outlaw's flanks and the pony edged closer to Falcon's horse.

"What time did Anya leave the party?"

"I don't know. I looked for her later but she was gone, not that I cared. She was a dud as a fund-raiser. She didn't even speak to the billionaire much less coax any money out of him for the film. I figured she got bored and left. Maybe she got lucky. Who cares? She wasn't my problem."

"Could you identify the other Russian woman from a surveillance photograph?"

Falcon made a kissing sound as he kicked his horse's sides. Both mounts broke into a canter. Davie grabbed the saddle horn and held on. Over the sound of eight hooves pounding the hard-packed dirt, she could just make out Falcon's reply.

"Probably, but it might be more efficient if I just told you how to find her."

21

FRIED BLONDE HAIR AND a black Brigid O'Shaughnessy pillbox hat with a veil that hung just below the first of her multiple chins—that's how Ray Anthony Falcon described the woman in the late-model black Mercedes S550 he had followed out of the Edison hotel valet area in the early morning hours on Sunday. He recognized the driver as the woman he'd seen arguing with Anya Nosova at the New Year's party. The car had a personalized license plate. As an actor, he was trained to memorize lines, so he remembered that it read MYILANA.

Falcon told Davie he'd gone directly home after leaving the Edison. He forgot his key, so his housekeeper let him in. They had a glass of wine and finally went to bed—together—at about six a.m.

Lana could mean anything but it sounded like a woman's name. Davie would run the plate as soon as she got back to the station, but on the way she decided to take a detour to see Spencer Hall at Hollywood Area Police Station. He would begin work at Pacific soon, and she'd prefer to get this over with before then.

Hall hadn't returned any of her calls for months and she had no expectations he would agree to see her now, especially since he had moved back in with his wife. His love life wasn't her problem, but given what Davie knew about the woman, his decision to reconcile seemed masochistic.

She texted him and asked to meet outside the station. She didn't want to go into the squad room and face people who may have heard the rumors about her. The only thing worse than answering well-meaning questions about her mental health from people who cared, was ignoring the hostile stares of the people who didn't.

A moment later, her cell phone *gonged*. Hall's text flashed on the display: SEE YOU IN 30. She was surprised and somewhat wary that he had responded so quickly.

Davie arrived in Hollywood a few minutes early and parked the Jetta on Wilcox in a neighborhood of small businesses and modest two-story apartment houses. The gnarled branches of the leafless trees lining the street reminded her of the fingers on a crone's bony hands.

Davie glanced across the street at the familiar red brick Hollywood Police Station. The building's floor plan was the same as Pacific's, but where Hollywood's detective squad room seemed cluttered and decrepit, Pacific's was as neat and orderly as a corporate boardroom, thanks to the efforts of a former captain who'd spearheaded the makeover. Davie doubted he knew about the box of bones from an old Jane Doe case that Detective Giordano kept under his desk, but she assumed corporations had a few skeletons hidden in their boardrooms too.

Two men argued in front of the bail bond office across the street from the station. When they spotted Hall exiting the front door wearing a badge and gun, they moved their dispute inside.

As Davie climbed out of the heated car, cold air seeped under her jacket like a stealth fog. Hall dodged a passing car and jogged toward her, flashing the boyish grin that had once made her heart race.

The two of them had worked well together. She didn't lecture him about eating junk food in the car. He didn't complain when she swabbed the steering wheel with hand sanitizer. Over time, the free flow of their conversation drifted to his troubled relationship with his wife. He was separated and had already hired a divorce lawyer, but his wife refused to let go. She was texting him fifty times a day and calling him at all hours of the day and night. At first, Davie just listened. Male cops loved to dish dirt about their wives and exes; it came with the badge. One night after work, she and Hall had gone to a cop bar after end of watch for some "team building." A few drinks later, they took the party to her place where, instead of comforting Spencer Hall with her words, she consoled him with her body.

At first she worried about their workplace romance, but she was single and his marriage was essentially over. The two were then assigned to different tables in the squad room. Neither had supervisory power over the other. Department brass understood that cops dated other cops and they mostly looked the other way.

The dysfunction caused by her parents' divorce had made Davie cautious about relationships. But over the next couple of months, she and Spencer Hall had spent most of their free time together, going to movies and concerts, and taking long drives along the California coast. She made him think. He made her laugh. She even took him to meet her grandmother, something she had never done before. Grammy loved him. That's when she realized she did too.

She'd thought the feeling was mutual.

She was wrong.

Her gaze glided down his familiar frame as he leaned toward the Jetta's fender. Davie grabbed his arm. Her hand lingered for a moment on the soft wool of his suit jacket, as she inhaled the scent of leather and Ivory soap.

Davie didn't want him to misinterpret the gesture, so she nodded toward the grimy fender. "This ride hasn't been washed since dinosaurs roamed the earth."

He nodded toward her clothes. "Looks like you had a run-in with a T. Rex yourself."

She brushed trail dust off her pants. "More like a run-in with an Outlaw."

"Good to see you haven't changed," he said. "I hear you're kicking ass on the Nosova case."

"Funny, I don't recall friending you on my Murder Book page."

The rugby scar near his right eye disappeared into the crease of his smile. "I stopped by Pacific yesterday to get my locker assignment. Vaughn was in the parking lot romancing a P-2, so I had a word with him. Watch out for that guy. He's a player."

She made a mental note to tell Vaughn to stop running his mouth about the case. "He's got my back. That's all I care about."

"Don't expect him to stick around to plan your retirement party."

"Not every relationship is meant to last."

Hall's thumb touched his gold wedding band. "You work a partnership until it lives or dies. That way you have no what-ifs, no regrets."

"You've been watching *Dr. Phil* again."

"I'm seeing a shrink but not the TV kind. I guess you heard Becky and I are back together. She wanted to take another shot at the marriage."

"Any fatalities?"

His smile seemed strained. "A few."

She heard the grinding of metal and glanced across the street to see a black-and-white roll through the station's security gate and disappear around the back of the building.

"Why Pacific?" she said. "You've avoided me for months and all of a sudden you want to be in my back pocket."

He ran his hand over the cowlick she suspected he would never tame. "It's closer to home."

"Well. Congratulations. I hope you two can work things out." She said the words but wasn't sure she meant them.

Neither spoke for what seemed like a long time. Hall was the first to break the silence. "Vaughn said your victim is Russian. About a year ago, the bodies of several Russian girls were found in Northern California. Turns out they were hookers working for the Russian mafia."

"What's your point?"

"The dump sites were all bodies of water. Your victim was found in the sewer. The two cases could be related."

She already knew about the Russian girls from reading department bulletins and resented Hall's presumption of ignorance.

"April 2015," Davie said, "a man fishing for bass in Clear Lake near Sacramento found the body of Tatyana Dashkov, age 19. She'd been shot in the head execution style. July 2015, two hikers spotted Larisa Kosikova, age 20, floating in the middle fork of the American River. She'd died of blunt force trauma to the head. October—"

"I know a guy at Robbery-Homicide with information about the case. I can put you two together if you're interested."

She didn't need his guy. She had her own contacts. "No, thanks."

He ignored her icy tone. "You have a suspect?"

"Why all this interest in my case?"

"Just making conversation."

"I didn't come here to brainstorm homicide theories."

He let out a frustrated sigh. "Look, Vaughn told me you think I started those rumors about you. I know how you feel—"

She cut him off midsentence. "You couldn't possibly know how I feel."

In reality, she had no thoughts at all, only a pain deep in her chest because she had liked Spencer Hall before she'd loved him, and now she'd lost not only his affection but also his friendship.

"Maybe not, but—"

"People are saying I panicked the night of the shooting and almost got you killed. That's crap and you know it."

He held out his hands, palms up, in a gesture of surrender. "It wasn't me, Davie."

She wanted to believe he wasn't talking trash about her, but after the shooting, Hall had abandoned her when she needed him most. She no longer trusted him.

"If not you, then who?" she said.

"I don't know."

Cold air seeped into her bones. "Right. Let me know when you find out."

She slipped into the front seat and cranked the Jetta's heater up to Hell. The tires screeched as she peeled away from the curb. In the rearview mirror, she could see Spencer Hall's gaze boring into the back of her head. Again she wondered why he'd offered unsolicited advice about the Nosova case. He was up to something.

22

WHILE SHE'D BEEN OUT in the field, somebody had used her desk again. The manuals on her shelf had toppled over like so many dominoes. She put them upright and went in search of the Russian translator. She found him sitting at an empty desk in Burglary. He was a probationer who looked eighteen but had to be at least twenty-one to be on the job. His father was a New Yorker born to Russian parents. His mother was from Moscow so he was fluent in Russian. The department paid him a stipend for use of his language skills.

According to the clock on her cell phone, the time in Kiev was ten p.m. the following day. It wasn't a good hour to call, but there was no good time to tell a parent his daughter was dead. She told the officer to put the call on speakerphone so she could listen to the nuances in the man's voice, rather than just having words interpreted by a rookie cop. She gave him a list of questions to ask and dialed the number Lucien had given her.

A man identifying himself as Anya's father answered on the third ring. He sounded sleepy or drunk or both. When the translator informed him that his daughter had been murdered, there was silence on the line.

The translator waited until the father processed the information before proceeding. What followed was a series of questions from Davie's list, followed by labored translations. The gist of the conversation was that the father had been a colonel in the Russian army and was now retired and living in Kiev.

"Ask him if he ever worked as a chef in Moscow."

After a brief conversation, the officer shook his head. "He said he's been in the military all his adult life. He's a soldier not a cook."

The father went on to explain that when Anya was sixteen, he and his wife divorced and she soon remarried another man. According to Colonel Nosova, Anya's new stepfather didn't want her around, so she stayed in Kiev with him but visited her mother in Moscow at least once a year.

"Ask if his wife ever danced with the Bolshoi or worked as a curator at the Louvre."

The officer posed the question, which was followed by a one-word answer she recognized without translation: *Nyet*.

Davie considered the parallels between Anya's broken family and her own. It made her feel that she and the victim shared a common history. Except Anya had lied to everybody about the details of her life. Her father was not a chef and her mother was not a ballerina for a Russian ballet company or a curator at a museum. And maybe Anya was not as naïve as everybody thought she was.

Colonel Nosova said his daughter was a good girl who wanted to make a success of her life. She had never been in trouble with the law. Eventually she became impatient with the gloomy Ukrainian winters and the dead-end life in Kiev. About nine months ago, she answered an ad in the local newspaper. Anya met with a woman who told her she would make a lot of money as a model in the US. The agency would pay for her airfare and all other expenses for the first three months. Anya would pay them back when the money started rolling in.

She had been excited, but her father was wary. His daughter was only nineteen. He seemed torn between holding on to the past and releasing her to find a future. In the end, he let her go.

The father couldn't remember the name of the woman who had made the arrangements but thought the agency was called Moscow Models. In the first four months Anya was in L.A., he didn't hear from her. He worried but thought she was just busy establishing her career. In the fifth month, she began to call once a week. There was nothing in their last conversation that caused him concern. When the translator gave the father Davie's phone number and told him how to arrange shipment of the body back to Kiev, Colonel Nosova's calm facade crumbled. Davie could hear him sobbing as the call ended.

Davie wondered what Anya had been doing in the four months between the time she arrived in L.A. and the date she had moved in with Troy Gallway. From the way her father spoke about his daughter, they seemed close, and yet she hadn't called him. That seemed odd— unless she'd been working for Grigory Satine, and he had prevented her from communicating with the outside world.

After the translator left, Davie searched the Internet and law enforcement databases but found no evidence that Moscow Models existed. The MYILANA license plate number Falcon had given her belonged to a corporation called Basic Imports located in the 4000 block of Sepulveda Boulevard. The vehicle was leased. When she cross-referenced the address, it came back to A to Z Liquors, not a modeling agency. Experience had taught her that hiding company ownership is child's play to the determined.

Her interview with Anya's father reminded her that she hadn't called her grandmother as she had promised. She checked her watch. One fifteen. Grammy should be back from lunch by now so she dialed her number.

Her grandmother's voice sounded breathless, agitated. "Rose Miller wasn't at lunch today."

"Maybe she wasn't feeling well."

"I think she died. I was looking out the window this morning and saw an ambulance drive away. It didn't use its siren."

"That doesn't mean Rose was inside." Davie meant the words to calm her grandmother even though her assumption was reasonable.

"After lunch, I asked the nurse what was going on. She told me Rose moved out. Rose Miller is my friend. She wouldn't move out without telling me."

"Why would the nurse lie?"

"They're all afraid to talk to us old people about death because they think we'll get depressed. Don't they know at my age I've learned how to mourn?"

Davie glanced up and saw Giordano limp out of Lieutenant Bellows's office.

"I'll find out about Rose and let you know."

"Can you take me to the funeral? I'd like to pay my respects."

"Sure, Grammy, but I have to go now."

"Back to work?"

"Back to work."

As soon as they finished their goodbye ritual, she called the manager of Grammy's assisted living facility and learned that Rose Miller had died in her sleep the night before. The funeral was the following day. Davie didn't want to tell her grandmother the bad news on the telephone, so she asked the manager to send somebody to her room to tell her the truth about her friend.

"Tell her I'll pick her up in time for the service."

Davie hung up the phone just as Giordano limped passed her desk. His face was flushed, as if his blood pressure were primed to explode. He slammed a stack of papers on his desk.

"You okay, boss?"

"Bellows says our homicide clearance rate sucks, and the captain is tired of being slammed by the command staff every time he goes to a COMPSTAT meeting. He wants us to review cold cases and pull together enough evidence to file with the DA's office."

COMPSTAT, short for Computer Statistics, was a program used to analyze crime trends and make division captains more accountable for lowering area felonies and misdemeanors in all categories. Those who attended the meetings dreaded listening to commanders berate them for any uptick in the city's crime rates.

"Does he know we just got two fresh homicides? How are we supposed to review cold cases?"

"He knows." Giordano pulled a notebook from the shelf above his desk. Under his breath, he mumbled, "Fucking crybaby."

"I have some new leads in the Nosova case."

"Good. Make an arrest and get Bellows off my ass."

"First I need to talk to somebody who knows about the Russian mafia."

"No shit. You think the mafia is involved?"

"Maybe. I'm not sure yet."

Giordano thumbed through an old-fashioned Rolodex he kept in his desk drawer. He handed her a card with a handwritten phone number on it next to the letter Q.

145

"Call Reuben Quintero. He's our go-to guy for all things Russian. He used to work Robbery-Homicide, but last I heard he was assigned to CCD. "

Davie thought of CCD as just another example of the department's fascination with alphabet soup. It stood for Commercial Crimes Division and was formed from a merger between the former Financial Crimes Division (FCD) and Burglary Auto Division (BAD), which everybody called BAD Cats.

Davie copied the number onto her telephone sheet and returned the card to Giordano. "Thanks, boss."

"Keep up the good work, kid. Let me know if you need help."

23

DAVIE WAITED FOR DETECTIVE Giordano to return to his desk before dialing Quintero's number. He answered after one ring. She briefed him on the case. "I'd like to show you some surveillance photos. See if you recognize anybody."

"Not this week," he said. "I'm getting ready to file a case I've been working on for months. Until that happens, I don't have time for anything else."

"I'm looking for information I needed yesterday."

"You hinterland dicks think you rule the planet. I got news for you: you don't."

She figured Quintero was a munchkin and the snub made him feel taller. She wanted to tell him that Giordano believed divisional detectives were the best in the department, but escalating the rhetoric wouldn't solve Anya Nosova's murder. She decided to save it for another day. Given Quintero's attitude, she was sure that day would come.

"A young woman is dead. I need to know who killed her."

Quintero blew a long stream of air into the telephone's receiver. "Be here by two or you'll be talking to the door."

She wondered if the door might be the lesser of two evils.

It took her forty-five minutes to negotiate traffic on the 10, not the twenty Quintero had dictated. She parked on the street across from the new Police Administration Building, an angular structure of smoky glass, sharp corners, and a maze of muted interior hallways. There was an underground garage, but it was off limits to all but the privileged and the powerful.

Quintero was waiting for her outside. She smiled when she saw that he was short. He was also wiry and intense, the sort of person who could pull an all-nighter cramming for a final exam without the benefit of caffeine. He had dusky skin and close-cropped black hair that reminded her of a harbor seal. She guessed he hadn't been a rookie for at least twenty years, but he looked as physically fit and healthy as an academy boot—except for the smokes.

He hunched against the wind to ignite a cigarette with a cheap plastic lighter. The smoke mingled with swirling dust, exhaust, and the fetid odor drifting from a homeless man sitting next to a shopping cart laden with treasure. A pile of butts, the same brand Quintero was smoking, lay scattered around the detective's feet. It reminded her, once again, that people were creatures of habit.

"I hear you used to work RHD," she said.

His eyes narrowed into slits, which made Davie think there was a story behind his leaving the unit that probably didn't include a happy ending. "Call me Q."

Not *you can call me Q,* she noted, just *call me Q,* like he thought of himself as a one-name celebrity. At least he hadn't asked her to call him sir. Maybe that came with Attitude 2.0.

"As I mentioned on the phone—"

Quintero cut her off. "Yeah, you told me. Here's a crash course on the Russian mafia. Back in the seventies and eighties, the Soviets relaxed emigration policies. They allowed some good people to emigrate to the US, but they also sent their prison population along for the ride. A group from Odessa settled in Brighton Beach and the Odessa mafia was born. They didn't expand to Los Angeles until the early eighties, but they've been making up for lost time."

"I can read all that on the Internet. What I want is recent department intel."

"Just because you have a dead Russian girl doesn't mean the mafia took her out," he said.

"The victim had a spiderweb tattoo on her elbow."

"That's a typical Russian prison tat. Those badniks love to ink their bodies. The images read like a memoir. I guess the Russians draw pictures on their skin because they can't write." The cigarette between his lips bobbed as he spoke.

Davie considered challenging Quintero's assumption, but she doubted that mentioning the works of Tolstoy or Dostoyevsky would alter his attitude.

"Anya Nosova doesn't have a rap sheet," she said, "and her father told me she was never in trouble back home."

"The mafia takes ink seriously. If your girl had an unauthorized prison tat, she might have been green-lighted for a hit."

"By the local *pakhan?*"

He raised his eyebrows, as if surprised she knew the Russian equivalent for godfather. "He'd kill her just to see if his gun was loaded."

"Who are the local players?"

Quintero inhaled smoke deep into his lungs. "There isn't much of a structure in L.A., not like in the old country."

"There must be somebody leading the pack."

He waited for two fresh-faced blue suits with shiny new badges to saunter by before he answered. "Grigory Satine. He owns a nightclub in West Hollywood called Perestroika."

Davie didn't tell Q that she had already spoken to Satine.

"What's he into?" she asked.

"The Russians usually stick to crimes like fraud and extortion. When Satine first put together his syndicate, he tried to sell drugs but he couldn't compete with homegrown street gangs."

"Is he a visionary or a doofus?"

Quintero swept the area with his gaze. "Look, what I'm about to tell you can't go beyond the two of us." He didn't wait for her agreement. Either he trusted her or he was unaccustomed to anyone challenging his authority. She guessed the latter. "That case I'm working on? Satine is my suspect. We've been conducting surveillance on his residences and businesses for months. We think he's hijacking trucks from the Port of Los Angeles. Other agencies are involved."

"FBI?" If the Federal Bureau of Investigation were involved, it could mean that Satine was transporting cargo across state lines.

Q's index finger wagged at her like a lazy metronome. "Forget it, Richards. I'm not authorized to say anything else. I can tell you we're working with a CI. And don't bother asking who it is. That's why we call them *confidential* informants."

A young Latina clutching the hand of a toddler ambled by and headed toward the Memorial to Fallen Officers.

"What's in the trucks he's jacking?" she said.

"Booze and cigarettes, among other things. We traced some of the cargo to Satine's nightclub."

"Sounds like an RSP case," she said. "When was the last time you saw anybody go to jail for Receiving Stolen Property? Satine will claim he bought the stuff from a seller he thought was legit. If you can't connect him to the theft, the DA's office will never file the case."

Quintero's cigarette had burned down to the filter. He took one last hit before crushing it with his heel near the other butts. "We have enough to nail Satine on Grand Theft. There could be other charges too."

"Any evidence he's branching out? Like prostitution?"

"Could be. He's a cog who wants to be a wheel. Our undercover team says there are always lots of pretty young girls hanging out at his bar."

If Satine were operating a call-girl ring, as she suspected, some of his hookers might be in the country illegally. If so, Immigration and Customs Enforcement, ICE, could be part of Q's law enforcement coalition as well.

Davie opened her notebook and showed him the snapshot of Nosova. "She look familiar?"

Quintero glanced at the photo and shook his head. Davie showed him pictures on her cell that she'd taken at the Edison. He watched over her shoulder close enough for her to smell the cigarette smoke trapped among the threads of his plaid tie.

Davie pointed to the photo of the woman Falcon had seen arguing with Anya at the New Year's party. "Know her?"

His fists clenched and then relaxed. "Lana Ivanov. She manages A to Z Liquors, another one of Satine's businesses."

Another puzzle piece had just fallen into place. The license plate on the Mercedes that Falcon had seen was MYILANA, a vehicle Davie had already connected to A to Z.

"A woman paid my victim's airfare from Kiev," Davie said. "She promised high-paying modeling jobs through an agency she owned. I can't find any evidence the agency exists. You think this Lana Ivanov is working prostitutes for Satine?"

"White slavery isn't my problem. Take it up with Vice."

Davie continued showing him the photos, pausing at the elevator shot of Satine with the bodyguards and the mystery man.

Quintero lit another cigarette. "That's Satine on the left."

"And the other guy?"

"He's a Russian arms dealer named Viktor Marchenko."

He told her Marchenko had been a colonel in the Soviet air force. After the Cold War, the military was short on money and long on equipment and weapons. Marchenko commandeered his first Ilyushin cargo plane loaded with AK-47s and rocket-propelled grenades without anyone even noticing. He sold the weapons and ammunition to third-world revolutionaries, mostly in Africa. Like any good capitalist, he used the profits to buy more planes and more weapons until he had a network of eager buyers all over the world. His net worth grew exponentially.

"The guy's a dirtbag," he said, "but he's also a billionaire. The Russian government considers him a successful businessman. Local boy makes good."

Davie wondered if Marchenko had been the target of Ray Anthony Falcon's fund-raising efforts or if there had been other Russian billionaires at Satine's New Year's party.

"Why was Marchenko meeting with Satine?" she asked.

"Everybody wants to know the answer to that question. So don't go charging into Satine's nightclub throwing your weight around. You'll screw up months of work. If that happens, I guarantee you people with juju will make you disappear."

A red and gray Metro Rapid bus whooshed by, launching a plastic grocery bag into the air. The homeless man teetered on the edge of the curb to stop its flight.

Davie ignored Quintero's threat. "Where's Marchenko now?"

"Stand down, detective."

Davie yanked the badge from her belt and thrust it within inches of Q's face. "Last time I looked we were working for the same outfit, so I'd like to know why you're obstructing a homicide investigation."

Quintero remained silent, weighing the consequences of helping her, which made Davie wonder if lack of team spirit had gotten him booted out of RHD.

"He's on his yacht anchored off Paradise Cove, but I'm warning you: don't go near him." The force of his words created a gust of cigarette breath.

Davie's gaze locked on his. She reached inside her jacket and held out a small metal box. "Breath mint, Q?"

"No thanks. Those things are loaded with sugar. It's bad for my health."

He turned and walked toward the main entrance of PAB. He reached the door at the same time as a man in his early thirties, blond and buff, wearing navy cargo pants and a polo shirt with an oval emblem sewn on the left side. The guy could have been any one of the nearly ten thousand cops on the job, but he wasn't. He was the driver of the cable van she'd seen parked across the street from her grandmother's place.

She watched from the shadows of the building as he flashed his department ID and slipped through security. Internal Affairs was housed in the building. Within IA were Force Investigations, Special Operations, and the Surveillance Unit. Davie figured that's where Blond and Buff worked, which meant that a fellow cop was following her. Davie couldn't understand why ...

Unless Malcolm Harrington had reopened her OIS case and launched a new investigation. She had to find out what was going on. And there was only one person she could trust to tell her the truth.

24

BUT AS SOON AS Davie left PAB and slid into the driver's seat of the Jetta, her phone rang. It was Cal Rogers, the Edison's Director of Security.

"I found the waiter from the video but there's a problem."

"Why am I not surprised?" she muttered.

"He's undocumented and scared shitless you'll have him deported if he talks to you."

"I'm not interested in his immigration status, only what was under that cart he was pushing."

"You'll need a Spanish speaker before you talk to him, unless you're fluent. I suggest you find one before the guy disappears. If you get in a bind, I can translate for you."

"That must have come in handy working county jail."

"You have no idea."

"You said you hated police work, but I get the impression you miss it."

He didn't answer right away. "Maybe a little. Look, I don't want to step on your toes, but I've already talked to this guy. He trusts me."

There were Spanish-speaking detectives in the squad room, but Davie didn't know how quickly she could find one who was available. Rogers was ready now, and she didn't want to risk the waiter getting spooked, so she decided to accept his offer. Finding out who was following her and why would have to wait.

Rogers told her Carlos Mata could meet them in West L.A. by the post office on Exposition. Mata and his uncle had a gardening job in Brentwood, so he couldn't stay long.

Davie ended the call and thirty minutes later, she parked the Jetta in the post office parking lot, located half a block from the 405 overpass. The area had once been a staging area for day laborers, but they had been chased away during construction of the Expo Line light-rail across the street. The tracks had been resurrected from a 140-year-old railroad that had once carried ore and sunbathers from Los Angeles to Santa Monica.

Cal Rogers was already there with a heavy-set Latino in his mid-twenties with doe eyes that reflected fear and crushing responsibility. They stood at the rear of a beater pickup with *Tree Removal* hand-painted in red on a plywood frame bolted to the truck's bed. A man, who Mata identified as his uncle, sat in the driver's seat with a baseball cap pulled low over his face. The uncle made no attempt to get out of the vehicle and Davie decided to let him be.

The sunlight exposed smile lines around Rogers's blue eyes and ignited the aroma of lavender on his skin. Despite the cold, he was wearing only a plaid flannel shirt and denim jeans but no jacket, which made him look like a Pacific Northwest logger.

She needed background information on Carlos Mata for her report, so she told Rogers what questions to ask and then listened to the exchange, watching the movement of Rogers's lips and tongue around the

Spanish tildes and softly rolled *R*s. She understood about fifty percent of the conversation, enough to know that Rogers had a gift for language.

A few moments later, Rogers turned toward her. "He said he crossed the Arizona border at Nogales about three months ago. The coyote drove him and about twelve other people to Los Angeles. He lives with seven other undocumented workers in his uncle's converted garage in Pico Rivera. His cousin works at the Edison and got him a temp job at Satine's party, using fake ID."

"Ask him about the cart."

Rogers asked Mata the question and translated his answer.

"He says he and his cousin were working in the kitchen when a woman came in. She was upset. His cousin speaks English, so the woman asked him for help. Some man at the party was bothering her and she wanted help getting out of the hotel without him seeing her. She didn't want to be followed."

Davie showed Mata the photo of Anya Nosova and asked if he recognized her.

He tapped the photo with his finger. "*Sí, sí. Es ella.*"

"Did she say who this man was?" Davie said.

Mata obviously understood the question, because he shook his head.

She glanced at Rogers. "How did he get her out of the suite?"

Rogers continued translating: "His cousin didn't want to get involved, but Carlos felt sorry for the woman. He hid her in the pantry until his shift ended. When no one was watching, he had her crawl onto the shelf of the cart and covered it with a tablecloth. Then he walked out the door of the suite and headed toward the main elevator. The woman's weight made the cart hard to push. The wheels kept catching in the carpet."

"Why didn't he take the cart down the service elevator to the main kitchen?"

Rogers rested his arm on the pickup's back panel and asked the question. "He says he didn't want to run into any of the staff. He was afraid they'd ask questions."

"The surveillance video didn't show anybody pushing a cart out the front door. Where did he take her?"

Rogers waited for Mata's response. "To the side door off the lobby. He helped the woman off the cart and watched her walked toward the parking lot. After that, he went home."

Davie remembered Rogers telling her there was no video camera trained on the side door.

Mata sank onto the bumper of the pickup. "*Su amigo*. He pick her up ... outside. "

Davie could barely hear his response over the noise from a passing cement truck. She waited for the dust to settle before asking her next question. "Did you see this friend who picked her up?"

Mata shook his head and made the sign of the cross. After a few more questions, it was clear that Davie had drained the man's reservoir of useful information. He hesitated when she asked for his address and cell phone number but finally gave it to her, explaining that the cell belonged to his cousin.

Davie knew that talking to her had put Mata at risk. She wanted him to know that it took guts to do what he did and she appreciated his courage. She also wanted to reassure him the LAPD would not hassle him about his immigration status. She didn't want to tell him with her limited Spanish for fear of mangling the words, so she asked Rogers to translate her thoughts.

"*Muchas gracias*," he said and reached out to shake her hand. Then he got into the truck and the uncle drove away.

Rogers walked with her toward the Jetta. She thought of Anya hiding under that kitchen cart and wondered who at that party had meant her harm. Lana? Satine? Both?

"I need to take another look at the parking lot video," she said.

Rogers stopped, forcing her to turn toward him. He stood with his feet apart and his thumbs hooked into the pockets of his jeans. A smile curved his lips. "I did that already."

He pulled two photos from his shirt pocket and handed them to her. One was of Anya Nosova getting into an older-model sedan.

"You can't see the license plate," he continued, "but the car is an Oldsmobile, a 2001 or 2002, I'd guess by looking at the taillights. I know because my granddad had one just like it. He thought the world ended when General Motors stopped making them."

Rogers should have told her about the car and the photo long before now. It was the first chink in the trust that she had built with him.

He seemed to notice her stony glare. "Look, Carlos told me the whole story when I spoke to him this morning. I figured it was your girl under the cart so I rechecked the parking lot video before I left the hotel."

"You could have told me that when you called."

His body tensed. "Sorry, detective. I was just trying to help."

He *had* helped her and she didn't want to appear ungrateful, so she softened her tone. "You have, but I'm not big on surprises."

"I'll remember that."

She turned her attention to the second photo. The camera angle was skewed so she couldn't see the driver. She glanced at the car, stopping at an image on the back windshield. It appeared to be a round decal of some sort. On closer inspection, she saw that it was a cartoon lion circled by the words: *Fairfax High School Class of 1983 Alumni Club.*

Davie turned toward Rogers. "Take a look."

"The decal? Anybody could have put that on the car."

"Are these the only photos you found?"

He nodded. "What are you going to do now?"

Davie checked her watch. Someone else she'd interviewed had mentioned a vintage Olds but she couldn't be sure of the connection until she made one more stop. "I'm going to the school library to look through a few yearbooks."

"If you have a name, why not run it through DMV and see if the guy owns an Olds?"

"The owner isn't the person I'm looking for."

"How do you know?"

She paused for a moment to weigh her response. "Minutiae."

25

FAIRFAX HIGH SCHOOL WAS in Hollywood Division at the corner of Fairfax and Melrose in midtown Los Angeles. Davie remembered when the area was considered the heart of the Jewish community, but she doubted that was still true. Most of her Jewish friends lived on the Westside or in the San Fernando Valley. She didn't know much about the school except that it had a reputation as a petri dish for leaders of the entertainment industry from actors to studio executives.

The rosy-cheeked librarian introduced herself in a Southern drawl as Leona Blanchard. She had a round face and full lips, the better to shush you with, Davie guessed. Blanchard told her that the Fairfax alumni association had created the decal she saw on the Olds several years ago for the Class of 1983's thirtieth reunion. A plastic ID that hung around Blanchard's neck on a lanyard clicked against the buttons of her maroon cardigan sweater as she pulled down the 1981, 1982, and 1983 yearbooks from a shelf in the reference section.

She motioned Davie to follow her to a wooden table in a quiet corner of the library that featured a half dozen students reading books and tapping on computer keyboards beneath sky-high ceilings. Above the book stacks were a series of wall pictures that included a Centaur, a covered wagon, and a guy wearing a space suit. Davie wondered if they had a unifying theme. If so, it was a mystery to her.

Ms. Blanchard set the yearbooks on the table. "Which one of our precious little darlings is in trouble now?"

"None of them at the moment."

Blanchard lowered her voice and leaned toward Davie's ear. "I've known a few most-likely-to-end-up-in-jail types, bless their hearts. I could be wrong, though." The knowing look on her face said *But that isn't likely.*

Blanchard pulled out a wooden chair and motioned for Davie to sit. Across the table, a teenage boy wearing a gray hoodie was slumped over a backpack, sleeping. Blanchard waddled over and nudged him awake. "Rise and shine, Henry." She winked at Davie. "If he starts snoring, just give me a holler." She turned and disappeared into the stacks.

As soon as Blanchard was out of sight, Henry lowered his head and appeared to fall asleep again.

Under the glow of fluorescent lights and surrounded by book dust and raging hormones, Davie opened the 1983 yearbook first. The pictures reminded her of her own high school annual. She wondered if all yearbooks looked the same: grim-faced kitchen staff, arty photos of campus buildings, and sports teams in crisp uniforms sitting shoulder to shoulder, hands clasped in front of them—different flavored dough formed by the same cookie cutter.

Davie returned her attention to the 1983 activities pages, scanning the photos and names. She was disappointed but not surprised that she didn't see one she recognized. She ran her finger down the list of names in the senior class section until she came to one she did know: Jeremy Forrester.

Anya's apartment manager, John Bell, had told her he didn't own a vehicle but that he sometimes borrowed an Olds from a friend named Jerry Forrester. She flipped to the section displaying pictures of the junior class, where she spotted Bell's photo. He was thinner back then, with thick brown hair. He wore heavy black-framed glasses that made him look nerdy. She remembered seeing snapshots of Bear and his cop friends from the early 1980s. Their glasses were wire-rimmed aviators.

She thumbed through photos of various extracurricular activities but couldn't find any shots of Bell. Since he seemed to have a passion for writing, she checked for his picture with members of the drama club or the yearbook staff. He wasn't there. Maybe his interest in writing was recent.

A bell rang. Davie looked at the clock over the doorway. 3:07 p.m. Soon students would rush out and the library would close.

Leona Blanchard strolled toward her. "You 'bout done here?"

"I need copies of a few pages. Then I'll be on my way."

"Whatever you say, dear. I'm just glad you found what you were looking for … whatever that was." Blanchard pulled a pad of Post-it notes from her sweater pocket and slapped one on each of the pages Davie wanted copied. Then she headed toward the checkout desk.

Davie was sure when she ran Jeremy Forrester's name through the DMV, it would show he was the registered owner of an Oldsmobile. She was also sure that John Bell had borrowed Forrester's ride last Saturday night and had driven to the Edison in answer to Anya Nosova's distress call. She needed to find out what had happened next. That meant having another conversation with John Bell.

This one would not be as cordial as the last one.

26

"**MALCOLM HARRINGTON IS A** cop-hating asshole." Detective Giordano's fists were clenched. A river of red crept up his neck.

Davie stood with her boss in the only place at the station where you could hold a conversation without being overheard—the parking lot. She had driven to the station after her library research, and had just told him about Bear's history with Harrington, her OIS case, the panic rumors circulating about her, and her suspicion that somebody from IA was tailing her.

"You're one of my peeps," he said. "Whatever's going on, I should have been told."

"Why would the lieutenant keep you out of the loop?"

"Because he knows I'd be pissed and he doesn't want to deal with it. Who could be bad-mouthing you besides Hall?"

Davie had already thought about the possibilities. A person couldn't work in law enforcement for as many years as she had and not irritate somebody—jealousy over a promotion, unequal case distribution, or some slight, either real or imagined. She searched her memory again but couldn't think of any enemies she'd made. There was nobody she knew of, other than Malcolm Harrington, who might harbor a grudge against her because of her father, but it seemed unlikely Harrington had started the rumors. Maybe she needed to think beyond the department. A civilian or somebody in the DA's office.

"I can't think of anybody. What now?"

"Do your job and don't let the IA tail know he's been made. I'm going to make a few phone calls."

Giordano walked toward the back door of the station. After a few steps, he stopped and turned toward her. "And if you need a department rep, ask me."

Giordano was warning her that the situation could turn ugly. If Harrington made some kind of case against her, she would be hauled before a Board of Rights. If that happened, she'd need an ally to represent her. She couldn't think of anybody better than Frank Giordano.

She watched as he put his cell phone to his ear and a short time later, she saw the index finger of his free hand stab the air. Whoever he was talking to, it didn't look like a happy conversation.

Giordano had told her to go about her business and she intended to follow his advice. She had to interview John Bell again so she returned to her desk and placed a call. There was a message on his machine that he'd obviously left for tenants. It said he would be gone until five p.m. If they needed help, they should call the owner.

Davie decided to call on Lana Ivanov, instead. She returned to her desk and grabbed her notebook and the Russian woman's DMV photo. Then she headed toward the car.

27

DAVIE WALKED ACROSS THE station's parking lot as fallen leaves cartwheeled across the blacktop, urged on by a chilly breeze. She backed the Jetta out of the space without fastening her seatbelt. She never used a belt unless she was in a high-speed chase, because it restricted her movement. Back in her patrol days, she and her partner had taken fire from Grape Street gangbangers. When she tried to draw her weapon, the butt caught in the seatbelt. She would never make that mistake again.

Black clouds bruised the sky as she drove out the Centinela gate and turned right onto Culver Boulevard, heading east toward Sepulveda. She glanced in her rearview mirror but couldn't spot a tail.

It took only ten minutes to reach A to Z Liquors, nestled between a Chinese restaurant and a dry cleaner. The place was a squat, one-story box with peeling paint and a yellow-and-red sign mounted above the door that read LIQUOR. Rusty security bars barricaded every opening, giving the place an edgy prison vibe.

The hinges of the wooden screen door groaned as Davie stepped inside the store. To her right was a display of packaged chips and nuts and a cold case filled with plastic tubs of what she assumed was food. Floor-to-ceiling wooden shelves held reclining liquor bottles. Some were coated with dust as thick as the fur on a caterpillar. Others looked like they had just rolled off a conveyor belt. She wondered if the booze Satine had hijacked was already rubbing shoulders with the grimy bottles she saw on A to Z's shelves.

On the left, a man dressed in black sat hunched on a stool behind a Plexiglas divider, guarding cases of cigarettes, high-end liquors, and a prehistoric cash register. Davie studied the contours of his face: hooded eyes, bushy eyebrows, coarse features, and scar across his cheek. He looked like the stunt double for Frankenstein's assistant from an old movie she'd recently seen on TV.

Not even the creaking of her weight on the wooden floor distracted the man from the video game he was playing. She pushed aside a round plastic jar of beef jerky and flashed her department ID through the opening in the Plexiglas. "I'm here to see Lana Ivanov."

The man stared at her with a dull expression.

"Lana Ivanov?" she repeated. "Is she working today?"

A moment later, Davie heard a woman's voice coming from the back room. The tone was raspy and low, as if she had smoked too many cigarettes. *"Borya, yést' li gdyé-nibút' ristarán nidalikó atsyúda? Ya óchin' khachú yest'."*

The Russian glanced toward the voice. *"Nylandt,"* he said and then took what looked like a slice of raw potato from a bowl on the counter and stuffed it in his mouth.

The door to the back room swung open and a plump woman sauntered into the store, filing the room with fumes from her flowery perfume. Her ample breasts and paunchy gut challenged the seams of a low-cut purple dress. Bleached hair rose from her scalp in short spikes that reminded Davie of wheat stubble after a harvest. Her complexion was florid despite heavy makeup. Davie recognized the woman from her DMV photo as Lana Ivanov.

Lana glanced at the man crunching potatoes and wrinkled her nose in distaste. When she noticed Davie, she seemed surprised to see a customer in the store. "*Zdrástvuytye*. Hello," she said. "How can I help you?"

Davie held out her ID. "Detective Richards, LAPD. Can we talk privately? In your office?"

Lana's eyes darted from her assistant to the back room. "No office. Is only storage. What do you want?"

"Information about Anya Nosova."

She shook her head. "I do not know this person."

"I have some photos that might jog your memory. They're at the station. I could drive you there. It won't take long."

"*Bayús' shto nyet*. I am working."

"What about your buddy over there? Can't he look after things while you're gone?"

"Boris speaks no English. Isn't that right, Borya?"

Davie remembered reading *War and Peace* in college with all those Russians and their multiple nicknames. She figured Borya and Boris were two variations of the same.

"Business looks a little slow. Maybe you could lock up for a while. You can ride with me. I'll bring you right back, I promise."

Lana raised her chin in defiance. "You arrest me?"

Davie gave her what she hoped was a look of incredulity. "Have you done something wrong?"

"In my country, police cannot be trusted."

"You're not in Russia anymore, Ms. Ivanov."

"Some things are same everywhere."

"Let me tell you how it works here. People with nothing to hide cooperate with the police."

In the silence that followed, all Davie heard was Borya/Boris crunching on potato rounds and the *pings* and *whooshes* from his video game. Occasionally he glanced at Davie but didn't appear concerned. She was glad he didn't speak English or he might have become a problem.

Lana turned toward the back room. "I make call first."

Davie wasn't about to let her go in that room alone. Lana might have a weapon hidden somewhere or she could simply cruise out the back door and disappear.

She stepped toward Lana. "I'll go with you."

Lana gave her a shrug. The presence of an LAPD detective didn't seem to intimidate her in the least. Davie wondered why she was so nonchalant.

The woman pulled a cell phone from inside her purple notebook and tapped a single digit on the keypad. Either the number belonged to someone she speed dialed often or someone she called in an emergency. Maybe both. She mumbled into the phone in English, not Russian.

"Policewoman is here. She take me to station." Without waiting for a response, she ended the call.

Davie motioned Lana into the front seat of the Jetta so she could watch her on the way to the station. When they arrived, Davie led her into the detective squad room and gestured for her to sit in one of the interview rooms, a small cubbyhole with a scarred wooden table pushed against the wall. Some detectives preferred the table in the middle of the room as a barrier between them and the suspect, but Davie believed the stress caused by invading a person's comfort zone produced better results.

The room also held two chairs. Davie gestured for Lana to sit in the plastic armless chair. The one closest to the door had a padded seat and armrests and wheels for mobility. Davie always sat in that one, both to establish dominance and to remain visible to other detectives in the squad room in case the interview went sideways.

"Those pictures I mentioned are on my desk," Davie said. "I'll get them."

As she left the room, she flipped a switch outside the door. If Lana tried to leave, she'd trigger an alarm that could wake the dead. Davie planned to let the Russian stew for a while, hoping she'd feel more talkative.

By the time Davie returned to the interview room thirty minutes later, the air smelled of sweat and rancid flowers. Lana sat perched on the edge of her chair, spring-loaded and ready to fire. Davie loomed over her, cradling the Anya Nosova Murder Book in her arm. She slowly leafed through the pages, pausing to study one entry or another. Most of the forms were still blank, but Lana didn't know that. She wanted to see how the woman reacted if she believed the evidence was piling up against her.

Davie lowered herself into the padded chair. "Do you know why I want to talk to you?"

Lana stared at the notebook. "About woman I don't know."

Davie leaned back in the chair. "How long have you managed Moscow Models for Grigory Satine?" Davie had no evidence there was a connection between Moscow Models and Lana Ivanov. She was bluffing, but Lana didn't need to know that, either.

The woman stared into midspace, her expression wooden. "I work in liquor store."

"Anya Nosova came to L.A. to be a model. Instead, I believe she became a prostitute." Davie pulled out John Bell's photo of Anya and held it up for Lana to see. "Do you remember her now?"

Lana looked at the ceiling, avoiding eye contact. "She is like many Russian girls."

169

Davie considered other possible victims of Lana's modeling scam and wondered if any of them had met the same fate as Anya had.

"What were you and Anya arguing about at the Edison hotel last Saturday night?"

"Edison? This hotel I do not know."

Davie rolled her chair closer to Lana but kept her tone soft and sympathetic. "I have a witness who saw you there with her. Saw your car. Remembered your license plate number."

Lana wrapped her arms around her chest and glance toward the door. None of this seemed to concern her. "This witness is mistaken."

Davie ignored the lie. "Look, if you hurt Anya, you should tell me now. Maybe it was an accident. You argued. Things got out of hand. You didn't do it on purpose."

Lana stared at Davie. "I know nothing about this Anya person. She is hurt?"

Davie rolled the chair within a hairsbreadth of Lana's knees and pulled out another photo. "Not hurt, dead. Somebody killed her and dumped her body in the sewer. She floated in shit for three days. This is what she looked like when they found her." Davie thrust a photo toward Lana that showed Anya's mangled body in the grinder at Hyperion Sewage Treatment Plant.

Lana recoiled. Davie wasn't surprised. The picture was gruesome. "Murder is never a pretty picture," she said.

Lana covered her mouth with her hand. Her eyes were moist. "Who give you permission to treat me like this?"

"I don't need permission. I'm investigating a homicide."

"I know your laws. You must get me a lawyer if I ask."

It irritated Davie that the first thing an immigrant learned when she came to this country was how to lawyer up.

"You're not under arrest, so I'm not required to get you a lawyer."

"But you keep me here." Her voice had become brittle and strained.

"I'm not forcing you to stay. I'll take you back to the store anytime you want."

"I want to go. Now."

Davie was disappointed but not surprised that Lana hadn't been more forthcoming. Grigory Satine had likely counseled her on what to say and do if the police came knocking. Lana had been smug at the liquor store and during the first part of the interview, but the autopsy photo had destroyed her cool, leaving Davie with the impression that she might not have known Anya was dead.

"I'll have one of our patrol officers drive you back to the liquor store."

Lana shook her head. "I take taxi."

Davie wondered why Lana had agreed to come to the station in the first place. She remembered Detective Quintero telling her he was working with a confidential informant from Satine's inner circle. She wondered if Lana Ivanov was that CI. If so, Davie suspected she would hear from Q, and soon. If not, Lana would likely report back to Satine and Marchenko that the police were closing in. Either way, Davie had a feeling all hell was about to break loose.

28

THE LIGHT WAS FADING as Malcolm Harrington jogged through the Santa Monica Mountains above Mountain Gate Country Club. Sometime during the previous mile, a runner's high had elevated him to a place that was as close to a religious experience as he was ever likely to feel. Still, he was anxious. Tire tracks rutted the access road, making the terrain hazardous. He could easily twist an ankle and fall. Someone would rescue him eventually, but there would be plenty of suffering until then.

As he headed up an incline, the cell phone attached to his water belt vibrated. He pulled it out and read the display. Blocked. Odds were fifty-fifty that the call was important so he slowed his pace, activated his earpiece, and answered with a crisp, "Harrington."

Internal Affairs investigator Alex Sloan chuckled. "You sound out of breath. Did I catch you in the middle of something?"

"I'm exercising. You should kick your nicotine habit and join me."

"An attractive offer, but I must decline."

"What did you dig up on Davie Richards?"

"You're not going to like it."

A cold wind coaxed the smell of sage from a nearby bush and chilled the film of sweat glazing Harrington's chest. "You disappoint me, Alex. I was hoping you'd have better news. "

"Look, I interviewed a shitload of people but for every one who thought Davie Richards was a prickly asshole, there were five more who believe she's Buffy the Vampire Slayer."

Harrington picked up his pace. "What about Spencer Hall?"

"He refused to be interviewed without his department rep present. I tried to get him to answer a few basic questions, but he was suffering from a bad case of CRS."

Harrington felt irritated. The police patois forced him to waste precious time searching his memory until he remembered what the acronym meant: can't remember shit.

Stress and exhaustion were making Harrington's breathing labored. "What about the grieving widow? Is she sticking to her story?"

"We both know the woman is lying. Richards is a crack shot. I found out she earned a Distinguished Expert Marksman and Sharpshooter medal. Somebody with a DX doesn't miss. No one will believe she aimed at Hall and hit the knucklehead husband instead."

"Mrs. Hurtado might create doubt about what happened that day."

"Not credible doubt. Let me tell you what's going to happen. The city will offer her a low-ball settlement just to get rid of her. She'll take the money and start looking for another mouth-breather to beat her up."

"What about interviewing the Hurtados' daughter?"

"Too risky. She's only five."

A sharp pain pierced Harrington's right knee. "If Davie Richards is mentally unstable, I want her off the streets."

"I've been sniffing around a couple of deputy DAs, trying to persuade one of them to file criminal charges against Richards, including Murder One Under Color of Authority. They tell me Force Investigations Division, RHD, the Chief of Police, *and* the Use of Force Review Board already investigated the case. The DA's office got the original paperwork six months ago. The DA reviewed the evidence herself and found no criminal wrongdoing on Richards's part. They think Mrs. Hurtado's new claims are crap."

"What about a lesser charge?"

Sloan sighed. "I have a few more people to interview. I'll let you know later this week if any of them drop the dime on her."

"That's not soon enough. If she poses a threat to the public, Chief Juno has to order a department shrink to evaluate her—immediately."

"One step at a time, Malcolm. We have to be methodical or people might think we have a hidden agenda."

Harrington was taken aback. His only so-called agenda was to save the city from another embarrassing and costly scandal. Still, given his troubled history with Richards's father, he'd be wise to consider Sloan's advice. He wanted everybody to understand that this investigation was not some twisted act of revenge against William Richards.

"I'll be waiting for your call."

Only a few more miles to go and he'd be at his car, but he wasn't at all sure he could go the distance. On a normal day, counting the beats of his running shoes hitting the dirt was a type of meditation. Today they pounded out a warning: *caution, caution, caution.*

29

JUST AFTER TEN P.M., Davie tucked the Smith & Wesson between the seat and center console of her Chevy Camaro and headed out of the station's parking lot. She turned right onto Culver and made her way to the entrance of the 405 and home.

While she'd been talking to Lana Ivanov, somebody had left half a dozen hang-up calls from a blocked number on her desk phone. Again she wondered if Ivanov was Quintero's informant. If Lana had called Quintero from the liquor store, he knew about the interview. Maybe he had called to complain, but that seemed unlikely. He would have left a message or gone over her head and talked to Giordano.

Just past Inglewood Boulevard, she glanced in her rearview mirror and noticed a black Mercedes a short distance behind her. *No big deal,* she thought. There were lots of them in L.A. As she merged onto the freeway a few blocks later, the sedan was still there.

Paranoia is a cop's best friend, so she slid the Rover under her right thigh in case she needed a radio. She doubted the driver was from IA's

Covert Ops team. They usually chose ordinary vehicles that a target was less likely to notice. But the driver might be a member of a local street gang that had recently issued threats against the LAPD. Several officers had been followed home. The department had warned all personnel to use extreme caution when leaving the station. Within a mile, the Mercedes changed lanes and fell back. Davie drew in a deep breath to steady her nerves.

Her serenity faded at the Sunset Boulevard exit when she saw the Mercedes again just two cars behind hers. If she used her radio to call for help, every black-and-white and airship in the area would descend on the scene Code 3, lights flashing and sirens blaring. That would be awkward if the driver were a wealthy CEO on the way home to his Bel Air mansion. The paperwork would take hours. There was only one way to find out if the sedan was following her.

She took her foot off the brake at the red light and rolled back until there was distance between the Camaro and the car in front of hers. When she saw an opening in traffic, she floored the accelerator.

Davie powered the car through the intersection and headed east on Sunset toward UCLA. Campus police were close enough to provide backup if necessary. Traffic was light, so she allowed the speedometer to inch up to eighty.

She ran the red light at Bellagio and turned right onto campus. The street was dark and deserted. She glanced in the rearview mirror and saw the Mercedes behind her, also turning. There was no doubt now; it was following her. Her pulse raced as she thought of all the criminals who had threatened her life over the years. There was one thing she knew for sure: if somebody in the Mercedes meant to kill her, she might go to the hospital but they were going to the morgue.

She accelerated the Camaro along the narrow winding street. She glanced in the rearview mirror and nearly collided with a construction barricade that blocked the right fork of De Neve Drive. It was too late to turn left. The brakes caught and the Camaro skidded to a stop. The Mercedes spun to a stop a few feet away.

Davie grabbed her weapon and the radio and shouldered open the car door. She tumbled onto the blacktop, scrambling into a shooting position, using the door for cover. The driver doused his headlights, but hers remained trained on the Mercedes.

All her senses were on alert as she surveyed the terrain for a campus cop patrolling his turf. She looked for an escape route in case the situation escalated, but her options were limited. All she saw behind her were eerie shadows looming in the dim light of the crescent moon.

She heard a car door open. The interior light in the Mercedes went on, illuminating two figures. Men. *Perfect targets*, she thought, *an amateur's mistake*. Every academy boot learned to disable the overhead light.

The man in the passenger seat got out of the Mercedes and closed the door. His leather soles scraped against the pavement as he walked toward her. She wrapped her hands around the butt of the .45 but left her index finger parallel to the barrel. She wasn't ready to shoot—yet. When her eyes adjusted to the dark, she steadied herself and aimed for the man's forehead.

"Police! Stay where you are."

"As you wish," he said in a cultured British accent. "But I'm not armed and you might want to hear me out before we end our *tête-à-tête* with bullets."

She grabbed the radio with her left hand. Made sure it was on the correct frequency and prepared to transmit. "Who are you?"

"My name doesn't matter. It's who I represent that will pique your curiosity."

Both hands returned to her weapon. "You have thirty seconds before all hell breaks loose."

"We monitor your radio frequency. You didn't call for help. We wouldn't have approached you if you had."

She changed her position to get a better shot. "Tick tock, my friend."

"You're investigating the death of a young Russian girl. My employer wants to assist you, if possible."

She glanced at the driver, but he made no effort to get out of the car. "Who's your boss?"

"I believe you already know his name. Viktor Marchenko. He knows yours, as well, and he's eager to meet you."

Davie figured her interview with Lana Ivanov might flush the cockroaches out from under the baseboards, but she hadn't thought it would happen so quickly. "Why didn't he just pick up the telephone?"

"He called you several times. You didn't answer."

Those hang-ups on her desk phone must have been from Marchenko. She wondered if Lana's call from the liquor store was to the arms dealer, not to Q. "If your boss wants a meet-and-greet, tell him to come to the Pacific cop shop."

"I'm afraid that's not possible. Mr. Marchenko has a phobia about police stations. If you feel more comfortable you can follow us in your own car."

Detective Quintero had told her the arms dealer was on a yacht anchored in Paradise Cove. She assumed that's where the interview would take place. "The Camaro doesn't float."

If the man was surprised that Davie knew about the yacht, his voice gave no indication of that. "You'll find the venue provides maximum privacy for your negotiations."

She heard movement behind her. Felt a jolt of fear. She glanced toward the sound but saw only a paper cup pushed along by a gust of wind. "Who said I'm negotiating?"

"I suggest you accept his offer while it's still on the table. That is, if you want to find out who killed Ms. Nosova."

"Why don't you just tell me now?"

"I'm afraid you'll have to ask Mr. M. I'm just the intermediary."

Davie's legs had cramped from tension and cold air. She altered her position again, this time to relieve the pain. "My partner and I can set up a meeting for tomorrow."

"Mr. Marchenko wishes you no harm, but he will only speak to you and only tonight."

Davie didn't like ultimatums. They disturbed the balance of power in the wrong direction, which could prove deadly. She was skeptical of Marchenko's information tease. He could be lying in order to lure her into a trap, but she just wasn't sure how that would benefit him. Eliminating one LAPD Homicide detective would not stop the investigation. It would only raise suspicion about his relationship with Grigory Satine. Despite the risks, if Marchenko had facts about Anya's murder, she had to talk to him. If he wouldn't come to the station, she would have to go to him.

She considered asking Vaughn to go with her, but it was past eleven and she didn't know where he was. He might be out working the Beau Fischer case. If so, she couldn't pull him away just because she questioned her ability to handle the interview alone.

"I'm calling in my position," she said. "If I don't check in within an hour, the LAPD is going to ruin your day."

"Code Six. Isn't that what you call it? We have no objection as long as you mention only the name of the yacht where you'll be. It's *Czarina*, by the way. I'll monitor the radio from my car in case you break the rules."

"I don't live by your rules."

"An even match, I'd say. Mr. Marchenko doesn't live by yours, either." He turned and walked toward the Mercedes.

"I'm bringing my weapon."

He pivoted toward her. "How many guns do you carry, detective? The one in your hand and maybe a second small revolver strapped to your ankle? I doubt my employer would be intimidated by your arsenal."

Davie knew he was right. From what Detective Quintero had told her, Marchenko was an international arms dealer. He probably had enough guns hidden aboard his yacht to outfit a small rebellion.

Once again, she considered her options. Then she pulled her cell phone from her jacket pocket and called Vaughn's number. The Brit had confirmed he was taking her to Marchenko's yacht. She left a message to send the cavalry to the *Czarina* if she didn't check in by 1:00 a.m. That gave her about an hour. Enough time to drive to Malibu, interview Marchenko, and get back to shore. Vaughn was compulsive about checking his cell phone, so she figured he'd get the message within the next few minutes. He'd be there if she needed him. At least she hoped so.

30

THE MERCEDES LED DAVIE not to Malibu but to a helicopter at Santa Monica airport. It was dark outside. She couldn't see the pilot, but she felt the power of cold air from the rotors swirling around her and wondered if she was making a mistake. Jason Vaughn would likely think she was crazy to interview an international arms dealer on a yacht at sea, alone, even if the man's employee had assured her safety.

Bear had always compared fear to opening a hatch on a submarine. Once the water started seeping in, there was no stopping it. Nature and training had conditioned her to control her emotions, because panic killed. She couldn't lose it if she hoped to solve Anya Nosova's murder.

So she tamped down her jitters and turned toward the Brit.

Close up, she was surprised to see his features were Asian plus some other gene pool she couldn't identify. He must have noticed she was staring at him.

"My mother is Mongolian. My father is Russian, but I was raised in London."

"How did you get involved with Viktor Marchenko?"

He smiled. "That's a long, complicated story best saved for another time."

She and the Brit boarded the helicopter for the short flight to the top deck of a sleek powerboat Davie estimated to be at least two hundred feet long. They disembarked, leaving the pilot behind, and descended two decks past a swimming pool and an al fresco dining area. Davie scanned every dark corner, looking for trouble. Once on the main deck, the Brit gestured her into an art-filled room that smelled of cigar smoke.

A heavy-set man sat on a mauve sectional couch in the middle of the room, smoking a cheroot. She recognized him from the Edison surveillance photos. The black mustache formed a bushy chevron on his upper lip that mirrored the scale of his coarse features and pillow lips. A plastic grocery bag slouched on the chair near his thigh. She wondered what was inside it.

The Brit whispered in Viktor Marchenko's ear and left.

"You have good flight?" he said.

Davie crossed her arms over her waist to control a tremor. Her right hand rested on the .45 holstered under her jacket, just in case the Brit had lied about Marchenko's benevolence toward her.

"I guess you couldn't afford a dinghy," she said.

He let out a wheezy laugh, a sound that reminded her of a cat coughing up a hairball. "I have big dinghy. Twenty-six feet. You want to see?"

Davie glanced toward the outsized windows that framed a Milky Way of lights along the shore. "I'll pass, thanks. Just tell me what you know about Anya Nosova."

He left the cheroot to smolder on the edge of a marble ashtray. "You do not know who kill her."

She glanced down the hall but saw no one else in the room. "You're psychic. Big deal."

Marchenko reached toward the carved wooden coffee table in front of him and lifted a bottle of Russian vodka from a crystal bowl packed with ice. He filled two shot glasses. "Sit. We drink. I tell you story."

Davie stood with her back to the wall, scrutinizing the entryways. "*Nyet* to the booze. Just give me the story."

Marchenko downed one glass of the vodka. "Grigory Satine did not kill this girl."

"That's not much of a story."

"This girl, she have no money. Grigory give her job because she is Russian."

"Did that job include forcing her to have sex with any dirtbag who had a credit card?"

"She is ambitious girl. If she is hooker, is her business."

A noise coming from the deck outside drew Davie's attention to the door. She turned and scanned the shadows, but the crescent moon provided too little light for detail.

Again, she focused her gaze on Marchenko. "And when she ran away he tracked her down and killed her as a lesson to his other girls."

The Russian downed the second shot of vodka. "Grigory is businessman. He did not harm this girl."

"Then who did?"

He wagged his finger. "I tell you. In one, maybe two days."

"What makes you think I won't find the killer myself?"

He picked up the cheroot and sucked it back to life. "Because you are not Russian."

"Here's what I think: you don't know shit."

"My people do not trust police, only other Russians. I help you. Only you. Is big deal. I make you famous."

"What do you want in exchange?"

"You and your LAPD stay away from Grigory Satine. Two days."

"Why two days? Is that how long it'll take you to finish whatever business you have with Satine with enough wiggle room to skip town and leave me with nothing?"

His expression was devoid of emotion. "We Russians keep our promises. This girl, she have boyfriend who gets her pregnant. When he finds out, he wants her dead."

Davie had no reason to trust Marchenko, but she kept her tone neutral. "Was he one of her johns?"

He shrugged. "I hear he is big important man."

She figured he couldn't be talking about John Bell, who by all accounts was a wannabe screenwriter and an all-around loser. "His name?"

"People in Russian community look for him. They will find, but not yet."

Davie walked toward the door and glanced outside. "Where's Satine? Why doesn't he speak for himself?"

"He is away on business."

"You keep track of him like you're his personal assistant."

The dim light in the room made Marchenko's frown seem puckered and shrewd. "I am only tourist."

"Just blew into town to visit Disneyland, right? What's the real reason you're pinch-hitting for Satine?"

"I do not want trouble with your LAPD. We Russians are blamed for everything. We are not perfect, but no Russian murdered this girl. You give me two days, I give you name of killer. After, if you want, I take you also to Disneyland."

If the Brit had found a way to hack into police radio communications, Marchenko might know Satine was under police surveillance. Maybe he hoped his offer to find Anya's killer would stall the investigation. Meanwhile, he could broker a business deal with Satine to arm local gangsters. Afterward, he'd pull up anchor and disappear. Even if she had the power to delay Quintero's investigation, making a deal with the Odessa mafia, even to solve a homicide, was something she couldn't do.

Davie checked her watch. Twelve forty-five. If she didn't check in with Vaughn in fifteen minutes, Marchenko would definitely have trouble with the LAPD.

"I have a better idea," she said. "We'll both look for Anya's killer. Whoever finds him first gets a pair of mouse ears and a front row seat to the Main Street Electrical Parade."

Marchenko eyed the vodka bottle and then poured himself another drink. "You Americans always the same. We talk *glasnost,* you talk guns."

The Brit had said Marchenko meant her no harm, but people lied. She calculated how long it would take her to hit the bottom of the San Pedro Channel with an anchor tied around her neck.

Marchenko smiled. "Is okay. I forgive you."

He reached inside the plastic bag that was beside him on the couch. Davie's hand tensed on the butt of her .45 as she watched him pull out a red beaded evening bag in the shape of a heart. She recognized it from Andre Lucien's description as Anya's missing purse. Pasha Kozlov had confirmed that she had left the purse at the Volga Bakery the night she disappeared.

"Where did you get that?"

"After New Year's party, Grigory stay at hotel. One, maybe two days. Later, he go to his car. He find purse inside."

"You're saying he was set up?"

185

He shrugged. "Like I tell you, we Russians are blamed for everything."

Marchenko handed Davie the purse. There was a bald spot on the flap where a thread had broken and beads were missing. Inside the purse were three twenty-dollar bills, a lipstick, and a silver locket. She wondered if it was the necklace Anya never took off, even when she was sleeping. She pried open the heart with her fingernail and noticed the mechanism meant to hold a picture in place had been torn off, as if somebody in a hurry had removed whatever was inside. She wondered who it had been—Anya or her killer.

31

IT WAS JUST BEFORE one when Davie left Viktor Marchenko's yacht. She checked her phone for messages. Vaughn had called a dozen times. She didn't want to listen to a lecture so she sent him a text, letting him know she was okay. His answering text consisted of two words she considered sweet talk between partners: FUCK YOU.

She could have waited until morning to interview John Bell, but she was juiced with adrenalin and eager to move forward on the case. She picked up her car at the Santa Monica airport and made her way to Bell's apartment in Westchester.

Bell didn't respond to the knock on his door. She wondered if he had passed out in front of his computer or if he'd stumbled to the market for another fifth of research bourbon. She knocked again, louder this time. Still nothing. She walked toward the side of his unit but saw no lights from where his bedroom would be. The prospect of a stakeout wasn't appealing, but she would wait all night for Bell to return if that's what it took to find out why he had lied to her about not seeing Anya after she left the apartment complex Saturday night.

Toward the rear, a six-foot metal fence surrounded a swimming pool. A faint glow radiated from the window of a building a few feet from the pool. The hum of machinery told her it was where the filtering system was housed. A shadow passed through the light from the window. She remembered that Bell had filed several burglary reports for thefts from the apartment's pool cabana. She decided to find out who was inside.

Davie followed a path along the fence until she came to a gate with a keypad. The gate was locked. The fence wasn't impossible to scale as long as she outmaneuvered the row of spikes at the top. She weighed the element of surprise versus ten minutes of online shopping in case she had to replace her damaged pantsuit and found a foothold in the railing. She slid down the other side and landed on the concrete below.

As she approached, she heard Bell's voice, loud and angry. Through the window, Davie saw him reading from pages held together by brass-colored brads. It looked like a screenplay, maybe the one about the detective who was afraid of guns. Bell had on the same plaid bathrobe he'd worn during their first interview. He wasn't wearing a hat, which exposed a long strand of hair sprouting from one side of his head, enough to cover his bald spot in an artful comb-over. He was leaning against a waist-high piece of equipment attached to a chimney that extended through the roof.

There must have been a leak in the system because water had pooled on the floor. A screwdriver lay idle near a tubular machine with bubbling liquid visible through a plastic cover. It appeared someone had tried but failed to fix the problem.

The motor's hum masked her footsteps as she opened the door and stepped inside the building. "Mr. Bell."

Bell whipped around, dropping the screenplay to the floor. His hand grasped at his chest. His hair flopped onto his cheek. It looked like the ear of a basset hound.

"You," he said.

"We need to talk."

There was a tremor in his voice. "I told you everything I know."

Davie kept her tone calm and controlled. "Except the part about Anya Nosova calling you the night she disappeared. Did you think I wouldn't find out?"

He pulled his bathrobe tight around his body. "I didn't do anything wrong."

She stood by the open door. If he decided to rabbit, she would be there to stop him. "You borrowed your high school buddy's Olds and picked her up at the Edison. A photo of Anya getting into the car was captured on the hotel's surveillance camera."

His voice was barely audible over the machinery noise. "I was only trying to help her." At least he'd dropped the flirty banter from the first interview.

"You may have been the last person to see her alive. You lied to the police about a homicide investigation."

"I didn't lie. I was protecting Anya."

Davie stood with her feet apart and her arms crossed. "There are three things you should know, Mr. Bell: you're in trouble; that trouble is bigger than any trouble you've ever been in before; and the only way out of that trouble is through me."

Bell slid to the floor in front of the pool equipment. His head collapsed into his hands. It was a bit of drama, but Davie let him have the moment.

"I'm sorry," he said.

"*Sorry* doesn't cut it."

He looked up. His face was ashen, highlighting the dark crescents under his eyes. "When you came to my door asking about Anya, I freaked. I didn't know she was dead. I figured she didn't want to be found, that she'd run away to start a new life."

"With the father of her child?"

He nodded. "She told me they were getting married."

"Why did she call you that night and not him?"

"I don't know. It doesn't matter. I would have done anything for her."

"Because you were in love with her."

His eyes were moist. "She wasn't interested in me except as a friend. That's life, I guess. I didn't know she was dead until I saw the newspaper. Foul play, it said. So Philip Marlowe."

"Why didn't you call me when you saw the article?"

"I was going to."

Davie raised her voice. "When, Mr. Bell?"

His jaw fell slack. "My heart's sort of broken right now. Some days I can barely get out of bed."

Davie knew the feeling, but she wasn't about to tell him that.

"What did Anya say when she called Saturday night?" she asked.

For the first time, Bell noticed his screenplay lying near his thigh, soaking up water. He rescued it from the puddle and swiped the stack of pages across his bathrobe. "She was hiding from a creep named Grigory Satine and needed a lift home."

"Where did you take her after you picked her up at the hotel?"

"I dropped her at Andre's apartment. I wanted her to stay at my place for the night, just to make sure she was safe, but she said no. I figured she wanted to be with her new boyfriend. She probably called him as soon as she got inside."

"Who was he?"

Bell rolled to his knees and braced one hand on the pool equipment. "I never met him. Obviously, he never came to Andre's apartment."

"She must have talked about him. What did she say?"

He placed the screenplay on top of the machine and stood. "He could have been the dictator of a banana republic for all I know or just some rich guy getting a little on the side. Anya wanted a man who could protect her. I got the impression she thought this boyfriend could do the job. He was older than she was but in good shape, from what she told me."

"How much older?"

He shrugged. "I'd guess at least over thirty."

"Sounds like you didn't think much of him."

"I didn't think he acted like somebody who was planning a wedding. I don't think he even loved her. He bought her stuff, but it was all cheap crap except for a silver necklace he gave her. Even that wasn't Tiffany."

"Was it shaped like a heart?"

He nodded. "She never took it off. Andre was so clueless he never once asked where she got it."

"Did you see her leave with the boyfriend after you brought her home?"

"What I told you before was true: I never saw her again. After I dropped her off, I took the car back to Jerry. We had a couple of drinks. I sort of passed out on his couch. I didn't wake up until noon the next day. I walked home."

Davie recorded Forrester's contact information in her notebook. She could find him using DMV records, but getting the details from Bell saved time.

"Anya's boyfriend must have taken her on dates," she said. "Did she ever say where?"

Bell stared at his soggy screenplay. "He took her out to eat a few times, mostly out of town. She was cagey about naming the restaurants. For all I know, they had Quarter Pounders in the car at some Pacoima drive-in. It was like he didn't want them to be seen together. I asked her if the guy was married, but she said no. He was single. He was also stupid. She was so beautiful. I'd want everybody to know she was mine."

"What else did Anya tell you?"

Bell tried to pry the wet pages apart, but the paper disintegrated in his hand. "He liked sports. Once he took her hiking in the Santa Monica Mountains because he liked to make love under the stars. She hated doing it on the hard ground, but she didn't tell him that, only me. I listened because I loved her, but it felt like a knife in my gut when I thought about someone else touching her."

"Sounds like you hated him. Maybe you hated her a little too. I understand how it could have happened. She told you too much, you couldn't stand it anymore. If you killed Anya, you need to tell me now."

Bell seemed crestfallen. "Have you ever loved somebody, detective? I mean really loved them."

"This isn't about my love life, Mr. Bell."

"Then I guess you wouldn't understand how I felt about Anya. No man could have ever loved her the way I did. I would have taken a bullet for her. I would never, ever have done anything to harm her."

Bell's words sounded like screenplay dialogue, but his passion seemed genuine. Still, his love for Anya didn't eliminate him from the suspect list. Davie had to corroborate his alibi with Jerry Forrester before that happened. If necessary, she would impound Forrester's car and have it tested for trace evidence.

If Bell was telling the truth, at least he had provided her with information about Anya's mystery boyfriend. In her head, Davie ticked off what she knew about him: older than thirty, physically fit, someone who wanted to keep Anya under wraps, possibly because he would be put in jeopardy if people learned he was dating a hooker. He was a cheapskate, so maybe he had a wife who managed the finances and would be suspicious if she saw any unusual credit card charges.

She wondered where Anya had met the guy. Was he a john? Had they connected at one of Satine's parties at the Edison? Cal Rogers had told Davie that Satine entertained everyone from business leaders to politicians. She thought about the LAPD business card left at the Volga Bakery. It seemed unlikely that anyone in law enforcement would attend a party hosted by a guy rumored to be a member of the Odessa mafia, but she couldn't exclude the possibility. Whoever the boyfriend was, his identify had been kept a well-guarded secret—one that Anya Nosova had taken to her grave.

"If your story doesn't check out, I'll be back."

Bell held his hands palms up. "All I have left is the truth. I've lost everything else."

Davie figured that line would likely make it into the script if it wasn't already there. The odds were against Bell's screenplay ever making it into theaters, which seemed like one more let-down in an already long list. Failure had a way of spreading like the plague, and she didn't want to be in its path if the wind veered her way.

She turned to leave and then stopped. "Why are you out here this time of night?"

"I can't do a read-through in my apartment. Tenants complain about the noise."

"What about Anya? Did she complain too?"

Bell didn't respond. He squeezed his eyes closed and then resumed sorting through his soggy pages. Davie left him like that and headed to the station.

The property room was closed at that time of night, but she filled out the form to book the heart purse into evidence and then locked it in her desk for safekeeping. After that, she headed for home.

32

AN ALARM PIERCED THE silence of Davie's darkened bedroom. It was an incoming call on her cell. She glanced at the clock. Three digits glowed blood red. 4:10 a.m. The caller ID read BLOCKED, which meant it was probably work related. The phone felt heavy as she fumbled it to her ear, knowing good news seldom came at that hour of the morning.

She muttered a groggy, "Who's this?"

"Get your ass out of bed. I have something you'll want to see."

Davie recognized the gravelly voice of Det. Reuben Quintero. She didn't attempt to mask her irritation. "You know what time it is?"

"Time for coffee, hotshot. We just served search warrants on three locations connected to Grigory Satine, including an apartment in Marina del Rey. And guess what? It was full of hookers and one of them knows your vic."

Davie swung her legs off the bed and planted her feet onto Alex Camden's Turkish rug. Her body felt stiff from the horseback ride the day before, but only slightly so. "Where are you?"

"Got a pen?"

She grabbed her notebook from the nightstand and jotted down an address on Lincoln Boulevard. "I'll be there in fifteen minutes."

The Bora Bora apartment building was ten stories high with lanais jutting from the façade where plants, folding chairs, and beach bikes were stored. Davie figured Satine chose the location because the marina attracted young people who might be less concerned about men parading through the hallways at all hours of the day and night.

Davie hadn't wanted to waste time picking up a car at the station, so she drove her Camaro, parking it curbside in the circular driveway between two patrol cars, so close the bumpers were almost kissing. The potential for scraped chrome might annoy somebody, but there was no street parking on this stretch of Lincoln. It was dark outside and she wasn't in the mood to hoof it back to the scene from blocks away.

As she walked toward the building, an onshore breeze rattled the fronds of three palm trees near the entrance. Polynesian torches flanked the door and batik curtains draped across the windows in lazy folds. That South Seas look seemed dated to her, but the sign on the door read LUXURY APARTMENTS—NO VACANCY, so maybe muumuu retro was making a comeback. For all she knew it had never left.

Three malnourished young women in various stages of undress stood outside the front door shivering in the night air, their hands cuffed behind their backs. A male whose raid jacket identified him as an Immigration and Customs Enforcement, or ICE, agent was standing guard.

A man well into middle age stood nearby wearing handcuffs, a wedding ring, and a pair of black thong underwear, the latter partially obscured by fifty pounds of paunch. He hung his head, likely assessing that skimpy V and wishing he'd reached for the boxers that morning instead.

A sheriff's deputy leaned against his patrol car, arms crossed and looking bored. Also milling around the area were several uniformed LAPD officers, including a female wearing a commander's star. The presence of top brass plus the unusual nighttime service of the warrant confirmed that this operation was a big deal.

Davie heard somebody call her name. She pivoted toward the voice and saw Detective Quintero striding toward her sporting an adrenalin-juiced smile. He issued a brief greeting and motioned her toward the building.

"What's with ICE?" she asked.

"Satine smuggled some of the girls into the States through Mexico. If any of them signed up of their own free will, they'll serve time for prostitution and then get deported. If not, they'll just get deported. It all works out in the end."

"Unless they end up dead."

"Occupational hazard. The witness is inside talking to one of my guys. Her name's Tatiana Bolshov. We had to call in a Russian interpreter. These lamplight loreleis don't speak much English. In their line of work, I guess the language of love is enough."

"I doubt *love* is the word you're looking for, Q. Dig deeper. I'm sure you can find something more appropriate."

Quintero gave her a sidelong glance, time enough to assess any damage his comment may have caused but not long enough to let her think he cared. "Beef me if I offended your feminist sensibilities. I was only joking."

"I would but you're not worth the paperwork."

He grinned. "Did you get coffee like I told you? Because if you did, you left your sense of humor at Starbucks."

They made their way through the lobby past a bank of mailboxes with a faux grass overhang and a chandelier made of seashells. Quintero eyed the six-foot wooden tiki guarding the elevator door and mumbled, "Ugly bastard," as he knuckled the up button.

"If I get even the faintest whiff of coconut air freshener," Davie said, "I'm taking the stairs."

"I got one of those little evergreen trees from the carwash hanging on my rearview mirror if that makes you happier."

"One more reason never to ride shotgun with you."

The elevator doors opened and they stepped inside the car. Quintero pressed the button for the fifth floor.

"What did you learn from the witness?" Davie asked.

"She claims she answered an ad for a modeling agency in a Kiev newspaper. But instead of making the cover of *Vogue*, she ended up blowing johns on a waterbed in Marina del Rey."

Davie raised an eyebrow to remind him how he had disregarded that information at their previous meeting. "Sounds like my victim's story."

"Look, I got no time for I-told-you-sos, so don't start with me, okay?"

"How did Satine keep the girls from walking away?"

"He took their money, cell phones, and if they had passports he took those too. Then he locked them up and threatened to kill their families back home if they tried to escape."

"So much for your theory that the girls were here willingly."

At the fifth floor, the doors opened and Davie followed Quintero onto the landing. "Were they ever allowed to leave the apartment?"

Quintero turned right down a long hallway. "Some trolled for clients at Satine's nightclub. Sometimes they got to leave with a john but only with an escort waiting nearby."

Midway down the hall, they entered an apartment with windows that overlooked traffic on Lincoln Boulevard. Three detectives wearing blue raid jackets with POLICE in white letters on the back and an LAPD badge stamped on the left front panel searched the living room. Davie saw nothing you might find in a home where real people lived, such as photographs or mail. Even the furniture looked rental.

"This one is two bedrooms," Quintero said, "but he had several other locations across the city. The setup was the same. The girls did their business in the master suite. When they weren't working, they were locked up in the spare bedroom."

At the end of the hall, Davie saw a door fortified with a dead bolt lock accessible only from the outside. As soon as Quintero turned the knob, the tangy stench of cigarettes, onions, and dirty bodies pushed against her as if it had been waiting for a chance to escape.

"I forgot to warn you," Quintero said. "Smells sort of ripe in here. That's why we closed the door. The windows are nailed shut and the girls didn't exactly have maid service."

Despite the hype on the sign outside the building, there was nothing luxurious about the bedroom where the girls spent most of their downtime. There was no furniture, only mattresses strewn across a stained beige carpet. Boxes of condoms and pizza boxes littered the floor. Davie noticed a cockroach suspended between death and deliverance in the jelly part of a half-eaten donut.

Quintero pointed to two black garbage bags in the closet. "Those belonged to your victim. Bolshov kept the stuff because she thought your girl was coming back. She was pretty broken up when she found out she was dead."

"What's inside the bags?"

"Mothballs and broken promises."

"Very poetic."

"I have my moments. All I found was a bunch of dirty clothes and a few knickknacks, but you're welcome to see for yourself."

33

IN CONTRAST TO THE squalor of the spare bedroom, the master suite was beautifully appointed. In addition to a king-sized waterbed, there was a matching dresser and end tables that held tastefully arranged items that made the place look like an upscale hotel room. The cloying aroma of vanilla-scented candles masked any stench that might escape the other bedroom.

Tatiana Bolshov had lied. She did speak English. Shortly after the translator told her Davie was investigating Anya Nosova's murder, Bolshov told the guy in passable English to leave the room. As soon as the door closed, she demanded a cigarette.

Davie stepped over a used condom and leaned against the wall. "They're bad for your health."

Contrary to what Quintero had told her, Davie saw no puffy eyes or tear-stained cheeks to indicate the girl was grieving over Anya's death. Bolshov sat on the king-sized waterbed with a black satin sheet swathing her body. The sheet added bulk and possibly warmth to her wraithlike figure, but it didn't thaw her expression, which was as cold and calculating as a feral cat scrutinizing lunch.

"You think I am afraid of cancer?" Her arms swept a wide arc to indicate the bedroom and presumably all that had gone on inside it. "After this?"

"Not to downplay what happened to you in this apartment, Ms. Bolshov, but you can't fix dead."

Bolshov stood, causing the waterbed to roll and pitch. She walked to the nightstand, dragging the sheet behind her. She searched inside a drawer until she found a stray cigarette.

"You have match?"

Davie shook her head. "Tell me about Anya Nosova."

She put the cigarette in her mouth unlit and eyed Davie with a cagy stare. "What will you give me if I tell you who killed her?"

"I can't give you anything but information. You'll probably not be charged with prostitution if you're here against your will."

She threw the cigarette on the carpet. "You think I am stupid? Even in Kiev we have lawyers."

"So what do you want from me?"

"I work for Grigory for six months. He owes me money. I want you to make him pay. Then I hire good lawyer to get me green card."

A large gilded mirror hung on the crimson wall behind Bolshov, reflecting her unruly thatch of toffee hair and the determined set of her bony shoulders. On the nightstand were tools of her trade: a jar of lubricating gel and an odd-shaped plastic object that reminded Davie of a corkscrew. Bolshov probably deserved compensation for that tool alone, but that wasn't her call to make.

"If you need financial help, there's something called the Crime Victim's Fund. You can apply. No guarantee you'll get anything, though."

"Anya has fur coat. I want that too."

So much for the hooker with a heart of gold, Davie thought. Claiming a dead girl's coat seemed like a petty prize. She wondered if Bolshov had squirreled away whatever was in those plastic bags expecting Anya to return, or if she had always meant to keep the items for herself. If there was a coat, Davie decided to search it thoroughly in case somebody had hidden the Czar's crown jewels in the lining—or maybe something more valuable, like a thumb drive that stored details about Satine's crime syndicate.

"The coat is evidence. When the investigation is over, it belongs to Anya's parents."

Bolshov plopped onto the bed, creating a tsunami of gurgling water. "Coat is old. Why would they want it?"

"If they don't, I'll add your name to the waitlist."

"I want to be on top."

Davie resisted the obvious comeback. "That depends on what you know about Anya's death."

Bolshov's expression hardened as she prepared to haggle for a better deal. "You will tell them I need victim money?"

"You have trust issues, Ms. Bolshov."

"In Kiev, the police cannot be trusted."

"This isn't Kiev."

She hesitated but apparently realized haggling over promises made and kept was the least of her worries. "Before Anya leaves us, she goes to a see a man at a motel in Hollywood. He beats her because she will not do what he wants. Somebody hear her scream and call police, but this man run away. Lana is waiting in car but she can do nothing. Police take Anya away. We never see her again."

"How long ago was that?"

She counted silently on her fingers. "Maybe five months."

Davie had checked law enforcement databases. Anya Nosova's name did not appear anywhere in those records. "Did she use another name when she went to see men?"

"Ask Lana. She give us all fake IDs and tell us to lie if police stop us."

"Did a detective ever contact her to follow up?"

"How? We have no phones. Anya would never give police this address. She would not tell them anything."

Out in the hallway, Davie heard the sound of heavy footsteps and low conversation, indicating the search was still underway.

"Why was Anya allowed to leave this apartment and you weren't?"

Bolshov's toe herded the fallen cigarette toward her. "Some men would not come here."

"What men?"

"Men who did not want to be seen. Men with wives. Men with money. Who knows?"

"There has to be more to it than that. Why was Anya so special?"

"She was smart girl. Men like her the best. She tell Grigory she can make more money if he let her come and go."

"So he said yes? Just like that?"

Bolshov closed her eyes and sniffed the tobacco. "What you think? He is stupid? She was never alone. Lana was always there."

"What do you think happened to Anya?"

"Maybe police kill her."

"Try again, Ms. Bolshov. What about Satine? Wasn't he upset when he lost one of his best girls?"

"I know what you think, but Grigory did not kill her. He did not know where she was."

"What if he found out?"

She shrugged. "You are detective. Is your job to know that." Bolshov punctuated her sentence with a grand gesture, whipping up another waterbed swell. The sloshing sound was starting to make Davie seasick.

"Did Lana keep a record of her customers? On a laptop or in a little black book?"

"For tax man, right?" Bolshov flashed a sly smile. "I have seen her with a book but it is not black."

Davie remembered the notebook Lana carried when she interviewed her at the liquor store. "Is it purple?"

Bolshov nodded. "The ink too. I think it is full of names and telephone numbers worth a lot of money."

Davie did the math. According to Anya's dad, she left for the US approximately nine months ago. Bolshov claimed that after living in the Marina del Rey apartment and servicing Satine's clients for four months, Anya was assaulted at a motel in Hollywood. She never returned to the apartment, but she did resume contact with her father.

If a man assaulted Anya in Hollywood Division, detectives from Major Assault Crimes would have investigated. Spencer Hall transferred to Hollywood MAC about that time, shortly after their officer-involved shooting. Even if Anya had given a phony name on the report, he might remember the case. As much as Davie dreaded the idea, she had to talk to him again.

Bolshov had never seen the john and could offer no further information. With luck, Quintero had found Lana's purple client book at one of the search locations. If so, Davie hoped to find the man's name and contact information inscribed inside in purple ink.

That is, if anything Tatiana Bolshov had just told her was true.

34

A FEW MINUTES AFTER Davie had concluded her interview with Bolshov, two patrol officers led the woman out of the apartment in handcuffs. Davie slipped on a pair of latex gloves from her jacket pocket
and dragged the bags of Anya's clothes from the bedroom into the
living room, where the air was less toxic. The sound of drawers opening and closing filtered in from the adjacent kitchen as detectives continued their search.

A killer had robbed Anya's parents of their child's future—a college graduation they would never attend and grandchildren they
would never spoil. Now their hopes and dreams had been reduced to
the contents of two plastic garbage sacks.

Inside the first bag, she found a photograph of a young couple on
their wedding day. Anya's parents, no doubt. Davie saw the resem-
blance to the girl in the man's almond-shaped eyes and in the woman's
long slim fingers, clutching her husband's arm. Another photo was an
eight by ten glossy of Anya. To say the pose was provocative didn't do

it justice. Her negligee was black and transparent. She was bending over at the waist with her thong-covered ass aimed toward the camera and her head canted to reveal a naughty expression on her face. The picture left no doubt as to why Anya was popular with her customers. Davie wondered if the photo had been used on a website that had since been taken down or was hidden somewhere on a darknet site that was available only with special software and authorization.

The bag also contained two ruffled dresses that looked like costumes for a revival of *Meet Me in St. Louis*. There were no labels inside the clothes, and the finish of the seams looked homemade. Davie imagined Anya's mother stitching the garments in a naïve misunderstanding of what life in L.A. was all about. In the bag were other outfits as well—sexy and revealing—for another life her parents didn't know about. Davie thought about the denim and black polyester in her own closet and wondered what value judgments someone might make about her under similar circumstances.

She tried to imagine her own mother hunched over a Singer, sewing clothes for her, but the idea was so farfetched it wouldn't come into focus even as a fantasy. Homespun couture wasn't part of Evelyn Cross's skill set. Her Neiman Marcus tastes on a cop's salary was the match that ignited the dry tinder of her marriage to Bear, eventually reducing the family to smoldering ashes.

Davie continued searching through Anya's clothing, hoping to find a mysterious key or a pawn ticket—anything that might lead to her killer. She found two crumpled cigarettes but nothing else. The second bag held a set of wooden nesting dolls similar to the one Davie's mother had brought back from St. Petersburg on her honeymoon cruise with husband number two. Davie disassembled the five dolls but found nothing hidden inside. She also found the fur coat with a label lettered in Cyrillic, probably brought to L.A. from Anya's home in Ukraine.

Davie slipped her hand inside a pocket and touched something square and rough. Pulling it out, she saw a small wooden box painted with the words *My heart belongs to you*. A flimsy metal hinge opened to reveal a red wooden heart nestled inside.

Hearts everywhere the bedroom wall of Anya's apartment, the silver necklace she never took off, and that red beaded purse that Davie had recovered from Viktor Marchenko. Now this. Anya had told both Gallway and Lucien that she had argued with her roommate, who later disappeared with all of Anya's personal property. That was a lie. Anya had left this apartment with only the clothes on her back. So except for the heart box in the pocket of her coat, she had collected the other heart items later. Davie wondered if Anya's mysterious boyfriend had given her all the heart-themed gifts. If so, he had likely known her when she lived in this apartment, working as a prostitute, and had continued to see her after she escaped.

Davie turned the box over and saw some sort of mark on the underside, but it was too blurred to read. She had a magnifying glass in her desk at the station but decided instead to take the box to the wonks at the Scientific Investigation Division. They could make the obscure seem obvious.

Quintero was still taking photographs in the second bedroom. She knew from experience he had also taken shots before executing the search warrant to create a before-and-after record. Department regulations required him to do that to counter any claims of damage from the property owner. Lawsuits and liability were part of a two-headed Troig that gave city officials the heebie-jeebies.

"I'm looking for a purple notebook full of names," Davie asked Quintero. "Did you find anything like that?"

"Nope."

She was disappointed but not surprised. According to Bolshov, Lana never let it out of her sight. "You can book these bags now."

"I'm not writing paper for dirty clothes, so unless you found stolen booze or cigarettes in there, forget it."

Davie knew taking Anya's possessions from the apartment without consent or without writing a search warrant specific to the bags could cause trouble. If something in there proved vital to her case, the defense could challenge the chain of custody. Then a judge might not allow the evidence into court, and Anya's killer could walk. Writing another a warrant and getting it signed would take time, though. Meanwhile, things had a habit of disappearing.

"I found a couple of cigarettes in one of the bags and they looked stolen."

Quintero rolled his eyes. "Okay, but you do the paperwork and take the crap with you. I'm not going to book it into Property."

She nodded. "Did you arrest Satine?"

"Can't find him."

"He may be out of town."

Quintero's jovial disposition melted away. "And just how do you know that?"

Davie had planned to share the information with Quintero. She just hadn't found the time. "Viktor Marchenko told me."

He whirled to face her. "What the—? You contacted Marchenko? When?"

"I didn't contact him. He contacted me. I interviewed him last night on his yacht."

A vein in Quintero's neck started to throb. "Why the hell didn't you tell me?"

"I'm telling you now."

He jabbed his nicotine-stained finger toward Davie's face. "Dammit, Richards. Marchenko's in the wind too. You just couldn't wait to talk to him, could you? Not even when I asked you pretty please."

She pushed his hand away. "He's probably headed for Mexico."

Quintero's face had turned a dangerous shade of red. "The Federales boarded his boat off the coast of Mexico a couple of hours ago. They didn't find shit. No Satine. No Marchenko. No whirlybird."

The helicopter was probably on its way to some remote airport connecting Marchenko and Satine to any number of possible destinations. Davie understood the radiating heat of Quintero's anger. She hadn't meant to compromise his case, but she would have been irresponsible to ignore an opportunity to interview Marchenko about Anya's murder.

"I didn't have time to call and ask your permission. What about Lana Ivanov?"

"We know where she is."

"And where is that?"

"Like I said, we know where she is."

"So she's your informant."

"You've got balls, Richards. You screw up my case and don't even say you're sorry."

"I didn't screw up your case. Marchenko made your surveillance team. He knew you were following Satine. *That's* why Satine split, not because I asked a few questions about a dead Russian girl."

Quintero paused for a moment, contemplating the possibility that the arms dealer had blown his team's cover. Davie figured things might get tense when he debriefed his people at the end of the day.

He turned and stomped out of the room. Over his shoulder he added, "You haven't heard the last of this."

35

DAVIE ITEMIZED ALL OF Anya Nosova's property on a department form. Then she sealed the garbage bags and loaded them into her car. When she arrived at the station, she booked the bags and the heart purse into the Property room. After that, she drove downtown and dropped the wooden heart box and broken cigarettes at SID. It was unlikely the techs would find traces of DNA or fingerprints on either, but she had to be sure.

Her watch read eight forty-five. Rose Miller's funeral was scheduled for ten a.m. at St. Monica Catholic Church in Santa Monica. Davie was exhausted from the early morning wake-up call, but she had promised Grammy she'd take her to the service, so she headed to West L.A. She arrived at her grandmother's apartment and found her dressed for travel in a purple knit dress that had been part of her wardrobe for decades and a black pillbox hat that Davie had never seen before.

"New hat?"

"I borrowed it from Mrs. Kimmelman. She told me Catholics have to wear hats in church, but I don't think that's true anymore. I never saw Rose in a hat except when she watched the Dodgers game on TV, but that was a baseball cap."

"Either way, you're covered. The hat looks great."

"Marvin Levine says it makes me look like a Shriner."

Davie held up the black wool coat her grandmother had worn to Poppy's funeral. "Marvin is full of shit."

Grammy guided her arms into the sleeves. "That's what I told him."

The last time Davie had been in a church was a year ago after her grandfather died. The atmosphere inside St. Monica's seemed tranquil until the pipe organ dirge draped her like a shroud. She believed death meant lights out. The end. No more pain. No more regret. But in the end, what did anybody know for sure? She wondered if Anya Nosova and Rose Miller had crossed paths in the afterlife and what they might have talked about.

There was a reception in the parish hall following the service, but Grammy didn't want to stay. She had paid her respects, she said, it was time to move on. Davie was glad because it was Friday. She'd been working the Anya Nosova case for three days, and she wasn't even close to an arrest.

The air smelled of eucalyptus and car exhaust as she guided her grandmother off of the curb and onto a broad crosswalk.

"I couldn't see much with these bad eyes of mine," Grammy said, "but the church seemed beautiful. Saint Monica's is Father O'Malley's church. Did you know that?"

"Who's Father O'Malley?"

"Bing Crosby. He played the priest in that picture *Going My Way*. The movie was filmed here. Mother took me to a matinee when I was eleven. It was my first visit to a movie theatre. Father was away fighting Nazis and we didn't have much money."

Davie steadied Grammy as they crossed the uneven grass on the way to the car. "You never told me that story before."

"There's a lot I haven't told you, Davie. Remember, I lived a whole life before you were even born. At times it wasn't easy, but I survived."

"I'm glad."

Grammy paused and faced Davie. "Sometimes you treat me like I'm fragile. I'm not, you know. I won't fall apart if you share the bad things in your life. It might even help you to talk about them."

"I wouldn't know where to begin."

"Why not start with that Harrington character. Maybe I can't see too well, but I can hear just fine. The TV news said he's the new police watchdog. I still remember what he did to your father. I'm afraid he could do the same thing to you."

"My boss is checking on the situation." Davie got them walking toward the car again. "He'll let me know if I should worry."

"Have you ever heard the phrase *trust but verify?*"

"Are you saying I shouldn't trust my boss?"

"No. I'm just saying, in the end, you can't rely on anybody except yourself."

Davie unlocked the car doors with her remote. "I can rely on you and Bear."

"Yes, because we're part of you. We're family."

She buckled her grandmother into the seat. "You're very wise today, Grammy. Must be the hat."

36

AFTER DROPPING GRAMMY AT her apartment, Davie returned to the station. As she entered through the back door, she saw Vaughn in the hallway outside the detective squad room. She wanted to tell him about the IA tail, but apparently he had just arrested a suspect in the Beau Fischer homicide and he was too busy planning his Detective of the Year acceptance speech.

"Who is he?" Davie said.

"Robert Foster, street name Rags."

"You get a confession?"

"The guy barely knows what planet he's on. He keeps jabbering about G-men and the Pentagon. Definitely fifty-one fifty."

The term came from the California Welfare and Institutions Code 5150, which allowed law enforcement to place a psychiatric hold on a person under certain conditions. It was cop shorthand for *crazy, nut job, wacko, bananas*. Lieutenant Bellows had ordered all personnel to use the term *mentally challenged*, but the old expression refused to die.

"What broke the case?"

Vaughn spread vapor rub under his nose to mask the odor of sweat, urine, and fear that hung in the air. Civilian personnel in Records had closed all doors leading to the hallway. They were unaccustomed to the perfume of the street.

"Eyewitness," he said. "Another junkie saw him kill Fischer in a beef over drugs."

"I hope you have more than the word of a heroin addict."

Vaughn brushed off her warning with a shrug. "There's more, but I think he'll plead once he gets over being mad at me. Right now he won't say a word."

That didn't surprise Davie. Vaughn's default setting for interrogating suspects was aggression, which often worked but sometimes backfired. Not everybody responded to his tough-guy posturing. Davie had accused him of watching too many bad-cop movies, but she knew her partner was wired to be a hard-ass, and he wasn't going to change.

"You want me to talk to him?

Vaughn hesitated, reluctant to cede power. "Go ahead. But you won't get anywhere."

Davie locked her weapon in the drawer of her desk. It wasn't allowed inside the booking area. The arrestee wasn't in the holding tanks visible from the hallway, so Davie tapped on the glass window. The jailer buzzed her in and pointed to a large room where a man lay slumped on a bunk under a mound of gray clothing. Davie recognized him immediately. Last time she had seen him was in front of the Inky Dink tattoo shop in Venice two days ago.

His fingers were laced over his head to form a protective shield. He was agitated, pleading for mercy from a god only he could see. Davie watched from a few feet away as the jailer unlocked the cell with an oversized key that looked like it belonged in a medieval dungeon.

Rags squinted at Davie. "Who's there?"

"It's Detective Richards. We spoke outside the tattoo parlor a couple of days ago. Remember?"

His body relaxed. "Hey, pretty lady. I didn't recognize you. I can't see too good without glasses."

The jailer roused Rags from the cot and led him to a nearby interview room that held a small table and two chairs. Rags gestured for her to sit across from him.

"I hear you're in trouble," she said.

He reached out and grabbed her hand. "I didn't kill Beau. Arnie dimed me, but it's not his fault. They made him do it."

Davie heard the jail's outer door open. She glanced over her shoulder and saw Vaughn step into the entryway and settle into the shadows out of Rags's line of sight.

"Who are 'they'?"

Rags withdrew his hand. "You know." He nodded toward the hallway but the direction was nonspecific. Davie was certain he couldn't see her partner or the jailer.

"You mean somebody in the police department, Mr. Foster?"

"You can call me Rags, because I know you."

She studied his face: skin weathered a reddish brown, unwashed hair the color of tumbleweeds, eyes gray and moist as river stones, reflecting that same flicker of intelligence she'd noticed in their first encounter. She wondered what kind of man he'd been before the drugs and the mental illness.

"Why would anybody make Arnie accuse you of murder?"

Rags tapped his fingers on the table as if he were typing a news story for an impossible deadline. "You can't trust cops."

"I told you the other day, I'm a cop too."

"You're different. You gave me a loan. Just so you know, I bought drugs with that money. I tried not to, but I couldn't help myself. I'll do better next time."

Fat chance, she thought.

"We all make mistakes." She leaned toward him, ignoring the pungent odor radiating from his clothing. "Tell me what happened between you and Beau Fischer."

He continued tap, tap, tapping. "Beau worked for the G-men."

"Sounds like Beau was a bad guy."

"The worst."

"I understand how sometimes you might have to kill a bad guy. Maybe Beau threatened you, pushed you too far. You had to kill him to protect your life. Is that what happened, Rags?"

Rags shook his head from side to side like the slow ticking of a metronome. "I didn't kill Beau."

"That's what you said before. So, who did?"

He was quiet for a while. Then he leaned toward her and whispered. "I typed a report."

Davie blinked. She had no idea what he meant. "What did it say?"

He drummed his fingers on the wood table in a dull staccato beat. "I saw the octopus and the blond seaweed. I saw him, too, in the alley. He wants to get rid of me because I know too much."

"What does an octopus have to do with Beau Fischer's death?"

"I know who killed her."

Vaughn was right. Rags Foster was certifiable. Deciphering his gibberish was taxing her patience.

"*Her*? You mean *him*. You know who killed Beau Fischer?"

"I figured it out later," he said. "It wasn't an octopus. She was a pretty lady, just like you, except not a redhead. She was a blonde."

"Are you saying Beau killed a blonde girl?"

He shook his head. "Not him. And she was already dead. Then she disappeared. Poof. Down the rabbit hole."

Davie's mind clicked back into high gear. The Hyperion engineer told Davie that Anya's body could have entered the sewer system in only two ways: either through an open pipe in a construction area or through a manhole. It was farfetched, but she pondered the possibility that Rags Foster had witnessed Anya's murder, or at least the dumping of her body—not down a rabbit hole but into a manhole in Venice, where Rags was known to hang out.

"Are you talking about the blonde girl they found in the sewer? Anya Nosova?"

Rags stopped tapping. His gaze darted from side to side, and then his eyelids opened wide. He seemed to have connected the dots in his scrambled brain. "I couldn't have saved her," he said.

Davie heard footsteps. She turned to see Vaughn walking toward the table. She shook her head to indicate the interview was still in progress. Vaughn ignored her.

"Time to go, Mr. Foster," he said.

Rags recoiled at the sound of Vaughn's voice. "Where are you taking me?"

"County jail, thirteenth floor. Great view. You'll love it."

Rags's breathing became shallow. "You took my watch cap. I need it back. It protects me again the forces of evil."

"You'll get it back. Later." Vaughn pulled cuffs from his belt and moved closer.

Davie stepped outside the interview room to block Vaughn's path, inhaling the odor of the menthol under his nose. "Rags and I are still talking."

"You're going to kill me, aren't you?" Rags shouted.

"I'll let the state handle that," Vaughn muttered.

"Help me, pretty lady."

She put her hand on Vaughn's arm, noting the smooth wool of his Italian suit. "I need to talk to you outside."

"Look, Davie," he said, "we can't keep Foster at the station. We don't have the personnel or the facilities to handle a fifty-one fifty. I need to book him into county jail so somebody can do a mental evaluation before he totally freaks out. If he goes off on us, I'll have to call an RA to take him to the mental ward of some hospital. Which means I'll be tied up there all night."

Vaughn was right. The rescue ambulance techs would provide medical aid, or more likely transport Rags to a hospital for observation. That could delay him, but letting Davie continue the interview was more important than his time.

"It may sound crazy," she said, keeping her voice low, "but I think he may know something about Anya Nosova's murder. I want to ask him a few more questions."

Vaughn sighed then slid the handcuffs into his jacket pocket. "Okay. Just don't take too long. Getting through downtown traffic is going to be a bitch."

Davie heard loud pounding coming from the interview room. She turned to see Rags "typing" on the wood table at a feverish pitch. His eyes seemed wild and unfocused. "Somebody help me. Please. I want a lawyer."

Shit.

Back in the day, the law allowed detectives to interview an arrestee after he invoked his Miranda Rights, but only if the questions were about an unrelated crime. A recent court decision had changed all that. Now that Rags had lawyered up, she couldn't ask him anything more about Anya Nosova. The man was obviously unstable, but if he did know something, whatever information he might have had was lost to her.

217

For every door that opened, another was slammed in her face. Davie left Rags to Vaughn without another word. She exited the booking area and headed for the squad room, hoping the warrant for Anya's telephone records had been returned and was waiting on her desk.

37

"HEY, RICHARDS."

Davie was in the hallway outside Records. She turned and saw the jailer holding up a property bag.

"Your partner was in such a hurry to beat traffic he forgot to take this."

The stench of sweat and decay radiating from that paper bag roiled her stomach. "I hope that's Vaughn's gym bag and not his lunch."

The jailer chuckled. "It's his suspect's watch cap and a couple of old newspapers. You want me to ship it to the county jail or are you headed that way?"

Downtown L.A. was out of her way, but delivering the property to the jail would give her a chance to check on Rags. She reached for the aromatic bag. "I'll drop it off on my way home."

When she returned to the squad room, she retrieved her gun from the desk drawer. She checked her desk but the phone company had not returned Anya's call records. The room was nearly deserted. She checked the sign-out sheet. Giordano was at a doctor's appointment, Garcia was on a regular day off. Vaughn and Montes were on their way downtown to book Rags. She assumed detectives from other tables were on follow-up calls or in court.

She slid Rags's bag under her desk. Then she picked up the phone and dialed Spencer Hall's cell. He had worked as a Hollywood MAC detective during the time Anya was assaulted. It was a long shot, but she hoped he remembered the incident or knew somebody who would. He didn't pick up, so she left a message.

While she waited for Hall's callback, she made notes on her interview with Rags. Maybe it was just wishful thinking on her part that Rags had information about Anya's killer, but she couldn't ignore the idea.

The stench from the property bag was fracturing her concentration, so she put it inside a large plastic sack she found in the cabinet under the shredder and sealed it with flex-cuffs. Five minutes later she went a step further and locked it in the trunk of her Camaro. She hoped the seal held and Rags's crap didn't stink up her car.

When Davie got back to her desk, the phone was ringing. It was Spencer Hall. She didn't waste time exchanging pleasantries.

"My victim was involved in an assault in Hollywood about four or five months ago. I'd like to show you her photo and see if you remember her."

"Come on, Davie. I have file drawers full of assault cases. Search DCTS if you want details."

The Detective Case Tracking System was a searchable database that held a detective's notes, witness statements, and other details about a case, including the final disposition.

"I couldn't find anything. She may have used an alias."

"Look, I'm at the DA's office dropping off a case. I'm too jammed to drive to Pacific today. Just email the photo. I'll look at it when I get back to Hollywood."

"We don't have a scanner here, and color won't show up on a fax," she said. "What if I meet you halfway?"

She could have scanned the photos from the app on her cell phone and sent them electronically, but she preferred to conduct important interviews in person, even when that interview was with a fellow cop. She wanted to watch Hall's expression when he looked at Anya's picture to see if and how he remembered her. Or maybe she just wanted to see him again.

He hesitated. "I can be at Café G'day in about twenty minutes."

The coffee shop had been a regular hangout in the early days of their romance. She'd prefer someplace neutral, but it was more important to show the photos to Hall than to nurse her bruised ego, so she agreed. She slipped the two photos of Anya into her notebook and headed to the parking lot.

On the drive to meet Hall, she detoured past A to Z Liquors, checking her rearview mirror for a tail. If anyone was following her, she didn't spot him. The liquor store now looked abandoned. Lana Ivanov and her buddy Boris were probably in Mexico on Marchenko's yacht or at one of Reuben Quintero's safe houses. She hoped Q wasn't still mad at her because she still needed access to Lana's purple notebook and hoped he knew where it was. After her meeting with Hall, she would have to call Quintero and make nice.

Café G'day was a small storefront on Pico Boulevard near Fairfax, dwarfed between a chain drugstore and a multistory office building. Maroon-striped awnings and wood-paned windows graced the façade. Inside, baristas served organic coffee to Millennials looking for a quaint Aussie-village experience in the middle of commercial sprawl.

The only other patron in the place was a young man wringing his hands over a computer screen. Hall was waiting for her on the patio outside. If the dark smudges under his eyes were any indication, he hadn't been sleeping well. She wondered if a guilty conscience was causing his insomnia. Two lattes sat on the table, one in a paper container, the other in a ceramic cup and saucer. Just like old times.

The metal chair scraped across the brick pavers as Davie sat a comfortable distance away from Hall. She accepted the ceramic cup he pushed toward her and noticed the barista had crafted a heart in the foam. It made her think of Anya Nosova.

Hall smiled. "Nonfat. Right?"

He already knew the answer, so she didn't bother responding. She pulled John Bell's photo of Anya from her notebook and held it up. "She look familiar?"

Hall studied the picture. "Yeah, I remember her. It wasn't my case, but I was there when patrol officers brought her into the station. She said her name was Tiffany something. Jones, I think. We all figured she was lying. Not many Russian girls with a name like that."

"You have a good memory."

Hall glanced at Davie. "Hard to forget a face like that."

"What was her story?"

"Boyfriend troubles. She was vague about the details."

Davie wrapped her hands around the cup to fend off the cold air, inhaling the fragrance of espresso and frothed milk. "Did she mention the boyfriend's name?"

"Nope. Said she didn't want to get him in trouble."

"Did she need medical treatment?"

"We asked, she refused. She had a bruise on her arm. Other than that, it didn't look like she had any serious injuries."

Davie took a sip of the latte. When she returned the cup to the saucer, she noticed the heart had dissipated into stringy trails of milk and foam.

"Did you figure her for a hooker?" she asked.

Hall seemed deep in thought. "Why? Was she?"

She held up the racy photo of Anya taken from the Marina del Rey apartment. Hall frowned, somehow disturbed by the image. Most cops on the job had seen dozens of smuttier pictures. Maybe he was taking the moral high ground now that he was back with his wife, but his reaction struck her as odd.

She ignored his question and asked another of her own. "Why did the officers bring her to the station?"

"I guess they thought she'd be more talkative."

"Where did the incident happen?"

"Some no-tell motel on Hollywood Boulevard, I think."

"Anybody follow up?"

"The case wasn't assigned to me, but I can tell you there was nothing to follow up on. The girl was uncooperative. You know the DA's office isn't going to file a case if the victim refuses to identify the suspect or testify in court."

A small brown bird landed on a table nearby and began pecking at the remains of a muffin on a plate. Davie studied its scrawny legs and thought of Anya's fragile limbs tangled in the jaws of the Hyperion grinder.

"Who picked her up from the station?"

"Nobody. She said she was a student at UCLA. The detective handling the case asked a couple of patrol officers to drop her off on campus."

"Where Troy Gallway found her and invited her to stay at his condo."

"Who?"

"Forget it. Too bad I didn't have this information earlier."

Hall's body tensed. "I told you she gave a phony name. How was I supposed to know it was the same girl? I've never seen either of those pictures before."

"Was she involved in other incidents?"

"None that were assigned to me."

Davie pushed back her chair and stood. The bird was startled by the noise and flew away with a small chunk of muffin still in its beak.

She put a five-dollar bill on the table to pay for the latte. "Thanks for your help."

Hall stood too. "Davie—"

"What?"

His lips parted, about to say something. Instead, he glanced toward the bird, but it had already disappeared. "Nothing. Good luck with the case."

On the drive back to the station, Davie thought about Hall's behavior. Gone were the sense of humor and charm she had once found so attractive. She reminded herself that he had the police commission's gun pointed at his temple just like she did. Added to that was the pressure of mending the relationship with his wife. Still, she was sure he had wanted to tell her something before she left the café. She wondered what it was.

When Davie returned to the station, several faxed pages were waiting on her desk: Anya Nosova's telephone records. Before she could flip through them, she sensed somebody walking toward her. She turned and saw Lieutenant Bellows.

He leaned on the wall partition of her cubicle. "Davie, I'd like to have a word with you in my office."

His tone was soft, almost fawning. Bellows had rarely spoken to her since she arrived at the division. When he had, he was businesslike, almost curt. He had certainly never used her first name before. His behavior didn't fit the pattern. Minutiae.

Something was wrong.

38

TWO UNIFORMED OFFICERS WERE already seated at the round conference table in Lieutenant Bellows's office. One wore the triple chevron of a Sergeant-1, the other's uniform sported captain's bars. Both men's facial expressions were rigid and unreadable. Bellows closed the door and lowered the mini blinds on his office window. That meant only one thing: he didn't want anybody in the squad room to see what was about to happen.

Bellows gestured for her to sit. The knife creases in his Class A uniform pants flattened as he lowered his trim five-eight frame onto the chair. She knew it was petty, but that small imperfection pleased her. The standard attire for detectives was a business suit. The department term was "soft clothes." Wearing the uniform was just one more way the lieutenant set himself apart from the people he supervised.

Bellows introduced the two men, a sergeant from Personnel and a captain from Internal Affairs. On cue, the sergeant flicked a piece of paper toward her, like he was skipping a stone across a polluted pond.

The gesture seemed dismissive and disrespectful. She didn't look down, not wanting to take her eyes off the men in that room. Her concentration was too fractured to read the words anyway.

"What's that?"

"A letter," the sergeant said, "advising you that you're being relieved of duty."

Davie could almost smell the pungent zest of ozone after a lightning strike. "Why?"

"The Inspector General has reopened your OIS case."

"The department already ruled the shooting was within policy."

"The victim's wife has offered new evidence. She claims you made false statements on the police report."

"What are you talking about?" Davie's voice sounded thin and brittle even to her.

"Mrs. Hurtado claims you murdered her husband and then lied about it."

She wanted to tell them the allegation was absurd, but she no longer had breath to support the words. She flashed back to the day of the shooting, to Mrs. Hurtado's bloody face, her hysteria, and her gratitude. The woman had thanked Davie over and over again for saving her life. Now she had changed her story, and it didn't take long to come up with a theory as to why—money.

"I recommend you get a department rep or a lawyer as soon as possible," Bellows continued. "For now, I need your department ID, your badge, and your gun, which I will give to the captain to hold. I'll have somebody box up the personal items in your desk. I'll see that they are sent to you."

Davie counted the number of "I"s in the lieutenant's monologue, but lost track. She figured Bellows loved statistics so much he could probably calculate the total, crunch the numbers, and come up with a theory for why everything was always just about him.

"What about Anya Nosova? While you waste time trying to put a case on me, the investigation stalls."

Bellows avoided her gaze by reshuffling some papers on the table. "I'll assign another detective to pick up where you left off."

"Nobody knows the case like I do."

Bellows's ramrod-straight spine radiated impatience, not empathy. "Your notes should be in the Murder Book. Somebody will figure it out."

Davie leaned into his personal space. "I didn't lie on that report."

"I'm not here to argue the merits of the evidence again you. You'll have a chance to defend yourself at your Board of Rights hearing." He held out his hand, palm up. "Your ID."

Davie wanted to slam Bellows against the wall, tell him she was being railroaded and that he was an asshole for not fighting for her. She studied his Beverly Hills haircut. It made him look slick and cunning—a villain in a movie thriller about the evils of Wall Street.

On a deeper level, she knew Bellows was only the messenger. Malcolm Harrington was to blame for this. It was now clear to her that he had a personal vendetta against her family. She thought about telling Bellows her theory, but that wouldn't change anything, except to make him think she was paranoid.

She pulled out her ID and threw it on the table, ignoring his outstretched hand. Next she gave up her badge.

"Hand over your duty weapon."

"The forty-five is my personal weapon. If you knew me better, you'd know that. The department-issued firearm is in my locker."

"The sergeant will accompany you upstairs to get it. Then he'll escort you out of the building." Bellows stood. "I think we're done here."

His tone was arctic. Davie wasn't surprised. His blood ran icy blue. The lieutenant worshiped at the altar of the Los Angeles Police Department Manual. She'd heard that his knack for playing politics had rocketed him up the ranks of the LAPD. He wouldn't let anything tarnish his resume, especially a lowly Detective-1. She might be the latest copper Bellows sent into the jaws of Big Blue Machine, but she wouldn't be the last. The lieutenant had developed a reputation for eating his young.

Davie knew how things went down from here. Friends would express sympathy, but eventually they would stop calling, afraid that whatever dirt clung to her uniform might rub off on theirs. For the first time, she understood how her father had felt after Harrington filed that civil lawsuit against him: shattered, betrayed, and pissed as hell.

Her gut felt raw. Time would tell if the wound was mortal. For now, all she could think about was surviving and finding a way to keep the department at bay while she continued searching for Anya Nosova's killer.

———

The next couple of hours passed in a myopic blur while Davie lay inert on her living room couch. Self-pity clung to her like a one-night stand that refused to go home. She avoided all the mirrors in the house because they reflected the gray complexion and lank hair of a stranger.

She replayed in her mind Lieutenant Bellows's smug words, the things she had said to him, and the clever, acerbic things she should have said, until she could no longer distinguish between reality and fiction. The sergeant had escorted her out of the station in front of her co-workers like a three-strikes felon.

At some point, the phone rang. It was Jason Vaughn.

"I just heard what happened. Bellows told everybody in the squad room not to contact you. I thought Giordano was going to ream him a new asshole. What's going on?"

"The suspect's wife in my OIS case changed her story. She now claims I made false statements on the police report to cover up the murder of her husband."

"Who's going to believe her?"

"Malcolm Harrington. I'll have to get a department rep or maybe an outside lawyer to sort it out."

"I've got your back, Davie. Anything I can do to help, just call."

After she hung up, she stared at the Wyeth watercolor, imagining she was the tree in the meadow, alone and stripped bare. Her cell phone rang several more times, but she felt too disengaged to answer it or to monitor her voicemail messages. The noise was intruding on her solitude, so when the phone trilled again late that afternoon, she was leaning over to turn it off when she recognized her father's number on the display. Curious, she took the call.

"Where the hell have you been, Ace? I heard what happened. I've been trying to reach you."

In a raspy voice she had not used in several hours, she said, "Screw the LAPD."

"You could, but all you'd get is a broken heart and a case of the clap. Look, the LAPD is just four letters in the alphabet. It's an organization made up of people, good ones and bad ones. Your job is to learn the difference between the two. By the way, you sound like Kermit the Frog."

"How'd you find out?"

"The better question is, Why didn't I find out from you?"

"I've listened to the lecture, now what do you want?"

"To tell you I'm in your corner and even after being out of that dysfunctional organization for fifteen years, I still know a few good people in high places who might be able to help."

"How? Lieutenant Bellows won't let anybody talk to me. They sure as hell aren't going to talk to you."

"Bellows can stick it up his ass. Nobody tells me who I can talk to. Look, Ace, you have twenty minutes to pull yourself together because I'm coming over and we're going for a ride."

39

APPROXIMATELY THIRTY MINUTES AFTER Davie ended the call with Bear, she watched from her front window as her father's black Chevy Silverado pickup pulled up to Alex Camden's security gate. She locked the door to the guesthouse and walked down the driveway to meet him.

Bear wouldn't tell her where they were going, but in case the destination required professional attire she had put on one of her black polyester pantsuits. She punched a security code on the keypad and the gates parted. Bear nudged open the pickup's passenger door and she climbed inside.

"You going to tell me where we're headed?"

"I don't want to spoil the surprise."

Bear maneuvered the serpentine streets of Bel Air until he reached Santa Monica Boulevard and then headed east. As soon as he turned into Century City she knew their destination and she wasn't happy about it.

"Please tell me you're not taking me to see Robbie."

"Your brother's a lawyer."

"He's an entertainment attorney. What are you thinking? He can sell my story to Disney?"

"I'm thinking he can give you free legal advice, which you need right now."

"I don't need advice from him, and I don't appreciate you putting me in this situation."

"Look, Ace, if you won't do it for yourself, then do it for me. Okay?"

As soon as Bear pulled into a parking slot, Davie got out of the truck and slammed the door. She headed for the nearest escalator, skipping two risers at a time to get to the top. She had just reached street level when Bear caught up with her. He was out of breath.

"Look, I know you're pissed, so I'm going to let you get it out of your system before we get to Robbie's."

She wanted to lash out at Bear, to tell him she understood her situation and didn't need him to explain the trouble she was in, but she knew he was just trying to help.

Davie hadn't seen her brother since her grandfather's funeral a year ago. She had never been to his office but she knew the firm was located in one of the Century Plaza Towers, which were patterned after the twin towers of the World Trade Center in New York. After 9/11, she'd heard that security at the L.A. Towers had been ratcheted up. Davie never associated those buildings with the New York counterparts. To her, the only twin towers in L.A. were the Twin Towers Correctional Facility.

Darkness had descended and the air had turned from crisp to cold as the Alaskan front continued to hold the city hostage. As Davie approached the south tower, she felt a strong wind funneling through the space between the triangular-shaped buildings. She remembered studying the Venturi Effect in a college physics class. As she recalled, it was something about how the velocity of fluid or air increases when it passes through a constricted area. She buttoned her jacket to keep the cold at bay. As she did, her hand brushed against her waist, a reminder that she was no longer authorized to carry a badge or a gun.

Once in the building, she and Bear had to clear two checkpoints before they were allowed into the elevator. They exited on the fifteenth floor and made their way to a set of double doors with brass letters that read GOLDEN & ASSOCIATES, LLC. Davie stepped inside a foyer with décor that was sleek and modern. The minimalist leather couches looked expensive but uncomfortable. Covering one wall was a large abstract painting that looked like Superman in a blender.

The receptionist was a woman in her twenties with opaque black hair accented with a shock of white on one side. She wore a black and white yin yang patterned dress that made her a ringer for Cruella de Vil from *101 Dalmatians*.

The receptionist's nostrils flared disapproval as she eyed Bear's faded jeans and worn leather jacket. Davie figured a woman who looked like a cartoon character had no right to judge.

"We're here to see Robert Cross," Bear said.

Davie noticed her father's jaw muscles twitch as he said the name, a reminder that Robbie had sided with his mother in the divorce and now used his stepfather's name. That move had devastated Bear, especially since Cross was the man who had destroyed his marriage.

The receptionist made a call and a few minutes later, Robbie sauntered into the area sporting a photo-op smile. Her brother hadn't inherited the recessive red hair gene as she had. His hair was a thick and glossy toasted brown with subtle blond highlights that could only have been achieved by a salon colorist.

Robbie was a flawless freak of nature who had decided early in life that good looks meant nothing more was required of him, so nothing was offered. Their mother's fawning had turned him into a narcissist who considered himself gifted even though Davie attributed much of his success to connections and dumb luck.

Robbie gave Bear a convivial slap on the back. "Welcome to my world." Then he moved toward Davie, arms outstretched, aiming to hug her. She stepped back, avoiding contact.

He smiled, amused by her snub. "I've booked the conference room so we'll have some privacy."

"I guess they haven't given you an office yet," she said.

Robbie winked. "I'm on a waiting list."

Slim, immaculately dressed in a designer suit and a Maui tan, Robbie looked ready for a power lunch or, as it turned out, a lowbrow meeting with his estranged sister. He gestured for them to follow him down a long hallway.

Davie guessed that "privacy" was his attempt at humor, because when they reached the conference room she saw that it was enclosed on all sides by floor-to-ceiling glass. Inside were leather chairs and a polished wood table. Davie figured the furniture cost more than the sum of all her possessions.

"Can I get you something to drink? Cappuccino? Perrier?"

Davie declined but Bear paused to think it over. "You got Diet Coke?"

Robbie flashed another high-beam smile. "It's the house specialty."

"No ice," Bear added.

Her brother picked up the phone and placed the order. Then he gestured for them to sit. Davie sank onto a leather chair, facing a spectacular evening view of West Los Angeles. Bear sat beside her. Robbie took up the other side of the table, facing the hallway.

"So, what's up?" Robbie said. "Dad said you were in some kind of trouble."

Robbie's tone was casual. Davie felt a slow burn on her cheeks, angry at Bear for bringing her here. The last thing she wanted to do was share her humiliation with her brother. It was bad enough that her fellow detectives knew. Telling Robbie the gory details about being relieved of duty was something she couldn't do, even in exchange for free legal advice. She didn't trust him. Maybe Bear had forgiven his betrayal, but her pardon had yet to be earned.

"No trouble that I can't handle on my own."

Bear shot her the stink eye.

There was a tap on wood and the door opened. It was Ms. de Vil, bearing a tray with a can of Diet Coke and a crystal glass.

Robbie gestured toward Bear. The woman teetered forward on five-inch platform shoes. She placed two napkins on the glossy wood table in front of Bear, one for the glass and one for the can. After fulfilling her waitress duties, Ms. de Vil stood near the exit, waiting for further instructions.

"Thanks." Robbie lowered his eyelids, giving everybody a clear view of his long lashes. It was a gesture that had sent several women in search of wedding planners. Robbie looked up and smiled. "Please close the door on your way out."

Davie felt a draft from the hallway as the door opened. When Ms. de Vil left the room, the door closed with a quiet *click*.

She rose from her chair. "Sounds like good advice. Maybe I'll take it."

Bear's fists clenched. "Knock it off, Ace. You're acting like a two-year-old on a car trip. Robbie, we need your legal opinion. Davie is being railroaded over some trumped-up charge that she falsified a police report. That's crap. If her name was anything other than Richards, the Police Commission would have signed off on her OIS case and moved on to something important."

"Aren't these issues usually handled within the department? I'm sure your Board of Rights rep can give you advice."

"She can't trust the department. If I know Harrington, he'll try to get the DA's office to file a case in criminal court and the command staff won't do shit to stop him."

"File? On what grounds?"

Bear caught the tab on the Coke can with his fingernail and flipped it back. "Who knows? Maybe murder charges. I wouldn't put it past him. The victim's wife has probably already filed a civil suit against the city. She'll say Davie killed her husband for no reason at all."

Bear and her brother had turned her into a spectator at a tennis match, watching them lobbing comments back and forth across the table. She crossed her hands in a T, like a basketball coach signaling for a timeout.

"Excuse me," she said. Both of them ignored her.

"Sounds like the widow is hoping for a big payday," Robbie said.

Bear poured the Coke into the glass. "Of course she is. That doesn't mean she won't be rewarded for her efforts. Meanwhile, Davie's career goes down the toilet."

"If that's the case," Davie said, "I need a criminal defense attorney, not somebody who negotiates the catering contract for *Die Hard 23*."

After a moment of silence, Robbie said, "I'm not sure if you re-member, Davie, but in law school I interned at the DA's office. I still have friends there."

"I didn't see much of you back then. Your choice, not mine."

"That's ancient history."

"Yeah, like your job at the DA's office."

He shrugged off her comment and continued his pitch. "Back then, I became friends with one of the filing deputies. She and I stayed in touch over the years. Her son just graduated from film school at USC. I got him a job at Sony. A few months back, she was elected L.A. County District Attorney. I donated to her campaign. If you'd like, I can call her, see if Harrington has played his hand. I know she'll take my call."

Bear's smile said, *See? I knew Robbie would come through for you.*

"That's great," Bear said. "When can you call?"

"As soon as Davie gives the okay. What do you say, Sis?"

She felt the skin on the back of her neck bristle as she heard the hissing of that *S* sound, like a snake preparing to strike. On the surface, his question seemed to be a polite request for permission, but she knew her brother. He had felt the power shift and was taking full advantage. What he really wanted was for her to beg.

Behind her, she heard men's voices in conversation as they walked past the conference room. Once they were gone, the room was dead silent. She glanced at Bear. His head was bent over. He seemed to be watching the bubbles in his glass. Davie studied her brother. They were different in every way. While she had inherited the square jaw and high forehead of her father, Robbie favored their mother. His aquiline nose and full lips made him look like a Greek god. Those genes also blunted many of life's disappointments.

Her gaze glided past her brother toward the window. In the distance she saw flickering taillights on the 405. Her lungs ached as she breathed in, watching the city she had sworn to protect and to serve.

She had no doubt that Robbie's relationship with the DA was solid. He was a narcissist, not a liar. She also knew this was a war and the person with the most information won. The more Davie knew about Harrington's battle plan and his vulnerabilities, the better off she would be. In the distance, the flashing light of an emergency vehicle caught her eye and she felt a power shift of her own.

"Thanks," she said, "but I can handle this myself."

40

NEITHER SHE NOR BEAR spoke on the drive back to Bel Air. Once inside her house, she spent the rest of Friday night and the following Saturday morning trolling for information on Malcolm Harrington. By mid morning the following day, the person she most wanted to speak with—Maria Luna—had not answered the three messages she'd left on her machine. She vowed to keep trying.

After living through Bear's legal troubles, she could imagine what would happen if Harrington filed criminal charges against her. She could lose everything, even her freedom. After a quick swim to clear her head, she sat on a deck chair near Alex's pool, huddled under a blanket, waiting for news.

Her cell phone rang. It was Cal Rogers.

"I called the station," he said. "Left a bunch of messages. Finally got some guy named Detective Vaughn. I didn't expect him to give me your lat-long coordinates but something in his tone made me worry about you. Good thing you gave me your cell number."

Davie didn't want Rogers to know she'd been relieved of duty. She hoped her partner had covered for her, said she was out in the field, a cop euphemism for *nobody's going to tell you anything so don't bother asking.* Rogers would understand that code.

"What can I do for you?" It sounded unnecessarily formal, but she couldn't think of anything else to say.

"I just wanted you to know I showed your girl's picture to everybody who works the front desk. Nobody remembers seeing her before last Saturday night."

Davie appreciated that he was trying to help, but he was no longer a sworn officer and any information he had learned from a third party would be considered hearsay in court. Pacific Homicide detectives would have to re-interview all potential witnesses.

"Heard any intel on Satine?" she said.

"No, but my boss finally got permission from corporate to release the surveillance footage without a warrant. I can bring the disk to you at the station."

She couldn't meet Rogers at the station. She wouldn't be allowed inside. The photos she needed were already on her cell phone, and accepting the disk might cause chain of custody issues later on.

"Drop it by the front desk," she said. "Tell the officer on duty to give it to my boss, Frank Giordano."

"Okay," he said, stretching out the word, "but I was hoping to see you. What about lunch? I know you're busy, but you have to eat."

At first, she hesitated, but she had nothing else to do. Maybe the distraction would be good for her. "Lunch could work."

Davie didn't want to run into people she knew, so she suggested meeting at a beachfront restaurant on Pacific Coast Highway near Sunset. She changed into jeans, a sweater, and her red Converse high-tops.

Just before noon, she parked the Camaro in the public lot adjacent to the restaurant. As she waited for Rogers to arrive, she thought about his name. You didn't hear Cal much these days, probably short for Calvin. She guessed he was named after his grandfather, the one with the vintage Olds. She imagined him as a farmer, living in Iowa, growing wheat or corn.

A few minutes into her fiction, Rogers arrived carrying a backpack slung across one shoulder. He stopped for a moment to study her hair. On duty she usually wore it twisted into a bun on the nape of her neck. That left nothing for a suspect to pull and no windblown hair blocking her vision. She wasn't on duty now, so she had unleashed her red mop to find its own path.

"Hope you don't mind," Rogers said, holding out the backpack. "I picked up some food. Thought we could have a picnic on the beach."

The air was cold but the sun was shining. They took off their shoes and hiked barefoot through the sand. They were alone except for a half dozen surfers in wetsuits braving the winter waves. Davie watched as Rogers spread a plaid wool blanket on the sand. He pulled plastic utensils and containers of food from the backpack in practiced moves. He poured chardonnay into two disposable glasses but she declined hers.

"You've done this before," she said.

"I like to eat outside. Everything tastes better." He studied her for a moment as he drank the wine. "You look stressed. What gives?"

Her dark glasses were still on because the sun was bright and she didn't want Rogers to see the vulnerability in her eyes. It felt so close to the surface she was sure he could touch it if she directed his hand.

"When you're standing alone in the victim's shoes searching for justice, the responsibility weighs on you," she said, hoping he'd buy that lofty response and leave it at that.

"How's the investigation going? Any suspects?"

She could tell by his expression he wasn't just making conversation. He wanted to know. Her lips parted to spill the truth about Harrington, the sharp creases in Lieutenant Bellows's uniform pants when he relieved her of duty, how close she felt to finding Anya's killer but was now sidelined while somebody else made the arrest.

Pride, or maybe duty, kept her from speaking the words. Good Homicide detectives didn't discuss an open case with anyone outside the department even if that person had once been in law enforcement. She wondered if Rogers's Grandpa Cal had ever taught him that old war slogan, "Loose lips sink ships." But Rogers's grandpa probably wasn't named Cal and in her gut she knew the reason for her silence lay in her own issues about trust.

"Still chasing leads," she said.

Rogers turned toward the water. The surface looked like an animated Monet painting, brush strokes of color that shimmered and moved. The sun had cast a shadow across his face, so she couldn't read his expression.

"These cases are always complicated," he said.

The mood lifted after that. Lunch was a salad and barbequed tofu that tasted like chicken. They watched the surfers paddle out on their boards to catch wave after wave. He didn't bring up Anya Nosova again. She was glad.

Rogers shared some memories about playing high school football. Davie glossed over stories about her dysfunctional family, preferring to tell him about her grandmother and how she had always been the stabilizing force in her life. She told him about a trip they were planning to Victoria, British Columbia, so Grammy could see the Butchart Gardens while she still had some vision left. For a time they stared at the water, saying nothing.

"Are you married?" It was none of her business but she was curious.

He sipped his wine without answering. In the distance she heard bits of surfer conversation fractured by the wind. It sounded like a radio off its station.

"Working nights doesn't leave much room for a family," he said. "I'm not really father material. What about you? Married?"

"Not even close." She wasn't sure why she'd been so emphatic. At one time she thought she was falling in love with Spencer Hall and might have married him had their relationship had time to develop.

Rogers glanced at his watch, saving them both from the embarrassment of further revelation. "I have to be at work in an hour. I'll give you a call if I find out anything more about the case."

He stuffed the blanket into the backpack and dropped the plastic dishes and empty food containers in a nearby trash can. Once they reached the parking lot, they brushed the sand from their feet and put on their shoes. Rogers walked with Davie to the Camaro.

He studied the car, admiring the finish. "I'm guessing this isn't a department ride. Looks fast."

"Zero to sixty in six-point-four seconds."

He put his hand on the back of her head and lowered his lips to hers. Startled, she pulled away before he could kiss her.

Judging a man's romantic intentions had never been her strong suit. She quickly thought back to the times they'd been together but couldn't remember any signals she might have given him that she was interested in anything but a professional relationship. But behaviors could be misinterpreted. She'd been guilty of that herself.

Rogers stepped away. "Can't fault a guy for trying. I like you, Detective Richards. I guess I just got carried away."

She tried to imagine Rogers in her life—chatting with Grammy next to her blue recliner, passing muster with Bear, spending the night in her bed in Alex Camden's guesthouse—but the images seemed out of focus. He was a good-looking guy, just not her type.

"No problem," she said. She got into the car and rolled down the window.

Rogers leaned toward her with his forearms resting on the door-frame. "Stay safe out there."

Davie assigned no particular meaning to his words. It was what people said to cops. "You too," she said as he straightened.

Rogers disappeared into the sea of parked cars. As Davie headed down the lane toward the exit, she saw him in the adjacent lot. There were plenty of open spots near the restaurant. She wondered why he hadn't taken one of them. Curious, she pulled behind a van out of view and watched.

Rogers opened the tailgate of a black SUV parked at the far end of the second lot. He threw the backpack inside the vehicle and closed the door. A moment later, he got behind the wheel and headed toward the exit. Davie rolled her car forward. As Rogers passed her row, she saw two safety seats in the back.

She tried to swallow but her throat was too dry. Rogers had implied he had no family. So why were there baby seats in his car? She considered the possibility he had nieces or nephews or that he transported children in connection with his job at the hotel. None of that seemed right. What made more sense, at least to her, was that Rogers had parked far away because he didn't want her to see what was in the back of his vehicle. If his plan included having more than a professional relationship with her, he couldn't let her know he had children and most likely a wife.

Everybody lied.

He had told her he was due at work but he'd been wearing jeans—not the attire for a job at an upscale hotel. It was possible he had another set of clothes in the car, but she doubted that. She could easily verify if he worked today or not, so she assumed that wasn't a lie. Perhaps he would go home to change.

Rogers turned right onto Pacific Coast Highway toward Santa Monica. Davie waited for a couple of cars to pass before she pulled into traffic behind him.

41

DAVIE FOLLOWED CAL ROGERS to an enclave of modest homes in Pacific Division's Mar Vista neighborhood. She pulled to the curb a block away and watched as he turned into a driveway behind a white Toyota Corolla. The front yard of the stucco bungalow was boxed in by a picket fence. A pink tricycle lay on its side in the yard. White plastic streamers spilled out of the handlebars and splayed across the fallow lawn. He got out of his car and used a key to open the side door.

Fifteen minutes into Davie's vigil, Rogers emerged from the house wearing a suit and tie. She waited until he drove away before getting out of her car.

As she strolled toward Rogers's bungalow, plotting her next move, she noted that the architecture in the neighborhood ran the gamut from Cape Cod to banana republic plantation house. One Colonial looked as if the residents had been away for a few days. Throwaway newspapers littered the yard and a small notepad lay on the porch.

She stepped onto the porch and grabbed the notepad, one of those giveaways Realtors used as calling cards. Moisture had curled the corners into a snarl. The black-and-white photo pictured on the header was of a woman with a pleasant face, but Davie guessed few people actually studied those pictures.

As she neared the front door of Rogers's house, she could hear a child throwing a tantrum. She rang the bell, and a pregnant woman answered the door. Soft blonde curls framed her face in contrast to the dark circles under her eyes. The woman looked like a former high school cheerleader who had retired her pompoms at least ten years earlier. A baby dressed in blue pajamas squirmed in her arms. On the living room carpet next to the couch, a toddler lay screaming.

Davie smiled. "Sorry. Did I catch you at a bad time?"

The woman smiled back. "The glamour of motherhood, right?"

Davie took one last glance at the name on the notepad and handed it to the woman. "I'm Margery Castle. I just stopped by to see if you're thinking about selling your home."

The woman accepted the notepad without looking at it. "Thanks."

The toddler began kicking the glass coffee table, a budding soccer player scrambling toward an unattended net. The force sent a basket of Crayolas skittering onto the carpet.

"You want me to hold the baby for a sec? If that glass breaks she could be seriously injured."

The woman glanced at the table in time to see another kick vibrate the glass. She thrust the baby into Davie's arms. He smelled like sour milk and baby powder. He stared at her, decided she was an alien life form, and began to cry.

The woman knelt beside the screaming toddler and handed her the notepad. "Chloe, look what Mommy has for you! A new coloring pad."

Davie scanned the living room. There were toys everywhere, un-folded piles of laundry and a half-eaten sandwich discarded on the couch. On one of the end tables was a wedding photo. Even from the door she could see the groom was a smiling Cal Rogers.

When the kicking stopped, the woman came back to the door and reclaimed the infant. She patted his back to calm his cries, which pro-duced a loud belch. "Sorry about that. You wanted to know about the house?"

"Just wondering if you're planning to sell."

"I get a lot of people asking me that. I always say no."

"No problem. I just thought—"

"But my husband *is* up for a new job. If he gets it, we'll have to move."

In the background, Davie saw Chloe pick up the sandwich, take a bite and throw it onto the carpet.

"My company has offices all across the country," she ad-libbed. "I could handle your sale here and help you find a new place. Where would you be moving?"

The woman hesitated. "The D.C. area but I can't tell you anything more. My husband thinks I'll jinx the deal if I talk about it."

Rogers hadn't mentioned he was planning to leave the state, which piqued her curiosity.

Davie made a zipping motion across her mouth. "I totally under-stand. When will you know for sure?"

The baby seemed fascinated by his mother's nostril. He probed until he found an opening and jammed his finger inside, which made her voice sound nasally. "Pretty fast. Maybe a week or so."

Davie silently thanked a fellow Burglary detective at Southeast sta-tion who talked endlessly about his problems finding a new house and selling his old one. "I can check the listings in D.C. and send you some properties in your price range. I can also research the market value of your current home."

The woman pulled the boy's finger out of her nose. "Maybe I should check with my husband first."

"You wouldn't have to bother him with it if you didn't want to. The report is no big deal. It's free and there's no obligation. If it isn't what you want, just toss it in the recycling bin. I only mentioned it because, in my experience, it's the woman who makes decisions about the family home."

The baby began to whimper. "Okay. Can you email it to me?"

"Glad to. By the way, I didn't catch your name."

"Norah Rogers."

Davie programmed Norah's phone number and email address into her cell phone. She figured if Cal Rogers's wife followed up with a call to Margery Castle, the Realtor wouldn't risk losing a listing. She would just pretend to have been a party to the conversation.

Davie sprinted back to the Camaro, thinking about what Rogers had told her at the beach: *I'm not really father material.* That was the moment he should have added, *I should know. I have two kids and another on the way and I stink as a dad.* Instead, he had withheld the truth. To Davie, that was the same as lying. And in her experience, one lie inevitably led to another.

She had let Cal Rogers's eagerness to help her with the Nosova investigation cloud her judgment. Before acting on her suspicions, she needed more information, and since she couldn't trust Rogers to tell her the truth, she would have to get creative.

As soon as she slid into the driver's seat, she pulled out her phone and called the cell number for Donovan Moran, a Los Angeles County Sheriff's Department deputy she had worked with on a Grand Theft case before transferring to Pacific. She doubted news of her suspension had carried as far as the LASD. If it had, Moran might refuse to speak with her.

She needn't have worried. When he answered the phone, he seemed cordial and welcoming. He was on his way to work but agreed to meet her for coffee before his shift. They settled on the playground at a shopping center called the Malibu Country Mart.

42

STRINGY CLOUDS STRETCHED OVER the shoreline as Davie cruised along Pacific Coast Highway past pale aqua lifeguard shacks and beach volleyball nets. Twenty minutes later, she arrived at the Malibu Country Mart. She remembered coming to the place as a teen. The restaurants were still there but the names had changed. The place had gone upscale—Beverly Hills at the beach. Even though it was January, a few leaves still clung to the trees. Strings of lights snaked around the trunks, holdovers from the holidays.

Moran was a compact man whose Kevlar vest made him look barrel-chested. Davie found him sitting at a picnic table with two cups of coffee, watching a couple of girls playing on the swings, squealing and pumping their legs toward the sky. One of the chains squeaked, adding to the symphony. They exchanged a few pleasantries before he glanced at his watch.

"Sorry, but I can only give you fifteen minutes. What's up?"

"I'm hoping you can find out why one of your jail deputies left the job."

"Probably because it's a shitty assignment. What's the name?"

"Cal Rogers."

Moran stared at her until she became uncomfortable. He broke eye contact to remove the lid from the coffee cup. "I've heard of him. Is this for a case you're working on?"

She let go of the breath she was holding. "For now it's personal."

"Has he been hitting on you? Because I'll tell you right now, he's married. At least he used to be."

She smiled. "Where were you a couple of hours ago?"

He brushed leftover crumbs from the table toward a squirrel that was begging for handouts. "Just so you know, what I'm about to tell you is a mix of fact and rumor, so don't take it as gospel."

"Understood."

Moran sipped his coffee as he waited for noise to abate from a small plane flying overhead. "Rogers had a reputation for hitting on anything with lady parts. When he worked the jail, there was a rumor he got serviced by a hooker waiting to visit her pimp."

"Was he disciplined?"

"The incident got a few eye rolls. Then it went away."

A breeze kicked up, brushing cold air across Davie's face. She wrapped her hands around the cup for warmth. "Sort of like, what happens in jail stays in jail?"

"Something like that."

"Then why did Rogers quit?"

Moran looked around to make sure nobody was listening. "He beat the shit out of an inmate. A couple of deputies pulled him off before he killed the guy. Rogers knew he'd crossed the line. He resigned a few days later."

"No charges were filed?"

"It happened around the time the Bedlam League story broke."

That story had made the front page of the *Los Angeles Times*. It was just one of many scandals that had tarnished the sheriff's department in the past few years. The Bedlam League was a gang of L.A. County Sheriff's Deputies accused of beating inmates and instigating fights in the Men's Central Jail in downtown L.A. She wondered if Rogers was a member of that gang or if he had just been swept up in the culture of violence.

"So the Rogers incident fell through the cracks?"

"One isolated assault was nothing compared to the Bedlam bombshell."

"The inmate didn't sue?"

"No time for that. He was treated in the infirmary and released the next morning. Jail overcrowding. Two days later, the guy was dead. Lit up in a drive-by." Moran checked his watch again. "If you want my advice, stay away from Rogers. He's bad news. And if this changes from personal to professional, call me. I might be able to connect you with people who know more than I do."

She lingered at the table after Moran had gone, nursing her cooling coffee. The obvious had been staring her in the face, but she'd ignored it because Rogers had once been in law enforcement. Rogers worked security for an upscale hotel. Hookers often hung out in hotels. Anya Nosova had attended Satine's parties, possibly many times after she arrived in L.A. Davie figured that's how Cal Rogers had met her—at the Edison hotel.

She understood how it might have happened. Rogers was married with two small children and another on the way. Every day he left two screaming kids and a harried wife to work as Director of Security in an upscale hotel where he hobnobbed with the rich and the beautiful. Anya was a stunning young woman. He'd told Davie none of the employees at the hotel had seen Anya before last Saturday night, but that was likely another lie. He may have just been attempting to sidetrack her investigation.

If Davie was right, that Rogers had met Anya at one of Grigory Satine's many parties at the Edison hotel, then Rogers could have known Anya back when she lived at the Marina del Rey apartment. Which might explain the heart-themed gifts she'd found both there and in Andre's apartment. Rogers had given them to her over the course of their relationship.

Davie thought about the generic LAPD business card used to collect Anya's heart-shaped purse. Rogers could have easily acquired one of those cards. Anya must have told Rogers she'd left her purse at the Volga Bakery. He had to get the purse in case there was anything inside that might lead back to him.

He must have panicked when he found out she was expecting a baby. A pregnant hooker was a threat to his marriage and that new D.C. job, especially if Anya pressured him to marry her.

As Director of Security, Cal Rogers had access to the parking garage at the Edison. He could have taken Grigory Satine's keys from the valet and planted the purse with the necklace inside Satine's car. Maybe he planned to make an anonymous call to the police, but Satine had found the purse before he could do that. Satine may have recognized the purse as Anya's and told Marchenko to give it to Davie, hoping it would serve as a bargaining chip to delay Quintero's investigation of the Russian.

Davie jumped when she heard a scream. Her gaze flew to the playground and she saw a woman attempting to coax a young girl down a yellow slide. The child seemed terrified, crying and shaking her head. Davie had known that kind of fear. It rocked your confidence to the core. The girl had a choice: face the unknown or retreat down the ladder to safety.

Davie faced that choice, as well. She wondered if there was still time to prove her new theory that Cal Rogers had killed Anya Nosova without destroying what was left of her career. She frowned when she glanced toward the slide and saw the mother guide her child down the ladder. Davie tossed the empty coffee cup in a trash can and headed for her car, knowing that, for her, retreat was not an option.

43

DAVIE LEFT MALIBU AND drove back to the guesthouse in Bel Air. She paced the floor, trying but failing to work off her escalating belief that Cal Rogers had killed Anya Nosova. Detective Giordano would assign another detective to pick up the investigation where she had left it, probably Vaughn since he was already familiar with the case. She thought about calling to tell him about her suspicions but hesitated. So far they were based solely on intuition and conjecture.

The department had schooled her to believe the foundation of a successful investigation was good note taking, but her chrono on the Anya Nosova case was in the Murder Book at the station. Davie sat at the kitchen table and jotted down every detail she could remember from her interviews and research. She could have used her laptop, but the ritual of scratching the pen across the paper gave her time to think.

Marchenko had told her Anya's boyfriend was somebody important. Bell said he bought her gifts but nothing expensive; i.e., nothing he'd have to pay for with a credit card that could be traced back to him. Bell also told her the guy always met Anya in out-of-the-way places and that he liked to have sex in the open air. She remembered something Rogers said to her at the beach, that he liked to eat outside because the food tasted better.

She lost track of the time she'd been bent over her pages, absorbed by Anya's story. Only the pain in her neck and shoulders hinted that it had been too long. She rose and headed to the refrigerator for a bottle of Pellegrino and to stretch out the kinks. When she opened the door, she smelled something rank. Her nose led her to the meat drawer where she found a piece of raw chicken that had been pushed to the back of the drawer and forgotten. The odor reminded her of how Rags Foster's clothes had smelled in the stuffy air of Pacific station.

That's when she remembered Rags's property bag was still in the trunk of her car. She had offered to drive it to county jail but Lieutenant Bellows had upended those plans when he called her into his office and relieved her of duty.

Davie pulled on a jacket and took the chicken out to the garbage can. On the way back, she grabbed Rags's property bag from her trunk and was heading inside when she saw Alex Camden walking toward her, carrying a large framed photograph of an old woman flying a kite.

"For me?" she said.

"An exchange. I have a buyer for the Wyeth. Didn't think you'd mind a change of scenery."

She didn't mind. In fact, she was tired of looking at that lonely tree. He followed her into the house and leaned the photograph against the wall near the door. Davie set the property bag on the kitchen floor.

Alex wrinkled his nose as he sniffed the air. "My dear Davina, what's that smell? It reminds me of a Pont l'Eveque cheese I once had at a Marseilles bistro."

She pointed to the bag. "That belongs to a homeless man who's probably still in county lockup getting his head examined. I was going to take it to him, but things went sideways and I forgot it was in my trunk."

Alex removed the Wyeth from the wall and hung the photo in its place. "How important could it be?"

She remembered how agitated Rags had been at the Pacific jail, begging Vaughn to give him back his watch cap. The bit about the white octopus tangled in blonde seaweed had made her wonder if he knew something about Anya Nosova's death, but given his fragile mental health there was no way to be sure.

"It seemed important to him. Besides, it's my duty to return personal property to the owner. I'll call my partner and arrange a pickup."

Alex studied the bag. "I wonder what's inside?"

"I wish I knew."

Alex reached into his pants pocket and pulled out a Swiss Army knife. He must have noticed the look of surprise on her face, because he held it up for inspection. "A gift from a well-wisher. One never knows what one might encounter in a yurt in Mongolia ... or in a property bag in Bel Air."

"I can't do that, it's—"

Alex interrupted. "It's what? Against the rules? *I'm* not bound by those rules. Let's just say I found the bag smelling up my guesthouse and decided to investigate the offending odor. Who would object?"

Davie could have told him that a lot of people might object. She thought about the consequences of opening the bag, but dismissed them all. It was more important to know if Rags's property held anything that could help solve the Nosova case than to worry about compounding her troubles.

"Wait." She went to her war bag on the floor of the bedroom closet and returned with two pairs of latex gloves. "We'll need these."

Alex's gloved hand cut through the flex-cuff on the outer bag and then the seal of Rags's property bag, releasing the tangy odor of sweat. Using his index finger and thumb, he pulled out a watch cap with Mylar strips duct taped to the yarn.

"Not exactly haute couture," he said, "but not without its charm."

"Rags thought the Mylar protected him from the forces of evil."

Alex held the cap away from his body, like it was a dead rat. "Don't we all wish it were that simple?"

Digging deeper, he found a grimy backpack containing drug paraphernalia and a copy of the *Los Angeles Times*.

She thumbed through the newspapers but found nothing that helped make a case against Cal Rogers. The stench of sweat drifting from the paper told Davie that Rags had probably worn it beneath his shirt to keep warm.

"You look crestfallen, Davina, but at least you know what was inside." Alex walked to a kitchen chair and sat. "Look, it's none of my business, but why don't you tell me the whole story. Beginning to end. Sometimes talking helps organize your thoughts."

Davie had worked alone since Vaughn had been assigned to the Beau Fischer homicide, so she hadn't talked to anyone about the case. She missed having a partner. Telling Alex would give her a chance to sort out the narrative of Anya's last days. Unlike her instinct to keep information from Rogers, she trusted Alex to keep things to himself. She quickly brought him up to speed on the investigation.

"Anya's telephone records were on my desk the day I was relieved of duty. Vaughn probably has them now. I believe they'll show she made a call to Cal Rogers from outside the Volga Bakery on Saturday night."

"But you can't be sure until you see the records."

"No, but I think Rogers was leading her on, promising to marry her, because Anya told the apartment manager that her secret boyfriend had proposed. Before she left for Satine's party, she typed a Dear John letter to Andre Lucien, letting him know she was leaving him. I'm guessing she called Rogers on Saturday evening, but he blew her off. The clerk from the liquor store heard her shouting at someone on her cell. Maybe she threatened to expose Rogers to his employer or Grigory Satine or whatever boogieman made him sweat."

"But you said that call took place *before* the party at the hotel."

Davie began to pace. It helped clarify her thoughts. "It did. Rogers may have thought the situation was handled, but I bet the records will show he got *another* call from Anya in the early hours of Sunday. Let's say this time he couldn't calm her down, so they agreed to meet. She'd gone home, so he drove to her apartment in Westchester."

Alex craned his neck to follow her as she paced. "I doubt he would have met Anya inside the apartment. She lived with another man and Rogers couldn't be sure the boyfriend wouldn't come home and find him there."

"You're right. He must have told her to come out to his SUV. They argued. Maybe he didn't plan to kill her, but he did."

"You said those manhole covers were heavy. Could this guy have lifted one by himself?"

Davie stopped pacing and leaned against the kitchen counter. "The Hyperion engineer told me most of them could be lifted by one person. Rogers is a strong guy. He beat up an inmate with his bare hands and nearly killed him. I think he's strong enough to lift a manhole cover and motivated enough because he had to dispose of Anya's body."

"And you think he did so in Venice, where this Rags person saw him. Why Venice?"

Davie thought for a moment. "It's not exactly on his way home, but not far off. Maybe he thought nobody would be out on the streets after midnight except cops and assholes, people he knew how to handle from his years in law enforcement."

"But Rags was there."

"And he saw everything." She was sure Hyperion maps would pinpoint manholes on the Venice streets near where Rags camped out. "I have to call my partner."

Alex picked up the Wyeth and headed for the door. "May the force be with you, dear Davina."

Davie's adrenalin felt charged as she reached Vaughn on his cell phone. "Did you get a DNA report on Anya Nosova's baby?"

"SID is backlogged. They'll get to it, but I'm not sure when."

"We might have a comparison."

"No shit."

"You don't know the half of it."

44

DAVIE BUTTONED HER COAT against a brisk onshore breeze. The sun had set, so she trained the beam of her flashlight on the trash can near the sand as Vaughn gloved up and extracted Cal Rogers's plastic wine cup. It was still where he'd dumped it after their picnic a few hours ago. The black-and-white had attracted a few stares from passersby but a plainclothes detective sorting through trash wasn't enough excitement to make them stay for the show.

Even though it was Saturday, Vaughn had arrived at the beach wearing his usual silk tie and Wall Street threads that hung model-perfect on his lanky frame.

The paper evidence bag crackled as he placed the cup inside. "I'll book this at the station. SID can pick it up and take it to their nerd cave."

Her hand shielded her eyes against the glare of a parking lot light. "Maybe you should take the plastic utensils, in case the cup doesn't have enough saliva for DNA testing."

Vaughn's expression hardened as he did a slow turn toward her. "You're off the case, partner. Stop micromanaging."

She had been relieved Giordano had passed the Murder Book to her partner. Vaughn had worked with her in the early stages of the investigation, so he knew almost as much as she did. What he didn't know, she had explained to him on the phone before he arrived. None of that meant she liked giving up control.

"We want the same thing, Jason."

He jostled the entire plastic bag out of the trash container with enough force to let her know he was annoyed. "Look, I know how you feel, but I'm on top of it, so chill."

She appreciated his attempt at empathy, but he couldn't possibly know how she felt. The department had suspended him for eight days for telling a dumb blonde joke; they had accused her of killing a man and lying about it on an official police report. Her suspension could land her in prison.

"I'm not worried."

He tied the trash bag with a plastic flex-cuff. "Any idea when you're coming back to work?"

She hesitated because the future was hard to predict. "My attorney's looking into that." She didn't mention that she had no attorney except for her slacker brother whose specialty was entertainment law. She figured that would only complicate the conversation and lead to questions she didn't want to answer.

"Like I told you before," he said, "if I can do anything to help ... "

A gull landed nearby, squawking for food.

"Thanks. That means a lot."

He attached an evidence tag to each of the bags. "Let's say they pull enough saliva off the cup to get a DNA profile and it confirms Cal Rogers is the father of Anya Nosova's baby. That still doesn't prove he killed her."

"He did it. Get a warrant. Search his house and his SUV. He may have killed her in the car. Search the laundry at his place for any clothes he may have worn that night. If you find anything, test it for trace evidence."

"Partner—"

"You already have Anya's phone records. I'm betting she called his number on Saturday night and again Sunday morning. And check with the Edison. See if Rogers ever used one of the guestrooms for an overnight stay with her."

"Davie, I'm not some rookie—"

"Interview hotel employees. Somebody saw them together."

Vaughn's body tensed as he jotted the case number on the tags. "The evidence is circumstantial. I'm not sure a judge will sign those warrants."

"Talk to Rogers's wife. She must have had some clue her husband was cheating on her. Wives always know, even if they don't want to admit it. She seemed afraid to cross him when I talked to her. Maybe she's looking for an excuse to tell somebody what a jerk he is."

Vaughn turned to face her. "His wife? You didn't tell me about that. When did you talk to her?"

The breeze whipped a lock of hair onto her face. She anchored it behind her ear. "Go to the no-tell motel where Anya was assaulted. The details are in DCTS under Tiffany Jones, the alias she used. Show the manager a six-pack that includes Rogers's photo. Maybe it wasn't a john who beat her up, but maybe Anya told the truth for a change and it *was* boyfriend trouble. Cal Rogers trouble."

"Whoa—"

"Take the same six-pack to County jail and see if Rags Foster can identify Rogers. I think he saw him dump Anya's body."

"Look, Davie, I'm beginning to think you have a thing for Rogers."

"That's ridiculous."

"Then what the hell's wrong with you? First you have a picnic on the beach with the guy, then you follow him to his house like some stalker. You find out he's married and all of a sudden he's Attila the Hun. You've gone off the rails. I'm worried about you."

"What the hell is wrong with you? I never hooked up with Rogers. He was somebody I met during a homicide investigation. Period. At least talk to Rags Foster."

Vaughn walked over to the black-and-white and put the evidence bags into the trunk. The Latex gloves snapped as he stripped them off and shoved them into a separate bag. "He's not in jail anymore. They kicked him loose."

Davie bolted toward Vaughn and grabbed his arm. "He bailed out? How? He's got no money and no address. Now the court has no way to contact a one-eighty-seven defendant."

Vaughn pulled his arm away, avoiding her gaze. "Rags isn't a murder defendant. He didn't kill Beau Fischer. It was a junkie named Arnold Waters."

She remembered interviewing Rags at the Pacific jail. He'd mentioned the guy who'd accused him of killing Fischer. Rags said he forgave Arnie because somebody pressured him to do it. She allowed herself a moment to wonder if that person was Jason Vaughn. Maybe he'd ignored key evidence in his eagerness to make an arrest.

"At least you made it right," she said. "You solved the case."

He put the unused tags in an envelope and threw it in the trunk. "It wasn't me. It was some Pac Pal soccer mom."

"What?"

"A couple of prep-school assholes from Pacific Palisades went slumming in Venice and started a junkie fight. They filmed Waters sticking a shiv in Fischer's gut. The mom was snooping in her boy-genius's cell phone and saw the action. She freaked and dragged the wannabe film-maker and his phone into the station."

Davie felt a jolt of apprehension. "Where's Rags now?"

"Probably back in Venice shooting up with his homies."

"He's a witness in the Nosova case. We have to find him."

"We?"

"Okay. You have to find him."

Davie walked to the Camaro and pulled Rags's property bag from the trunk. She handed it to Vaughn. "Here's his watch cap. Once he sees you're returning it, I think he'll trust you enough to talk."

Vaughn slid the foul-smelling bag into the trunk and slammed it shut. "I appreciate everything you've done, Davie, but you have to trust me now. Stand down. If you don't, you're going to end up with ten pounds of shit in a five-pound bag."

She stared at him for a moment. "Will do."

That lie would likely get her into deeper trouble, but there was no way she was going to stand down until Cal Rogers was locked up for the murder of Anya Nosova.

Her partner would be busy writing search warrants and finding five booking photos that looked enough like Cal Rogers to make up a six-pack. Finding Rags Foster would be low on his list of things to do, but it topped hers. When he worked at the jail, Rogers had demonstrated he was capable of violence. If he found out Rags Foster had seen him dump Anya's body, he might try to eliminate Rags as a witness. She had to find him.

As soon as Vaughn headed back to the station, she took out her phone and dialed the number for the public defender's office. Even though it was Saturday, she left a message for Rags's lawyer. She spent the rest of the day searching for Rags at homeless shelters and alleys near Venice where he was known to hang out, but it wasn't until Sunday morning that she found him.

45

RAGS FOSTER'S LUCK WAS finally changing. The people at County jail had given him a yellow uniform and put him in a special observation module called the ding tank, because that's what they called people like him—ding-a-lings. They also gave him medication at the pill-call window, which made him sleepy and unsteady on his feet. Then on Saturday afternoon, the tall detective—Rags remembered his name was Vaughn—came to the jail with Rags's attorney and told him Arnie had confessed to killing Beau Fischer, which meant Rags was off the hook.

Detective Vaughn looked mad about that. Rags could have told him that all those fancy threads he wore didn't make him right about everything. The pretty lady detective hadn't come with him to the jail. Too bad. Rags liked her. She didn't treat him like a nobody who had no history or no place in the world. Plus, she'd given him money. That showed she had heart.

Once Rags was free, his public defender drove him to the homeless shelter in Venice. She gave him a disposable cell phone with prepaid minutes in case she needed to contact him to testify against Arnie. Before he got out of her car, she slipped him five twenties. He guessed it was because she was still young enough to believe people deserved a second chance in life. He hoped she'd stay nice forever but doubted that she would.

Rags was still at the shelter on Sunday morning when he saw Detective Vaughn walk through the front door and start talking to the lady at the desk. He tried not to listen, but his ears perked up when he heard them mention his name. He hated it when people talked about him when he was close enough to hear. Like he was invisible. Reminded him of doctors yapping in the elevator about people's private medical problems.

He thought about running away but knew he'd waited too long when Vaughn come over and sat down on the bench next to him. The detective handed him a bag with his watch cap inside and said he wanted to talk about a girl named Anya Nosova.

The pretty lady detective had mentioned that name the day he got arrested. Rags knew right away she was talking about the dead girl he'd seen in the alley. Killing her was evil. The man should have to pay for what he did. When Vaughn told him there was a way he could help, Rags didn't even have to think about it. He was onboard.

Later, with a business card in his hand and a new story in his brain, Rags was back on the streets of Venice crouched under the eaves of a dental office just east of the roundabout, sheltered from a needling rain. It had been rough the past few days, but his mind was clear now. He felt better, even though the medications the doctors gave him had slowed his reflexes and dulled his thinking. That worried him because he needed to concentrate if his mission were to succeed. Warmed by a blanket he'd borrowed from the shelter, he pulled that business card from his pocket and squinted as he entered the telephone number on the keypad of his cell phone. He hoped the conversation was brief because it hurt to bend his scarred arms for too long.

After three rings, a man answered. Rags's future depended on this call, so he struggled to remember the words the detective had helped him rehearse.

"I was in the alley when you dumped that girl's body in the sewer," he said. "I saw everything."

For a moment all Rags heard was the clang of raindrops on the metal drainpipe above his head.

"Where are you?" The voice sounded as jagged as shards of glass.

"In Venice but I've been thinking about moving to Mexico. Just need a little traveling money."

"How much?"

Rags felt relieved that the man had given in so easily. He didn't like conflict, preferring quiet negotiations. Only he couldn't remember the amount the detective told him to ask for, so he just blurted out a number. "Twenty grand should do it. Just enough to start over."

As soon as he said the amount, he knew the number was wrong. He regretted his error. The girl's life was worth more than that.

"Fine."

Rags wondered how the man could get that much cash together so soon. He hoped the offer wasn't a con. Maybe the man didn't intend to pay or maybe the man even planned to kill him. Rags didn't want to die, but he wasn't afraid of the Grim Reaper, either. He had faced greater challenges in his life. Still, if he had to cross over, he hoped they'd cremate him. He hated the cold and couldn't bear the thought of being buried in the bitter ground.

He closed his eyes to think about the dangers of his mission. It wasn't too late to hang up. He could use the money in his backpack for bus fare to San Diego and still have a little left over to slip across the border into Mexico. Live on the beach. He knew enough *habla español* to get by. He imagined filling his belly with fish tacos as a Mariachi band coaxed love songs from their violins and *guitarróns*. Maybe he'd even meet a good woman who would heal his wounds and make him whole again.

Rags knew that dream would evaporate the moment he opened his eyes. Mexico couldn't happen until he executed the plan. There was one big thing in his favor. This time the powerful forces were aligned with him, not against him. They wouldn't allow him to fail.

"Meet me where you dumped the body," Rags said. "I'll be in the alley for twenty minutes, no more. If you don't show, I'll tell the cops what I saw."

Rags's heartbeat hammered his chest. He hoped his words had sounded tough and convincing, but he couldn't be sure because of the medications.

"It'll take me at least thirty minutes to get there."

Rags almost said "no way," but he finally agreed because he prided himself on his willingness to compromise, especially over a measly ten minutes.

"Aren't you going to ask me what denomination of bills I want?"

"Yeah, sure ... lay it on me."

Rags waited as a car sped past the dental office, its tires kicking up rooster tails from the wet pavement. "A thousand in twenties, the rest in hundreds. I'm on foot and you'd be surprised what a heavy burden money can be."

After Rags ended the call, he thought about all the things that could go wrong. Maybe the man would come with a gun. *Too noisy*, he thought. A knife then, or a baseball bat. He imagined the SUV rolling to a stop in the alley. The driver would pull the bat from the front seat and walk toward him, widening his stance, bending his knees, and slowly raising the bat above his head.

Rags guessed the first strike to his head would make a hollow sound like somebody dropping a watermelon in a grocery store aisle. The man would swing the bat again and again. Three strikes. Out.

He shook his head to purge those bad thoughts. He shuffled toward the beach, drawing the blanket around his body to quell the chill. He had a feeling it was going to be a long day.

46

EARLY MONDAY MORNING, DAVIE'S cell phone rang. It was Jason Vaughn.

"Please tell me Rogers is in custody," she said.

"Not yet."

Davie's shoulders tensed. "What's happening?"

"I showed Rags a six-pack yesterday, just like you said. He pointed to Rogers's DMV photo and said he saw him dump the body of a young woman down a manhole in Venice. He couldn't identify Anya as the victim, but he was sure about Rogers. He remembered his face and described what he was wearing. He's an iffy witness, but his statement was enough for the judge to sign a warrant to impound Rogers's SUV."

"Where was it?"

"Parked in the Edison garage, but Rogers must have seen us show up, because he split before we could talk to him. The bell captain saw him get into a cab shortly after we got there. A couple of blue suits followed me to Rogers's place, but his wife told us she didn't know where he was."

"Find anything in his vehicle?"

"The techs found traces of blood. Somebody tried to clean it up, but they didn't do a very good job. It's too soon to know for sure, but I'm guessing it's Anya's. They also found some red plastic beads. Not sure what that means. Maybe nothing."

"They're from Anya's purse. It's booked in the Property room. Rogers picked it up from the Volga Bakery on Monday. He must have broken one of the threads before putting it in Satine's car. Did any of the other forensic evidence come back?"

"No hits on that heart box from the Marina del Rey apartment, but they got a sample from the hairs on the brush you collected. They also got Rogers's saliva from the plastic cup. The lab did a rush job on the DNA. I just got the results. You were right. Rogers is the father of Anya's baby. That could explain his motive for killing her."

"What about Rags Foster?"

"One of the undercover vice guys posed as Rags, just like we planned. He sat in the alley for almost two hours. Rogers didn't show. The only thing our guy got was hypothermia. And by the way, Rags's public defender wasn't happy that we used him as a decoy. I told her he only made a phone call but she didn't like it."

"Where is he now?"

"He's safe. He wouldn't go back to the shelter, so we checked him into a motel and told him to stay put. A couple of our guys are stationed outside. If he tries to leave, they'll do their best to talk him out of it."

"So Rogers was a no-show. Any idea where he is?"

"We can't find him, but his wife's Toyota is missing. We've notified local airports, Amtrak, and border agents for both Mexico and Canada. Right now I'm running down leads from the tip line."

"Anything promising?"

"A couple of calls are worth looking into. A guy claims he saw Rogers sailing a boat out of Marina del Rey and a clerk at a sporting goods store says a man matching Rogers's description bought a couple hundred dollars worth of survival gear."

"He's outdoorsy, likes to hike. He may be headed to the mountains."

"I've got it covered, Davie."

"I know you do."

She should have felt better about being right but instead she was left with a sense of loss that somebody else had taken over her investigation.

"What can I do to help?" she said.

"Nothing if you ever want to work as a cop again. Trust me on this, partner."

Vaughn promised to keep her updated before ending the call. She glanced out the window toward Alex Camden's house. The place was dead quiet. He had left on a buying trip to Asia and wouldn't be home for two weeks. Even the dogs were gone, staying in Thousand Oaks with Camden's aunt.

The width of the guesthouse was less than twenty-five feet. She paced the distance several times, wondering where Rogers was and what his next move might be. Would he leave town or make a last stand somewhere? She didn't think he'd turn himself in, and she didn't believe he sailed off into the sunset. A sailboat was too slow and too easy to track. The sporting goods tip sounded more promising. There were dozens of vacation cottages in the mountains where he could hide, at least until the owners showed up.

Her nerves were frayed. She decided to go for a swim to work off the tension. In her bedroom, she opened the drawer where she kept her swimming suit. Her hand reached in to pick it up and then stopped. She had never felt afraid living here alone—until now. Despite the tony neighborhood and the security gate, she felt vulnerable. It could take days or longer before they found Cal Rogers. She couldn't hide inside the house forever with a gun by her side—a gun she was no longer permitted to carry, no less—but for now she decided to stay inside,

If Rogers hadn't kept his appointment with Rags it was likely because he sensed a set up. He'd worked in law enforcement and once you developed a cop's paranoia, it wasn't easy to shake it off. Sometimes it was the only thing that kept you alive.

Rogers must have wondered how a homeless junkie got his telephone number. If he had bothered to ask, she hoped Rags remembered the story she and Vaughn had concocted—that he'd memorized Rogers's license plate number and later gave someone at the shelter fifteen bucks to buy the registered owner's address and phone number from the Internet. Davie had hoped Rogers would believe that story, but apparently he hadn't.

It seemed unlikely that Rogers would come after her, but just to be cautious, she made sure the doors and windows were all locked. Then she turned the TV to a news channel and waited.

————

After thirty minutes watching TV coverage about everything but the search for Cal Rogers, Davie needed a break. It was almost one o'clock and she couldn't remember how long it had been since she'd eaten. Food didn't sound appealing but her body needed fuel in order to function. She was on her way to the kitchen to make a sandwich when her cell phone rang. She muted the sound on the TV and answered the call.

"Davie." It was her grandmother. She sounded breathless.

She felt a surge of guilt. With everything that had happened, she couldn't remember the last time they'd spoken.

"Sorry I haven't called, Grammy. Too many things going—"

"Help!"

She looked at the number on the phone's screen. Blocked. A feeling of unease washed over her. "Grammy, what's wrong? Did you fall? Whose phone are you using?"

"A man came to my apartment. He put a rag over my mouth and dragged me out the back door."

Davie's mind was unspooling. She struggled to rein in her thoughts. "Where are you, Grammy?"

"In a car. On a freeway, I think. We're going fast. I punched him, Davie, but I couldn't stop him."

Davie's pulse raced as she sprinted into the bedroom in search of her gun. "Who's with you? Let me talk to him. Okay?"

A moment later, she heard Cal Rogers's voice. "I know you told me you didn't like surprises, but I couldn't resist. You didn't tell me your grandmother is as beautiful as she is smart. I'm so glad to finally meet her. We'll all be together soon, just the three of us. That should be fun."

She opened the drawer of the bedside table and pulled out the Smith & Wesson, checking the chamber to make sure a cartridge was in place. Her first impulse was to say, *If you harm her in any way, I will make you pay,* but from what little training she'd had in hostage negotiating, she knew to avoid threats that might escalate the situation.

Her tone remained calm but her body was a taut wire. "All I want is for everybody to stay safe, Cal."

"Me, too, Davie. By the way, if you're considering a career change, my wife thinks you'd make a great real estate agent."

She used her shoulder to hold the phone to her ear while she strapped on her gun belt. "How did you know it was me?"

He chuckled. "Norah tells me everything and she has a great memory for details. She described everything about you from your red hair down to those red sneakers. We'd just been together, so I knew right away it was you. You screwed up my plans big-time, so I'm counting on you to help me through this rough spot."

"What do you want from me?"

"I need to take a trip abroad, but the economy sucks. Got any spare change? A lot of it."

"I'll see what I can do. Where do you want to meet?"

"Do you have a pen?"

He rattled off an address in Chula Vista, a town near San Diego close to the Mexican border. Crossing into Mexico was a good bet for Rogers. Extradition was iffy, especially if the DA's office decided to seek the death penalty for Anya Nosova's murder.

"Just the three of us, Davie. Got that? I wouldn't want anything to spoil the day."

"Let me talk to my grandmother."

His tone was mocking. "What? I can't hear you. Davie, are you there? I think I'm losing the connection."

The phone went dead.

47

DAVIE PRESSED REDIAL BUT her call wouldn't connect to the blocked number. She didn't know what Rogers expected of her. She couldn't access any significant amount of cash on such short notice. All she had was a couple thousand dollars of emergency earthquake money hidden in a bag of green peas in the freezer compartment of the refrigerator. That would have to do. She pulled out the bag and set it on the counter.

She had been suspended from the department and was no longer authorized to carry a weapon, but she'd be crazy to go after Rogers unarmed. Back when she'd been a probationer, her training officer had told her it was better to be judged by twelve than carried by six. That still seemed like sound advice. She threw on her Kevlar vest and slid her Smith & Wesson into her belt holster. At the last minute, she strapped a .38 snub-nose revolver to a holster on her leg. It wasn't good for distances, but it might come in handy for close encounters.

Once in her car, she entered the Chula Vista address into her cell phone's navigation app. As she headed toward the Sunset entrance to the 405, she reached Jason Vaughn.

"I've located Rogers," she said. "He's holding my grandmother hostage. They're on their way to the Mexican border."

"What the hell? How do you know?"

"He called. He wants money. I'm driving to meet him."

"What?! No! Where are you?"

"On the freeway, headed south."

"Go home. Let us handle this."

She maneuvered the car into the fast lane. "If I don't show up at the meeting place, he'll kill her."

"Stall him. Tell him you got hung up in traffic. Just give me time to call Chula Vista PD. See if they want us to send a SWAT team and a hostage negotiator."

"Call anybody you want, but I'm going to Chula Vista."

He blew out a blast of air. "Okay, but keep in touch. I'll call you with the plan."

She grabbed the 12-volt phone charger from the glove compartment, attached her phone, and plugged the charger into the cigarette lighter. She didn't know how long Rogers had been on the road, but it would take her at least two hours to get from Bel Air to Chula Vista. She inched the Camaro's speedometer to eighty, hoping that number would hold all the way to her destination. If she had to slow down, she would. If the Highway Patrol pulled her over for speeding, it would only waste time while she explained the situation.

As she drove south, she considered the possibility that Rogers might have access to a powerboat. A vessel in open water, even a fast one, was easy to track, so she placed that option at the bottom of the list. Chula Vista was close to the border. A better plan for Rogers would be to force

Davie to drive into Mexico with her grandmother riding shotgun and Rogers in the trunk of the car. She and Grammy would look like tourists on a winter vacay. It was unlikely border agents would stop them or search their car.

If that was the plan, she doubted Rogers would cross at San Ysidro. Too many eyes watching, too many potential delays. He might choose a smaller border town like Tecate. Then she realized the option was unworkable. She and Grammy could get tourist cards at the border, but they'd need passports to complete the transaction.

As Davie passed the exit for Pacific station, she realized Rogers must have considered the possibility she would notify authorities he was holding her grandmother and that Davie would come to the meeting place armed. She wondered if he'd even be there when she arrived. Maybe he'd call again with another address or leave a message somewhere ... or maybe he had no intention of returning Grammy alive.

Her hands felt numb from gripping the steering wheel. She shook each one until feeling returned. If Rogers harmed her grandmother, all bets were off. Neither her career nor her personal safety mattered. She would take him down any way she could.

Vaughn said he would call her with the plan. She hoped for Grammy's sake it was a good one. By the time she had cruised past the last exit to Long Beach, she had formed a backup strategy of her own.

48

THE ADDRESS ROGERS HAD given Davie led to a boarded-up gas station just outside of Chula Vista. She scanned the surrounding area but didn't see Rogers or any evidence her partner and the cavalry had arrived. Just to be cautious, she watched for a few minutes before getting out of the car.

A note was taped to the front door of the station, a notice for a weight-loss product. A phone number was printed on tear-off strips at the bottom. She flipped the note over but saw nothing on the back. She made her way around the building, checking the doors. They were all locked. Back in the car, she called Vaughn.

"I'm at the location. Nobody's here. Where are you?"

"Just outside of town, but Rogers hasn't been there. Chula Vista PD has had eyes on the place for the last two hours. Their captain cleared SWAT to help but he wants to run the show. Our guys arrived by airship. They're at a staging area nearby, waiting for instructions. Have you called Rogers?"

"His number's blocked. I can't get through."

"He'll contact you again. If he gives you another address, let me know. If we can't get a visual on your car, we'll use your cell to track you."

She ended the call and waited. A pool of water had formed around the package of peas but the cash was in a separate bag so it wouldn't get wet. The money was still cold when she pulled it out. She was about to look for a place to dump the peas when Rogers called. In the background her grandmother's voice sounded raw and panicked.

"Help me. I don't know where I am."

Davie's pulse raced. "Hey, Cal, I'm in Chula Vista. Where are you? Look, nobody's been hurt. You've done a good job keeping things under control. Drop off my grandmother at the nearest hospital so we can talk without—"

Rogers interrupted. "Did you have a pleasant drive?"

"You know, lots of traffic. Let me talk to my grandmother."

"Maybe later. I'm annoyed with you right now. It was supposed to be just the three of us, but I see you brought the Keystone Kops."

"There's nobody here but me and a few tumbleweeds."

"Don't lie to me. I've been watching. A couple of hours ago the place was crawling with Chula Vista PD."

"Everybody just wants to make sure things turn out okay." She craned her neck to look for any sign of her partner, but saw no police vehicles approaching.

"They'll turn out if you do what I say. There's a throwaway cell in the trash can by the street. Take it and leave your phone there. Once you've made the switch, I'll call and tell you where to go. And remember, I'm watching. If you signal your buddies or communicate with them in any way, you will never see your grandmother alive again. Got that?"

"Whatever you say."

Davie searched the horizon for places where Rogers might be hiding. There were commercial buildings along the street but none over three stories. She doubted he'd risk staying in the area, but she couldn't be sure. In case Rogers had binoculars or some sort of scope trained on her, she had to be cautious. She found the trash can and leaned inside. As she did, she called Vaughn again. As soon as he answered, she started speaking.

"I don't have much time. I'm ditching my phone for one of his. Can you follow my car without attracting attention?"

"Did he give you the next destination?"

"No. Just follow me. I have to go. He may be watching."

"Will do, Davie. Be careful."

As instructed, she left her cell inside the trash can along with the peas and returned to the car. A short time later, Rogers called.

"Turn right out of the parking lot. Stay on the phone. I don't want you making any calls."

He didn't mention anything about the extra time she'd spent leaning into the trash can talking to her partner, which meant Rogers hadn't been watching her as he claimed. He was probably already at the secondary location.

For the next eight miles or so Rogers monitored her progress over the telephone. Following his instructions, Davie called out landmarks as he directed her farther into hills that were green from the recent rain. She listened for her grandmother's voice in the background but heard nothing more from her. She kept checking her rearview mirror but saw no sign she was being followed. Even if SWAT were tracking her, they wouldn't have much time to set up a perimeter once they arrived at the destination—*if* they arrived.

The sun had just begun drifting toward the western horizon as Rogers told her to turn onto the road leading to Lower Otay Reservoir. A sign announced that fishing licenses could be purchased at the concession stand. Another read that the area was closed on Mondays. Rogers had likely been there before and knew the place would be deserted.

She felt the Camaro's wheels bump along a gravel road lined with overgrown brush until the road curved into a paved parking lot where she saw a boat ramp sloping into the reservoir. There was a small building at the water's edge—the concession stand. A dock housed a smaller building with a sign that read BAIT SHACK.

A white Toyota Corolla was parked in front of the building. It looked like the same car she'd seen in the driveway of Rogers's Mar Vista home. A red plastic fuel container stood near the trunk. She wondered if he planned to torch the small building with her and Grammy inside, then take the cash and disappear.

She heard Rogers's voice though the phone's receiver. "Park next to the Toyota. Leave your weapons in the car and come inside the building."

That wasn't going to happen. There was no guarantee her grandmother was still alive. Even if she were, Davie wasn't going to gift Rogers with two hostages instead of one. She would keep him engaged until he surrendered or help arrived.

Just before the curve, Davie made a sharp left turn, angling the Camaro across the road to block Rogers's exit and to provide cover for her. She threw the money on the ground and slipped out of the car, covering the phone's mouthpiece to muffle the sound of the door closing. With the phone anchored between her shoulder and her ear, she slid the Smith & Wesson out of its holster.

"I brought money, Cal, just like you asked. It's only a couple of grand. That's all I could pull together on such short notice. Before I give it to you I need to make sure my grandmother's okay."

Davie slid to the ground, prone on the dirt with her legs splayed and her elbows digging into the soil. Rocks scraped against her Kevlar vest. She juggled the phone and her pistol, moving through the dirt until she could see underneath the car. From there, she had a clear shot of the front door of the concession stand.

"A couple grand's not going to get me far," Rogers said, "Come inside and we'll talk."

"Be happy to, but first send my grandmother out where I can see her."

"I'm not going to bargain with you, Davie. Do it. Now!"

Davie weighed the pros and cons of doing what he asked and decided instead to distract him with the money and keep him engaged. She set the phone on the dirt and rolled into a crouch. She threw the plastic bag toward the concession stand. It landed on the ground a few feet short of its target.

She retrieved the phone and continued the conversation. "You see the money, Cal? It's just outside the building."

In the long silence that followed, she imagined Grammy dead and buried in a shallow grave somewhere in the desert. The door of the concession stand finally opened and Grammy stepped outside. Rogers's left arm was looped around her waist, using her as a shield. The phone was in his left hand, inaccessible and useless. In his right hand he had what looked like a Glock 19. Grammy's hands were primly folded in front of her, like a church lady at Sunday service. When Davie took a closer look, she saw that her wrists were tied. She counted breaths to control her anger.

Davie moved toward the back of the car. Rogers couldn't use his cell at the moment, so she ended the call. Then she called her partner.

"We know your location," he said. "We're close by."

"I have to watch Rogers. I may not be able to pick up the phone, so I'll set it to speaker so you can hear what's happening."

"What's he doing now?"

"He's in the parking lot with my grandmother and a gun. We're talking." She set the phone on the trunk of the car with the line open.

"Davie, are you there?" Her grandmother's voice sounded thin and brittle.

"I'm here, Grammy. Everything's going to be all right."

"I'm scared. This is like the bad thing that happened to you before."

Davie remembered how upset Grammy had been when she found out about the officer-involved shooting. Even all these months later, Davie still remembered the coppery odor of blood spilling from Abel Hurtado's body.

"No, Grammy, this is different. But that turned out okay too. Remember?"

"I told you," Rogers said. "She's fine."

"What's the plan, Cal?"

"The plan is I take your car. Then granny and I drive across the border."

"You're taking a big risk. What if you don't make it?"

"Got a better idea?"

"Take me instead."

He laughed. "Try again."

"What about Norah and the kids? If something happens to you, how will they manage?"

"You think they'll do better with me on death row?"

"It might not turn out that way," she said. "I'm not sure what happened between you and Anya. Maybe her death was an accident."

"She got knocked up and claimed I was the father. She was a hooker. It could have been anybody, but it was my life she wanted to ruin. I couldn't let that happen."

Now was not the time to tell him that DNA proved he was the father of Anya's baby. "I'm sorry you had to go through that, Cal. It must have been stressful."

"Cut the lame bullshit. Move away from your car. Leave the keys inside. If you do as I say, I'll drop grandma off somewhere in Mexico. You can pick up her up there."

"She needs a passport to get a tourist card."

"I have her passport. Before we left her place, I told her you needed to check the expiration date for that trip you two were taking to British Columbia. Your grandma can't see worth shit but she remembers where her stuff is."

Grammy looked weak, on the verge of collapse. Help was on the way. Until then, she had to keep Rogers talking.

"What's the gas can for?"

"It's a long way to the border. I don't want to stop and refuel."

"We need to figure out exactly how this is going to work."

"I told you how it's going to work. You do what I tell you to do. Period."

Rogers was struggling to keep her grandmother upright. As he reached down to pick up the money, Grammy drove her heel into his shin. He groaned and let her drop to the ground.

In the distance Davie heard what sounded like the rotors of a helicopter. She glanced up and saw an LAPD airship heading toward the reservoir. In a moment, the SWAT team would rappel down cables and set up a perimeter. She craned her neck toward the road and saw a cloud of dust from multiple vehicles driving toward her. Rogers saw and heard too. He tried to pull Grammy to her feet, but she had gone limp. The roar of the airship overhead made it hard to hear. Air turbulence sent leaves and dust swirling around her.

The sound of her voice seemed husky and fractured. "Cal, we can work this out. Put down the gun and we'll talk."

Davie heard boots slamming against the ground and men's voices. Dust coated the back of her throat. Help was close but not close enough. She shut out the noise and tried to focus on only one thing—the threat.

Rogers lowered the gun toward her grandmother's head. "Too late for that. You should have followed directions."

Davie steadied her hands on her weapon. There was only one shot she knew would stop him. She aimed, slid her index finger from the barrel to the trigger, and fired.

Rogers slumped to the ground.

As she approached, she saw a trickle of blood seeping from a hole in his forehead. Grammy lay next to him, fragile and still.

Vaughn's voice came from somewhere behind her, muffled by the ringing in her ears from firing her gun. "I'll take over from here, Davie. You look after your grandmother."

Davie's hands trembled as she lifted Grammy's head off the dirt and cradled it in her lap. There was a pulse, weak but steady. She was untying the rope that bound her grandmother's wrists when she felt Jason Vaughn's hand on her shoulder.

"Hang in there, partner," he said. "The EMTs are here."

Davie rested her cheek against Grammy's forehead and waited.

49

MALCOLM HARRINGTON PARKED ON a residential street at Mountain Gate near the trailhead, eager for his run. It had been a week since Alex Sloan called to tell him Davie Richards had killed again. Not that Harrington was pleased about the loss of life, but the detective's actions strengthened his case against her. She was out of control. He'd been justified in having her relieved of duty.

The sun was out, but the air was cold. He locked the car doors and began to jog. Except for a middle-aged woman walking a golden retriever, he was alone on the trail. He kept a steady pace until around mile three, when a pebble began rubbing against his heel. He sat on a rock and pulled off his shoe.

"Nice day for a run."

He swiveled toward the voice and saw a woman standing on the path in front of him, sporting a cloud of red hair. He hadn't seen Davie Richards in fifteen years, but she didn't look much different from the teenager who'd sat behind the defense table every day in a courtroom in downtown L.A. Those green eyes of hers were still shooting death darts at him. He felt blood flow to his head, pressuring the walls of his skull. For a moment he thought an aneurism was exploding in his brain.

She hadn't followed him. He would have noticed. Her denim jeans and heavy sweater were not conducive to jogging. Judging from the boots she wore, she must have hiked down to the path. There was an access road above the trail where she could have parked a car. He had no idea how long she'd been tracking him or if she was armed. All he knew was that they were alone in the middle of nowhere. If she meant him harm, there would be no one to help him.

Until he could determine her intentions, he decided to keep a measured tone. "What are you doing here?"

"I have a message for you. From Maria Luna. Remember her? It took me a while to track her down, but she finally agreed to talk."

It startled him to hear Davie Richards speak that name. After the verdict in her father's civil trial, he'd never heard from Luna again. No Christmas cards addressed to him at the firm, telling him how Daniel was doing and thanking him for his heroic efforts on their behalf.

Harrington tapped the pebble from his shoe and slipped it back on his foot in case he had to run. "I haven't heard from her in fifteen years. What could she possibly have to say to me now?"

He tensed as Richards stepped closer.

"She said my father told the truth on the witness stand. Her son had a gun in his waistband that day. He was reaching for it when my father shot him."

"No gun was found."

"Daniel threw it in a storm drain. It was dark. In all the confusion, nobody saw it there. When his mother came to see him at the hospital, he told her where it was and how to dispose of it."

Harrington monitored her position as he tied his shoe. "Do you expect anybody to believe you?"

"They don't have to believe me. They just have to believe Maria Luna." The woman's eyes narrowed. "She said you never asked Daniel to testify about the gun, probably because at some level you knew the truth and couldn't allow a client to perjure himself on the stand. She told me all you seemed to care about was nailing my father and getting a big payoff. She didn't care about my dad, but the money sounded good to her, so she kept quiet. If I recall, even though you lost, the publicity surrounding the case launched your career."

"She's lying."

Richards moved closer until she was looming over him.

"You ruined my father's life back then because you didn't ask the right questions. You're doing the same thing to me now. What's the plan, Harrington? Are you angling for your next job? A tough-on-crime candidate for mayor? Or maybe senator?"

"Speculation and innuendo."

"Maria Luna thought you had a thing for her."

Harrington crossed his arms to ward off the morning chill. "I would never jeopardize my law practice by coming on to a client, nor would I betray my wife. We've been happily married for twenty-five years."

He knew "happily married" wasn't entirely accurate. There had been dark days. But wasn't that true of all marriages? Maybe he'd admired Luna, but only because he would never see her dressed for bed in flannel pajamas that had been through one too many wash cycles. In his mind's eye she would always appear in a short skirt that exposed her toned legs. She would smile at him with those brilliant white teeth. He remembered her glossy lips barely moved as she held a rosary in her hands and prayed for justice for her son, even though Harrington knew it was her lawyer in whom she'd placed her faith.

But she had *never* told him about the gun.

"You have to win, don't you?" Richards said. "Nothing is more important, not even your reputation."

"A trait I share with many successful people. So what?"

"Your need to win at any cost is what makes you dangerous. You hated my father because you believed he got away with attempted murder. It turns out you were wrong—he was innocent. But that was the first big case you lost, the one that stung the most. You're using me to settle the score."

"Your father shot a man and lied about it, just as you did."

"Both cases are based on fiction by people who just wanted to make a few bucks."

A chill had settled into Harrington's muscles. "Why are you telling me this? Why not just hold a splashy press conference with some ambulance-chasing lawyer?"

"Not everybody borrows a page from your playbook."

His right leg began to tingle. Sitting in one position on the sharp edge of a rock had cut off his circulation. He stumbled to his feet, ignoring the needling pain. "You've made a huge miscalculation coming here."

"Ironic, isn't it? All your crusading against the police department and it turns out you're as dirty as the worst of them."

Harrington turned toward his car. "This conversation is over."

"Don't you want to hear what else I have?"

"Stay away from me or I'll get a restraining order."

He ran the first few yards, listening for the sound of footsteps but heard nothing to indicate she was following him. She had gall, accusing him like that. He thought about the cases he'd lost in his career, not many, but he admitted that none of them had caused him as much pain as losing the case against William Richards.

It troubled him that Maria Luna had withheld key evidence and that he may have transferred his hatred of William Richards to the detective's daughter. His entire career had been dedicated to the pursuit of justice, but now he wondered if Davie Richards was right. Had he subconsciously tried to punish her as a last-ditch effort to wipe out that humiliating loss? He had known the evidence against her was thin, but he hadn't followed the Police Commission's recommendations or listened to Alex Sloan's warnings, because he truly believed she had lied on that police report. He still believed that.

Twenty minutes later, he sat in the car to catch his breath, warming his hands in front of the heater. Then he turned the wheel and headed back to his office.

———————

"Excuse me, sir." Maggie Perez stood at the threshold of Harrington's office, wringing her hands. "One of Mayor Gossett's people just called. The mayor wants to see you."

Harrington's watch read 10:17 a.m. He had just arrived at the office from his run, having showered and changed into his suit at the gym. He was eager to review the latest investigative report on the Davie Richards case, which was waiting for him on his desk.

"I have a meeting in half an hour. Tell him I can rearrange my schedule but not until this afternoon, sometime after two."

"He wants to see you now. His car is waiting downstairs to pick you up. It sounded urgent."

The anxiety in Perez's voice made Harrington's pulse quicken. He took a deep calming breath, hoping she had misjudged the threat in the mayor's summons.

"Call Alex Sloan. Tell him we'll have to reschedule."

Harrington locked the Richards report in his desk drawer. He grabbed his overcoat from a rack near the door and headed downstairs, where he found Mayor Lloyd Gossett sitting in the backseat of an SUV parked in a red zone. The mayor's driver and another member of his security team sat up front.

Harrington slid into the back next to Gossett, inhaling the fragrance of the mayor's citrus cologne. Next to him on the seat was what looked like an iPad with a black cover. Gossett didn't look him in the eye, which was troubling. Instead, he studied a contact sheet full of glamour headshots. Harrington assumed they were from the recent *People* magazine photo shoot. Gossett tapped his knuckle on the closed privacy window and the driver pulled into traffic, but he didn't go far. He made a right turn and immediately pulled up to a two-hour parking meter, leaving the engine running.

Harrington was pleased. At least this meeting would be a short one.

The side street was lined with trees, forming a canopy that blocked the light. To the right, ivy snaked up the facade of the building. To the left, razor wire coiled atop a wall that guarded a parking lot. All at once, the scene made Harrington feel claustrophobic. He stared at the sheen on Gossett's manicured fingernails and waited for the bomb to drop. It didn't take long.

Gossett put a photographer's loupe to his eye and studied each picture. "I've been in conference all morning with the DA, the City Attorney, and the President of the Police Commission. We have what you'd call a situation."

Harrington clasped his hands together to hide the onset of a slight tremor. "What's going on?"

Gossett's body was as still as a Sphinx. The car's heater had elevated the temperature in the SUV to high noon in the Sahara. Harrington began to sweat. He considered removing his overcoat but didn't want to appear weak.

"The Davie Richards case, that's what."

Harrington wondered if Richards had contacted the mayor about Maria Luna's bogus gun story, but he didn't see how she could have done that so soon. He and Gossett were friends and even he had trouble getting the man's attention.

"You appointed me to investigate police misconduct, Lloyd. That's what I'm doing. Some cases are more challenging than others."

"Malcolm, it appears you forgot to tell me there wasn't a case against Davie Richards six months ago, and there isn't one now. You had her relieved of duty without cause. The voters might think you abused your authority. They hate that. The City Attorney says if she files a civil suit against the city, he'll have to settle. If he doesn't, a jury could award millions, which will mean budget cuts for everyone, including me. Do I have to tell you how annoyed that would make me?"

Harrington leaned forward to catch Gossett's eye. "The victim's widow claims Richards lied on the police report."

The mayor's focus remained on the contact sheet. "Ah, Mrs. Hurtado. Earlier this morning I arranged for an Internal Affairs detective to interview the woman. He found her packing to move to Texas with her new boyfriend. The investigator enlightened her about the penalty for perjury. After hearing that, Mrs. Hurtado seemed confused about her lawsuit against the city. Claimed she doesn't remember hiring a lawyer."

The odor of the mayor's cologne in the overheated car was now making Harrington feel nauseated. "There are other witnesses."

"Like who?"

"All in good time."

Gossett circled one of the photos with a grease pencil and held the contact sheet toward Harrington. "What do you think of this one? Do I look sexy enough for *People*?"

"I wouldn't know."

Gossett moved on to study the next sheet. "I warned you not to mold the facts of this case to fit your conclusions."

"Cool your jets, Lloyd. No criminal charges have been filed against Richards."

"And none will be filed. Shut this thing down."

"As soon as the investigation is—"

Gossett slammed the contact sheets onto his lap. "Do it now, Malcolm, because we both know there's more to the story than Davie Richards's OIS case."

That's when he realized Gossett knew. Somehow Davie Richards had gotten to him. Harrington hoped his voice sounded confident. "It's about exposing cops who break the law."

The mayor slipped the loupe into his jacket pocket and turned toward Harrington. "It's about *you*, Malcolm. You're obsessed with the Richards family. I'm worried. I think you need professional help."

Harrington's pulse quickened. "Don't be ridiculous—"

"Take a look at this." Gossett opened the cover of his iPad, exposing a video clip. "This arrived in my private email account yesterday."

The mayor pressed the arrow in the center of the frame and the video began to play. Harrington saw an older but still recognizable Daniel Luna speaking to the camera, admitting he had a gun the night William Richards shot him and that he intended to use it to kill the detective, if he'd gotten the chance.

After thirty seconds, Harrington had heard enough. "Have you asked yourself what motivated Daniel to confess now? I suspect Davie Richards paid him to make up that story to get herself off the hook."

Gossett closed the lid of the iPad, silencing Daniel's voice. "Luna is facing felony drug charges. I guess he figures after fifteen years nobody cares about William Richards's civil case, so he has nothing to lose by confessing, and maybe his cooperation will nudge the DA to downgrade the charge to a misdemeanor."

"Davie Richards has no authority to promise Luna anything. No wonder he decided to fabricate—"

"Get out of the car, Malcolm. Now. I need to fix this mess you've created."

Gossett's words felt like a punch in the gut and the coldness in the mayor's expression told him the sentiment was real. He opened the car door and staggered onto the sidewalk, glad to be away from the heat and the smell of citrus. Gossett's SUV pulled away from the curb.

Harrington stood motionless under the mesh of leaves and branches that covered him like a shroud. For the first time in years, he didn't know where to go or what to do.

50

ANOTHER WINTER COLD FRONT had blown into town. Lawyers, bankers, and file clerks cranked up car heaters as they inched through the early-morning chill toward the Meccas of commerce—downtown L.A. and Century City. Undocumented day laborers huddled at staging areas, hoping for a day's work for a day's pay. Shelter employees nudged the homeless from their warm beds and cast them onto Skid Row streets to fend for themselves until nightfall. Grape Street gangbangers plotted burglary capers over latte macchiatos at Starbucks.

Davie Richards sat at her desk in the Pacific Division squad room, applying hand sanitizer to her desk telephone receiver. It had been nearly two months since she'd entered the station and there was no telling how many people had used her phone during that time. For good measure, she swabbed the desktop and the drawer handles too.

The books on the shelf above her workstation had fallen over again. She had meant to buy bookends but never got around to it. Maybe she'd go shopping after work.

She had left a message for Jason Vaughn the night before to let him know she'd be back at work. He was in training for the next two weeks but invited her out after end of watch to celebrate. He promised there would be team building and adult beverages.

Several people came to her desk and welcomed her back. Lieutenant Bellows wasn't one of them. He was with the Captain at a COMP-STAT meeting, spinning tales of lowered crime rates and patting himself on the back for solving the Beau Fischer and Anya Nosova homicides. She doubted he'd bother to mention the detectives who had done the actual work.

The Police Commission had finally ruled the Hurtado OIS case was within policy, clearing her of all wrongdoing. Everything had moved quickly since the case had been thoroughly investigated months before, and for that she was grateful.

After the Daniel Luna video surfaced, Malcolm Harrington resigned as Inspector General of the Police Commission to "spend more time with his family." She wondered if he planned to return to his former law firm and start suing the LAPD again. Maybe Mrs. Hurtado could be his first client. There might even be some gold to mine by investigating the death of that inmate Cal Rogers had assaulted in County jail.

A gust of air brushed past Davie's cheek. She turned to see Detective Giordano wearing a starched white shirt and a tie with palm trees and ukuleles on it. She hoped it wasn't his retirement tie. Life on the Homicide table would not be the same without him. She stood as he reached out to shake her hand. At the last minute he pulled her into a hug that nearly squeezed the air from her lungs. The move surprised her. There was an unwritten rule in the station that hugging could be misinterpreted as sexual harassment and therefore was strictly *verboten*.

He gave her a stern look as he let her go. "Good to have you back, kid."

Most cops go through their entire careers without firing a weapon in the line of duty. Davie knew she was an outlier and that knowledge weighed heavily on her. After Rogers's death, she questioned whether she had the temperament to be a cop or even to own a gun. She worried what would become of Norah Rogers and her children, and felt shattered that her work had jeopardized the life of her grandmother. Guilt strained all her relationships, and she realized once again why the department forced cops to see a psychiatrist after a shooting. Justified or not, killing another human being messed with your head.

She had been relieved of duty a second time for shooting Cal Rogers, pending an inquiry by the Force Investigation Division and an evaluation by a department shrink. FID detectives presented the case to the DA's office, but only as a formality. The shooting was justified and they declined to file charges.

Giordano told anybody who'd listen that she deserved the Medal of Valor for what she'd done, but the department still gave her an eight-day suspension without pay for the unauthorized use of a weapon while relieved of duty. Giordano had no control over the process but he stood by her throughout the ordeal and lobbied the Captain and Lieutenant Bellows to expedite her return to Pacific Homicide.

"Thanks for everything you did for me," she said. "I'll never forget it."

"Like I told you before, you're one of my peeps." Giordano walked toward his workstation. "I also want you to know I smoothed things over with Detective Quintero. He was mighty pissed you messed with his case. I took him out for a few beers and an attitude adjustment. He's fine now. Q's a good guy. You should call him and make nice in case you have to work with him again."

She nodded. "Will do."

"How's your grandma?"

"Doing better every day. Thanks for asking."

"Rags?"

She shook her head. "Gone."

"He'll turn up."

Davie wasn't so sure. It troubled her not knowing where he was. She just hoped he was in a safe place.

Giordano snagged a package from his desk and handed it to her. The wrapping paper had cartoon cars on it and looked like a committee had assembled it.

"What is this?" Davie worked off the bow and slid her finger along the seam to loosen the tape.

"Just a little something."

Inside, swaddled in tissue paper was a set of heavy stainless steel bookends, each forming the numbers 187—the penal code for a homicide.

"A few of us chipped in and had 'em made," he continued. "We got tired of the mess on your desk—not to mention all the racket your crap makes when it falls over. Now maybe we can have some peace and quiet."

Her chest felt tight as she set the bookends on her shelf. "I don't know what to say."

"Don't waste the oxygen. You have work to do. The watch commander just called. We have a body at Mar Vista Gardens. If you're lucky, it'll be a heart attack. Take the green Crown Vic. Keys should be in my desk drawer."

"Who's going with me? Garcia?"

"He's in court."

"Montes?"

"Broke his arm last night at his son's soccer game. And no, he wasn't punching out the coach. He was reaching in the cooler for a beer and fell off the bleachers."

She nodded. "Don't worry. I can handle it alone."

"No need for that. Bellows gave us Detective Hall on loan from Burglary. He'll be your partner until Vaughn gets back. You got a problem with that?" He didn't wait for a response. "I didn't think so. Go work your magic, kid."

Davie was walking to the kit room to check out a fresh battery for her radio when her cell phone, which Vaughn had rescued from the Chula Vista trash can, *pinged* with an incoming text. It was from Spencer Hall: I HAVE THE CAR KEYS. MEET ME AT THE GARAGE.

Davie grabbed the battery and a notebook from her desk and made her way to the parking lot, past a crop of low spiky weeds that had erupted at the base of a cinder block wall. Just past the bank of fuel pumps, she found Hall washing the car.

When he heard her footsteps, he glanced up. "Since we're working together again, I thought we'd celebrate with a clean ride. Just like the old days."

Water bounced off the windshield like a vintage Los Angeles rain. A fine mist drifted over and settled on her face. "The old days are gone, Spence."

He turned the faucet off, dipped a brush into a bucket of soapy water, and began scrubbing the tires. "Just so you know, Malcolm Harrington got nothing from me. I told his rat squad I wouldn't speak to IA without my department rep. If Sloan had bothered to call back, I would have told him there was nothing to say that wasn't on the police report you wrote. Guess he didn't want to know the truth."

Davie grabbed a chamois off a shelf and swept water off the front windshield. "You could have warned me."

Hall turned the water on again and hosed off the tires. "Sloan ordered me not to talk to you. I had no choice."

Davie paused. "You always have a choice."

"Look, the department put us both through hell. The shooting was righteous. Everybody knows that now."

"Except for the people who think I panicked. The rumors will follow me my whole career. Nobody will want to work with me."

Hall hung up the hose and turned to her. "I think it was Becky."

Behind him, dark cumulus clouds had muscled out all but a few patches of blue sky.

"What does your wife have to do with anything?"

"The other night when I got home, Becky was hammered. She started busting my chops about you."

"Did you remind her you were separated and headed for divorce before we got together?"

"She knows that, but she brought up those rumors about you. Said at least she never tried to kill me like you did. I told her that story about you panicking at the Hurtado place was bullshit. She just smirked like the whole thing was a big joke. That's when I knew there was something she wasn't telling me."

"This is all very interesting but—"

"Becky's a gossip and a lot of her friends are married to cops. It's not hard to imagine she helped spread those rumors. She might have started them herself. I doubt she understood the trouble it would cause. When I told her you could have gone to prison, she wouldn't even look at me. She seemed sort of shocked."

"Sort of?" Davie threw the chamois at the bucket. The slam-dunk splashed soapy water onto Hall's suit pants.

He brushed away the suds. "Okay, you're pissed. I get that."

"Why not just *ask* her if she started the rumors?"

"I did. She wouldn't answer me, not even to deny it. That told me everything I needed to know. Remember a few weeks ago when we were talking outside the station? I said you work a partnership until it lives or dies. That way you have no what-ifs, no regrets." He met her eyes dead on. "I worked the marriage with Becky. Twice. But now I know I can't trust her. When there's no trust in a relationship, there's nothing. Last night I walked out."

"Give it a week. You'll be back."

"Not this time. Look, Davie, I'm sorry. I made some bad decisions. I wish I could change things, but I can't. Right now, all I want is to be your partner, even if it's only for the next couple of weeks. Let me try to make it up to you."

Davie felt a mix of emotions she couldn't quite sort out. "Working with you on this wasn't my decision. Somebody made it for me. For now, we're stuck with each other. Let's keep it professional."

Hall emptied the contents of the bucket into a nearby sink. "I told Lieutenant Bellows about Becky. I asked him to pass it up the chain of command. Not sure he will, but I wanted you to know."

A patrol car pulled up behind them, waiting for a wash.

"We have a body in Mar Vista Gardens, Spence. Give me the keys. I'm driving."

About the Author

Patricia Smiley (Los Angeles, CA) is a bestselling mystery author whose short fiction has appeared in *Ellery Queen Mystery Magazine* and *Two of the Deadliest,* an anthology edited by Elizabeth George. Patricia has taught writing classes at various conferences throughout the US and Canada, and she served on the board of directors of the Southern California Chapter of Mystery Writers of America and as president of Sisters in Crime / Los Angeles. Visit her online at www.PatriciaSmiley.com.